With a degree in English and American Literature, Julie Haworth worked as an English teacher for a number of years, specializing in working with learners with literacy difficulties, before launching her own freelance copywriting business. She is a member of the Romantic Novelists' Association.

Also by Julie Haworth:

Always By Your Side
New Beginnings at the Cosy Cat Café

Bea's Book Wagon

JULIE HAWORTH

SIMON & SCHUSTER

London · New York · Amsterdam/Antwerp · Sydney/Melbourne · Toronto · New Delhi

First published in Great Britain by Simon & Schuster UK Ltd, 2025

1 3 5 7 9 10 8 6 4 2

Simon & Schuster UK Ltd, 1st Floor
222 Gray's Inn Road, London WC1X 8HB

Simon & Schuster Australia, Sydney
Simon & Schuster India, New Delhi

www.simonandschuster.co.uk
www.simonandschuster.com.au
www.simonandschuster.co.in

The authorised representative in the EEA is Simon & Schuster Netherlands BV, Herculesplein 96, 3584 AA Utrecht, Netherlands. info@simonandschuster.nl

A CIP catalogue record for this book is available from the British Library

Paperback ISBN: 978- 1- 3985- 4818- 3
eBook ISBN: 978- 1- 3985- 4819- 0
Audio ISBN: 978- 1- 3985- 4820- 6

Typeset in the UK by M Rules
Printed and Bound in the UK using 100% Renewable Electricity
at CPI Group (UK) Ltd

To Mum and Dad
For always encouraging me to follow my dreams.
Love you lots xx

CHAPTER 1

'Bea!' a voice boomed through the flimsy partition wall of Bea Miller's office cubicle. 'I said two sugars!' it continued, becoming gradually louder. Bea could hear Brendan's footsteps getting closer as he marched towards her desk in the dreary, uninspiring office space she shared with a dozen other lacklustre staff. The fluorescent tube-lighting strip buzzed above Bea's head and she blinked, attempting to refocus her gaze in its harsh glare.

'Sorry, I must've given you Dave's,' she said, flashing a half-smile at the pasty, thirty-something man standing in front of her, wearing a cheap nylon suit. He placed a chipped 'World's Best Boss' mug – the irony of which wasn't lost on her – down on Bea's desk. The milky, beige, determinedly sugarless liquid slopped over the sides, spilling onto her workstation. Bea grabbed a tissue and began mopping up diligently.

'How long have you been here now, Bea? Five months?' asked Brendan, tapping his foot against her desk.

'*Five months too long*,' she muttered under her breath.

'Sorry?'

'About that, yep,' said Bea, nodding absentmindedly as she threw a sodden tissue into the bin.

'And is it really too much to ask that you know how I take my tea?'

Bea hesitated. What she really wanted to tell Brendan was that he should be making his own damn tea. She was pretty sure 'general dogsbody' wasn't in the job description the temp agency had sent across when she'd signed up for a job as a PA in the sales department of Hobbs & Partners. Brendan Fuller was head of the sales team, and he possessed a totally skewed sense of self-importance for someone who was essentially managing a team of cold callers, most of whom were barely out of school. The power really had gone to his head.

'And Bea!' shouted Brendan, even louder, this time slamming a pile of papers down on her desk. 'I asked for the *February* sales figures, not January.'

'Really? I could have sworn you said January—'

'Oh, you could, could you?' he grunted.

'Well, yes . . .' Bea *knew* she was right, she *knew* the mistake was Brendan's, not hers, but it wasn't worth antagonizing him further, not while he was in this mood.

'How about you stop questioning me and get things right for once? Is that really too much to ask?'

'Actually, yes it is!' said Bea, loudly. She'd had enough,

she wasn't taking any more of Brendan's abuse. She might need the money, but no temp job was worth this every day.

'What did you say?' said Brendan, staring at her, eyes wide.

'I said, I'm sick of taking this from you, Brendan. The way you talk to me isn't okay and I'm done,' she said, folding her arms.

'*You've* had enough?' replied Brendan, incredulous.

'Yes, I have!' she swallowed hard, the entire office was looking at her now. She saw Kieran, the new trainee, throw her a thumbs-up from across the room. 'You can stick your job, Brendan, I'm worth more than this,' she continued, pulling on her jacket and grabbing her bag from under the desk. 'I quit!'

'Yes, Bea!' yelled Kieran, clapping wildly.

'Too late,' said Brendan through gritted teeth, 'you're fired.'

'Whatever,' Bea shrugged, 'you're not my problem anymore, Brendan,' she said, turning on her heels and walking out of the office for what would be the last time, adrenaline coursing through her veins.

She'd finally done it, she was free.

'What have I *done*?' said Bea, as she sat slumped at the bar in Lagoon Lounge two hours later. She'd walked straight into the first place on Hastings' High Street that served alcohol, and the tired-looking bar, decked out in blue velvet upholstery, was the closest to the office. She'd immediately ordered a shot of tequila and then called her best friend, Jess, to come and help her drown her sorrows.

Bea and Jess had met on the first day of secondary school, and the pair had been firm friends ever since. Jess lived in the nearby village of Blossom Heath, just five miles from Rye, where her parents, Ted and Maggie, ran the village store. Despite the fact that the journey from the village took nearly thirty minutes, in true best-friend style, Jess arrived at the bar in record time.

'Oh, you hated that job anyway,' said Jess, setting another round of drinks down at their table. 'Brendan sounds like a total arse.'

'Oh, he is, but I still shouldn't have walked out like that. I've only just moved back to Rye . . . to Mum and Dad's.' Bea said, dropping her head into her hands. 'What are they going to think? I've already failed in London and now I can't even hold down a job here.'

It was almost four years since Bea had left university, finishing her degree in English Literature from Birmingham with honours. To say things hadn't exactly gone to plan since then would be an understatement.

She'd moved to London – Essex to be exact; she was so far out on the Central Line it didn't even count as London – to look for a job in publishing. It had always been about books for Bea, ever since she was tiny. If her mum, Carol, was to be believed, she was reading as she soon as she could talk.

Carol had worked at Rye library for close to thirty years and Bea had lost track of the hours she had spent there as a child, her nose buried in a book. It was the place that had first ignited her love of stories, and when her mum had been diagnosed with cancer when Bea was ten years old, it was books she had turned to, to help her through those dark days. The time she'd spent in Narnia, Wonderland and at Hogwarts had helped her cope. And, when Carol had recovered, books had remained Bea's sanctuary; they were the place she retreated to when the real world got too much, and she knew that, whatever she ended up doing, it would have to involve literature in some way.

It hadn't been as easy as that, though. Bea had lost count of the number of applications she'd submitted to publishing houses during her time in London, although it must fall somewhere in the thousands. She'd had a few interviews, which got her hopes up, but they'd all come to nothing. She'd been pipped at the post by candidates with 'more experience' or 'a better fit' . . . whatever that meant.

It was soul destroying.

How was she supposed to get experience if she couldn't even get a foot in the door?

Last year, she'd been offered an internship at a small independent house, but when she'd crunched the numbers, she'd realized living on a budget of zero in London wasn't practical, so she'd had to turn it down.

Where did these companies find people who could afford to work for free, anyway?

'Hey, coming back home isn't a failure. You were there almost four years, it's not like you gave up easily,' said Jess.

'I had no idea how competitive it was going to be. I've lost count of how many interviews I went to. Hundreds?

Thousands?' she said, shaking her head. 'There are only so many rejections I could take.'

'It's tough out there. Even tougher in creative jobs. Remember how long it took for me to get that first gig in graphic design, even with my degree? It's hard to catch a break.'

'It really is. I floated from one temp job to another, getting nowhere fast. It doesn't help that Archie's totally killing it either; he's raking it in in that IT job. He's got his own place and a mortgage – it's hard not to feel like I'm coming up short.'

Archie, Bea's older brother, had bought a house at Meadowgate Mead, a new-build estate on the outskirts of Blossom Heath, a couple of years ago.

'IT jobs pay well, it's no surprise that he got that mortgage,' said Jess. 'And, anyway, it's not a competition.'

'It feels like it is.'

'You've got savings, though, haven't you? Could they tide you over for a bit, until you find something else?'

'I could probably make them stretch for a couple of months, but after that, I'm screwed . . .'

'Oh Lovely,' said Jess, rubbing her friend's back. 'To be honest, I'm amazed you lasted this long with Brendan. He sounded horrendous.'

'He really was,' Bea groaned, rubbing her temples.

'And you've still got that volunteer job at the library, right? You're enjoying that?'

'Yeah,' said Bea, mustering a weak smile. As soon as she'd

arrived back in Sussex, Bea had wasted no time in signing up to volunteer at her local library. Her three-hour weekend shift there was the highlight of her week.

'That's something, then,' said Jess with enthusiasm.

'I guess,' said Bea, downing another shot.

'Hey, go easy,' said Jess. 'You don't want to do something you'll regret.'

'I already have,' said Bea, her voice hollow, 'I've quit my job, remember?'

'Good point,' said Jess, nodding. 'Well, you don't want to do anything *else* you'll regret. I think the job thing is enough for one day. Why don't you give the temp agency a call? I'm sure they can find you something else.'

'Good idea,' said Bea, squinting at her phone before dropping it onto the floor with a thud.

'Maybe,' said Jess, scooping up the phone, 'wait until the morning, when you're more . . .'

'Sober?'

'Exactly. There's no rush, is there?'

'No, it can wait. Brendan's probably already told them I'm useless.'

'Do you want to come back to mine and we can make a plan? You can figure out what to say to your parents?'

'Yes, please,' said Bea, fishing the keys out of her purse. 'Can we stop off for supplies?'

'Supplies?'

'If we're making a plan, we'll need the essentials: wine, crisps *and* chocolate!'

'Whatever you say.'

'You have to eat the chocolate *and* the crisps at the same time, though. And it has to be cheese and onion.'

'If I have to,' Jess nodded, helping Bea up from her seat. 'Maybe we should get you some coffee too?'

'I knew there was a reason I liked you, Jess Harrison,' Bea slurred, taking her friend's arm. 'You're one of the good ones.'

'Oh, don't worry, I know,' said Jess, steadying Bea as she stumbled towards the door.

'What shall we have next? Bea asked, looking at the selection of bottles lined up on Jess's kitchen counter. 'Tequila or vodka?'

'God, not more tequila, it's disgusting,' said Jess, pulling a face.

'We should eat something,' said Bea, pulling apart a family-sized bag of crisps and throwing them into a bowl. 'Line our stomachs.'

'I think it's a bit late for that,' said Jess, lying back on the sofa. 'The damage is well and truly done.'

'It can't hurt,' laughed Bea, setting the crisps on the coffee table and sitting down. 'I've seen a TikTok that will change your life,' she continued, opening a slab of Dairy Milk. 'The trick is to eat it at the same time, like this,' she said, shoving a couple of squares of chocolate into her mouth along with a handful of crisps. 'It shouldn't work, but it does,' she said through a mouthful.

'Here, let me,' said Jess, doing the same. 'Oh my god, that's amazing,' she said, closing her eyes. 'How have we never done this before?'

'I know, right?' Bea nodded, taking another handful.

'Who came up with this idea?'

'Who knows? But it's all over TikTok.'

'Well, whoever it was, it's delicious. Good spot, Bea, you're a genius!'

'I am, aren't I? Far too good for the likes of Brendan!' said Bea, puffing out her chest.

'Exactly,' said Jess, raising a glass.

'You know, he reminded me a bit of Trunchbull . . .'

'Trunchbull?'

'Miss Trunchbull? From *Matilda*?' said Bea, nudging her friend gently. 'The awful headmistress, remember?' Bea loved comparing people to characters from the stories she adored, especially the horrible ones.

'Ah, yeah! God, he sounded awful!' said Jess.

'I know, I should have quit ages ago . . .' said Bea, thinking about how much Jess reminded her of Amy March from *Little Women*: artistic and kind, sassy and fiercely loyal. Yes, Jess was definitely an Amy through and through.

'Well, you've done it now, that's the main thing.'

'I have, haven't I? It feels . . .' Bea paused, trying to find the right word, '*liberating*.'

'God, I wish I'd been there. I'd have loved to have seen the look on his face.'

'It was priceless,' said Bea, smiling. 'He tried to fire me, but I'd already quit – in front of the whole office, too!'

'That took guts, Bea, I'm proud of you,' said Jess, pulling her into a hug. 'You were too good for that job.'

'I was.' She slumped back into the sofa cushions and took another sip of her drink. 'Although . . .'

'What?'

'What am I going to do now?' she said, panic rising in her chest.

'Well . . .'

'Jess, what the *hell* am I going to do?' Bea asked, bolting upright, clutching one of the cushions desperately. 'Mum and Dad are going to be fuming. What am I going to say to them?' Her breathing was speeding up, her alarm evident.

'Bea,' said Jess, taking her by the shoulders, 'you're panicking. Take some deep breaths,' she said, modelling breathing in and out slowly. Bea followed suit.

'Okay,' she nodded, blowing out a long, deep breath.

'There, that's better,' said Jess, encouragingly. 'How are you feeling now?'

'Better, thanks. Sorry, today's been a lot.'

'I get it. It'll be fine though, Bea, I promise.'

'Actually, I had an idea recently . . . you'll think it's silly, though . . .' Bea said, shaking her head.

'Course I won't. Go on, tell me!'

'Okay,' said Bea, taking another deep breath, 'I was thinking about setting up an online shop, selling books. A bricks-and-mortar bookshop would be my dream, but I guess I never thought it was . . . *realistic*, so publishing seemed the most obvious path to take,' she shrugged.

'I tried applying for bookshop jobs in London, too ... Waterstones, Foyles, loads of independents, but even that was super competitive.'

'Okay,' said Jess, sitting up straight. 'Well, you've always been book-*obsessed*, I can totally see you doing that.'

'Can you?' said Bea, hesitating. She hadn't given the idea much serious thought, but perhaps she should? 'So, I was thinking about having a stall at local fairs ...'

'And?'

'Well, I was at the farmer's market the other day and they had one of those coffee bars – a converted horsebox, I think it was – and I was wondering, well ...' She breathed in deeply. 'What if I did the same, only with books?'

'A mobile bookshop?' asked Jess, setting down her glass.

'Yeah, exactly.'

Jess stared back at her for a moment.

'It's a mad idea, isn't it?' said Bea, shaking her head.

'Mad? Absolutely not!' said Jess, seriously. 'I think it's bloody brilliant!'

'You *do*?'

'God, yes! It's a great idea! You should totally do it!'

'Really?'

'*Definitely*! There's nothing like that around here. It would have a real novelty-factor too—'

'That's what I was thinking,' said Bea, animatedly. 'I could travel to all the local villages – none of them have bookshops – and there'd be no rent to pay, not like with a high street shop. What's the worst that could happen?'

'Exactly! If it didn't work, you'd just pack up and move on to the next place. What have you got to lose?

'That's what I thought,' said Bea, buzzing with excitement. 'I've got some savings – how much could a horsebox cost anyway?'

'There's only one way to find out,' said Jess, grabbing her laptop, '*eBay*!'

'I could get an old one and do it up,' said Bea.

'I'll help. I could design your logo and paint it across the sides; give it a proper glow-up,' said Jess, spreading her arms wide. 'Whatever you like!'

'Let's have a look,' said Bea, tapping away at the keyboard.

'How much are they?' Jess asked, peering across at the screen.

'Hmmmm . . . more than I thought,' said Bea, her face falling a little.

'Yeah, but those have already been done up, look for the ones that haven't.'

'Cheaper . . . *much* cheaper,' Bea said, scrolling down the page. 'Hang on, this one looks good,' she continued, tilting the laptop towards Jess. 'It needs work, but it looks pretty sturdy.'

'There you go! It says it's perfect for a conversion, too. Can you afford it?'

'Barely,' said Bea, biting her lower lip. 'It'll wipe out most of my savings, but I'd have a bit left to give it a revamp and buy some stock. Just think how cute it would look with a pretty, pastel paint-job and some fairy lights around the door!

I could have beanbags inside and macramé on the walls. It would be *dreamy*,' she swooned, lost in the picture she was creating in her mind.

'You only live once!'

'Exactly, and I am here for it!' Bea said, her mouse hovering over the *buy it now* button.

She hesitated.

Was this complete madness? She'd given the idea no real thought, and here she was, about to sink every penny she had into buying a beaten-up horsebox. But she had to do *something* to get herself unstuck. She didn't have a job right now, anyway, so what was there to lose?

She had to be brave.

She took a large swig of her drink. 'I'm doing it!' she said, decisively, clicking her mouse and completing the sale in an instant. 'There! Done!'

'This calls for a celebration,' cheered Jess. 'More tequila!'

'Yes! I'll put some tunes on!'

As they danced around the living room, 'I Gotta Feeling', by the Black Eyed Peas, blasting out at full volume, Bea relished the fact she was now the proud – if terribly drunk – owner of a pre-owned horsebox.

CHAPTER 2

Bea woke early the next morning with light flooding through her bedroom window. She shoved her pounding head back underneath the pillow.

'Oh, God,' she groaned, her mouth parched. She reached out to feel around for a glass of water on the bedside table. '*Eurgh*,' she grunted, massaging her forehead. Exactly how much had she drunk last night? The last thing she remembered was dancing around Jess's living room to 'I Gotta Feeling'.

She rubbed her eyes and pulled herself up into a sitting position. '*Oh, God,*' she whispered, as she remembered she'd quit her job yesterday. What had she been thinking?

She could hear her parents moving about in the kitchen downstairs, and a knot formed in her stomach. There was a muffled cry of '*See you later, love,*' shouted upstairs to her as the front door clicked shut behind them. It was Friday morning; her parents were off to bowls club.

She slumped back down on the bed. How on earth was she going to tell them? she wondered.

Bea's duvet was strewn with empty bags of crisps, and her laptop, which was still running, was covered in cheese puffs.

'Jeez,' she groaned, stretching an arm out towards it. The screen sprang to life. *eBay?* She hardly used the auction site anymore, not since she'd made a spur-of-the-moment drunk purchase and ended up with a dozen copies of *It's A Wonderful Life* on DVD in the middle of August.

She clicked into her account to look at her purchase history.

What?

She rubbed her eyes and looked again. It must be a mistake, it had to be. She hadn't been *that* drunk last night, surely?

Bea refreshed the page. It made no difference, the purchase from yesterday was still there, clear as day.

11.37pm Vintage Double Horsebox Trailer in need of refurbishment / Perfect for food truck conversion. £2500.

No, no, no, no, no! It *had* to be a mistake. An amount like that would wipe out her savings; she'd have almost nothing left. She didn't even own a car to tow the damn thing, for God's sake! She'd have to email the seller and get the transaction cancelled, get her money back. It'd be fine. No need to panic.

But just then, a scene from last night flashed in her head. She was sat on the sofa with Jess, who was telling her what a great idea it was: a mobile bookshop she could take on the road …

A mobile bookshop? Is that what she'd intended the horsebox for? Sure, she'd *thought* about it after she'd seen that converted one at the farmer's market, but she wouldn't actually *buy* one. That would be crazy, wouldn't it?

She pushed the laptop away and sank back into her pillows. Her head was thumping; she couldn't think.

Exasperated, she hauled herself up and padded down to the kitchen, found a box of paracetamol and swigged a couple down with a glass of water. If she could just clear her head, perhaps that would help her to remember exactly what had happened last night.

Her mum had left a note on the kitchen table: *Gone to bowls, see you later. Can you unload the dishwasher?*

She'd have to call Jess. Hopefully, she could shed some light on the eBay situation.

Bea refilled her glass with water and headed back upstairs, settling herself under the covers. Jess picked up after a few rings, sounding even worse than Bea felt.

'Hello?'

'Jess, it's me,' said Bea.

'Why are you awake already? I feel terrible.' Jess croaked. 'How much did we drink last night?'

'*Way* too much judging by my purchase history on eBay.'

'What are you talking about?'

'Did I say anything last night about a horsebox?'

'Oh, yeah,' said Jess, slowly, 'you were going on about that for ages. You'd seen a food truck in Rye, and you said it would be the perfect way to sell books. I thought it was a great idea—'

'I've bought one.'

'What?'

'A horsebox.'

There was silence down the line.

'Jess? Are you still there?'

'Bloody hell, Bea!'

'I know.'

'How much was it?'

'Two and a half grand.'

'*How* much?' Jess gasped.

'That's nearly all my savings gone.'

'Christ! What are you going to do?'

'Try and get my money back, obviously. The seller's in Blossom Heath . . . Millcroft Stables.'

'No way!' said Jess, 'that's Charlotte's place.'

'Who's Charlotte?'

'She's lovely. Comes in the shop all the time. I used to go riding at her stables when I was a kid.'

'Do you think she'll give me my money back?'

Jess paused before answering.

'Maybe, but . . .'

'What?'

'What if it's not actually a bad idea?'

'Spending my life savings on a wreck of a horsebox – yeah that sounds like a genius plan,' said Bea, her voice laced with sarcasm.

'But what if it's a sign, Bea? You've always wanted your own bookshop.'

'But I don't know anything about running a business, it was just a drunk, spur-of-the-moment idea—'

'And sometimes those are the best kind!'

'I don't know, Jess . . .'

'The stables are literally just down the road, Bea, that can't be a coincidence—'

'So, what, you think it's all part of some grand plan that the universe has for me?'

'Yes? Maybe? Oh, I don't know . . . but manifesting is a real thing, loads of people are into it.'

'I'm not sure drunk-buying a horsebox is the same thing.'

'All I'm saying is, why don't we go and have a look. Talk to Charlotte. You might regret it if you don't.'

'But where would I even keep a horsebox, let alone refurbish it? It looks like it needs tons of work; I wouldn't know where to start. And I'll need to buy stock too, I don't even own a car to tow it either.'

'Hmmmmm . . .' said Jess, thoughtfully. 'Who do I know that's good with their hands and has tons of storage space, *acres* of it in fact . . . Nathan!'

Nathan Chambers was Bea's childhood boyfriend. They'd met at secondary school and dated right through to the final year of sixth form. He lived and worked at Three Acre Farm on the outskirts of Blossom Heath. He'd been her Dawsey Adams, a farmer with a poetic soul, just like in *The Guernsey Literary and Potato Peel Pie Society*. She'd thought they'd be together forever, but life had other plans.

'Jess, no,' said Bea.

'I'm sure he'd be happy to help, he's a good friend and you've been hanging out loads since you got back from London.'

'Don't you dare, Jess.'

'Too late, I've already sent him a text.'

'Jess!' Bea shrieked, as she heard the ping of Jess's phone.

'He said yes! We've just got to let him know when to meet us at Charlotte's.'

'Oh, for fuck's sake, Jess!'

'You email Charlotte and find out if we can go over there today.'

'Can I have time to get over my hangover first?'

'Of course, I'm not a monster. I've got a good feeling about this, though, Bea, I really have.'

'I wish I could say the same,' replied Bea and, as she hung up the phone, she was pretty sure that the queasy sensation in her belly wasn't entirely due to how much tequila she'd drunk last night . . .

When they pulled into the yard at Millcroft Stables later that day, Bea saw a woman she assumed must be Charlotte, in the courtyard, brushing down a handsome chestnut stallion.

'I hope you're right about this,' Bea whispered to Jess as they got out of the car.

'Hi, Jess!' called Charlotte, looking up. 'And you must be Bea,' she said, striding across the yard towards them.

'I am,' said Bea, smiling nervously. 'Thanks for finding time to see us today, I hope my message made sense.'

'I'm guessing the horsebox was an impulse buy?' said Charlotte.

'Drunk buy, more like,' said Jess.

'Jess!' said Bea, nudging her friend in the ribs.

'It's fine,' said Charlotte, 'it's a lot of money, I totally understand that you'd want to see it in person. If it's not right for you, I'll cancel the sale, no problem.'

'That's really generous of you, thanks, Charlotte,' said Bea, beaming at her.

'Here's Nathan,' said Jess, gesturing towards the old Land Rover that was pulling into the yard.

'Morning, all,' said Nathan, brushing his floppy brown hair out of his eyes. 'So, you've bought a horsebox, eh?' he said, beaming broadly at Bea.

'Why don't I take you to see it? It's in the back field,' said Charlotte.

'That would be great,' said Bea. 'Thank you.'

They followed a path through paddocks filled with horses swishing their tails and flicking their ears in the morning sun.

'Aw, they're gorgeous,' said Bea, as she reached out to pat a pretty, grey mare who had poked her nose through the wooden fencing. 'Are they all yours?'

'Duchess is,' said Charlotte, nodding towards the grey horse, 'but most of the others are here on livery, only six . . . no, five, are my own,' she continued, correcting herself.

'I was sorry to hear about what happened to Apollo,' said Jess, softly. 'He was a gorgeous boy.'

Charlotte had lost her champion stallion last year in an accident on the road, and it had hit her hard.

'Thanks, Jess,' said Charlotte, forcing a half-smile. 'I still miss him every day, but it's getting easier. Here we are,' she said, pointing to the next field, 'that's the horsebox.'

'Great, thanks,' said Bea, her heart sinking as they got closer.

This was what she'd spent her savings on? It was a wreck. The paintwork was cracked and peeling, there was moss growing out of its roof and rust around the wheel arches. It had most definitely seen better days.

'It needs a bit of work,' confirmed Charlotte, reading the look on Bea's face. 'It hasn't been used for a while, so it's just sat here gathering dust and moss by the looks of things, I'm afraid.'

'Well, you did list it as vintage,' said Bea, forcing a smile.

'Let me open it up so you can have a look inside,' said Charlotte, swinging open the doors and lowering the ramp.

'It's very roomy,' said Jess, encouragingly.

'It's got a divider to take two horses, but you can remove that easily, depending on what you're planning to use it for,' said Charlotte.

'And what exactly *are* you planning to use it for?' asked Nathan, raising his eyebrows.

'Promise you won't think I've gone completely mad?' said Bea.

'Depends . . .' said Nathan, looking serious.

'A mobile bookshop,' Bea blurted in one quick breath.

'A bookshop?' said Charlotte, eyes wide. 'Interesting.'

'But what about your job?' asked Nathan.

'Bea quit yesterday,' said Jess.

'What?' said Nathan, his head snapping in Bea's direction. 'You *quit*?'

'Erm . . . yeah,' Bea whispered.

'Why don't I leave you guys to it?' said Charlotte. 'Take a look around, have a think, and come and find me back at the yard when you're done.'

'Great, thanks,' said Bea.

'Wow, quitting's a brave move,' said Nathan, turning to face her.

'I guess I'd had enough, Nate,' Bea shrugged. 'I just couldn't stick it anymore.'

'Hey, I'm not judging,' he said quickly, holding up his hands, 'you've gotta do what's right for you. So, the bookshop idea? How did that come about?'

'Well, I'd been thinking about opening an online store,' explained Bea. 'A sort of side hustle I suppose, and I thought maybe a mobile bookshop could work.'

'Right, okay . . .' said Nathan.

'And then I got really drunk with Jess last night and woke up to find that I'd bought a horsebox to turn into a bookshop. *Ta-dah!*' she said, sweeping her arms out in front of her.

'Wow, that upscaled fast,' Nathan laughed.

'So, what do you think?' said Bea, looking at him.

'What do *I* think?' said Nathan. 'How am I involved in this exactly?'

'Well, look at the state of it.' Jess chimed in. 'Do you think Bea's going to be able to turn this into a bookshop on her own?'

'No,' said Nathan, flatly.

'And who do we know that's handy, local and has loads of space to store it while it's being converted?' Jess asked.

'Don't feel like you have to say yes,' Bea said, quickly. 'But you know more about this kind of stuff than I do, Nate. Is it possible, do you think? I mean it *looks* pretty dire to me.'

'Well,' said Nathan, circling the horsebox slowly. 'It's mostly cosmetic, I think,' he said, stepping inside and bouncing up and down. 'The structure feels solid,' he continued, tapping the walls.

'Really?' said Bea, excitement bubbling up in her stomach.

'And we could store it at the farm, no bother. I've got a spare barn,' said Nathan.

'Did you say *we*?' asked Bea. 'Does that mean you'll help?'

'Of course I'll help,' said Nathan, his face splitting into a grin.

'Are you sure?'

'I *want* to, okay? I can't sell books, but I can help with the refit of this, no problem,' said Nathan.

'And how long will it take, do you think?' asked Jess.

'Hmmmm . . .' he said, thoughtfully. 'A few weeks, maybe? If we do it in the evenings and weekends, you'll be surprised how quickly it'll come together.'

'That soon? Wow! Thanks, Nate, that's amazing,' said Bea, throwing her arms around his neck and squeezing him hard.

'My pleasure,' said Nathan, his cheeks colouring. 'How are you going to tow it, though? Have you forgotten that you don't actually own a car?'

'I've got a plan: I'm going to ask Archie if I can use his – he barely uses it, it's just sat on his driveway,' said Bea.

'Great idea!' said Jess.

'There's so much else to think about, though,' said Bea. 'I don't have a business plan, I've wiped out my savings and I've got no idea how to get started.'

'I know it seems like a lot,' said Jess. 'But you'll figure it out.'

'Do you think I could ask Tori at the Cosy Cat for some advice, Jess? She set up the cat café last year, didn't she? I've only met her a few times, but you know her pretty well,' said Bea.

'I'm sure she'd be happy to help, I'll give you her number,' said Jess.

'I'll ask Charlotte if she'll give me a few days to think about it before I go ahead,' said Bea.

'She did say she'd cancel the sale if you're not sure, so I reckon she'll give you some leeway,' said Nathan.

'Looks like I've got a plan then!' said Bea. 'You know what, though? I think I might already have a name,' she said, nodding towards the trailer.

'What is it?' asked Jess.

'Bea's Book Wagon!' said Bea, looking at them expectantly.

'Ooooh, I love it!' said Jess, with a gasp of delight.

'You realize now it has a name you'll have to go through with it?' said Nathan.

'I'll start thinking about a logo, too,' said Jess, mulling it over. 'I'll get my sketchbook out when I get home.'

'Let's not get ahead of ourselves,' said Bea, seriously. 'This is all still hypothetical right now.'

'Hypothetical, yeah, right,' Jess sniggered. 'As if.'

'I've still got to talk to Mum and Dad – as far as they're concerned, I've still got a job at Hobbs & Partners!' said Bea. 'That's going to be a fun conversation.'

'Ah,' said Nathan. 'How do you think they'll take it?'

'God knows, but I don't think they're going to be happy,' Bea said, shaking her head.

But, as Bea walked back through the paddocks towards the stables, she realized that she'd already fallen more than a little in love with Bea's Book Wagon.

CHAPTER 3

Bea jumped out of Jess's car, before her friend was late for her shift at Harrison's, and hurried towards the one and only bus stop next to the village green. She glanced down at her watch: 4.03pm. She only had four minutes to wait for the bus back to Rye, to face the dreaded conversation with her parents.

In all the excitement at the stables, she'd almost managed to forget just how apprehensive she was about breaking the news to them that she'd quit her job.

Bea stuck out her arm when she saw the bus approaching, hopped on board, found a vacant seat and reached into her bag for her book. A bus journey meant only one thing: pure, uninterrupted reading time. Utter bliss.

She opened the pages of a pastel pink copy of Jane Austen's *Sense and Sensibility.* She'd lost count of how many times she'd read it, and owned several copies, but this one was a special edition with beautiful, gold-sprayed edges, which she hadn't been able to resist adding to her collection. Bea had stopped counting exactly how many books she owned years ago, her passion taking up most of the floor space in the tiny box room at her parents' house. She was always searching through crates at fairs and flea markets, and she'd found some real gems over the years. To say it had become a bit of an obsession was an understatement.

She found the page marked by a pretty boho bookmark and smiled to herself before starting to read. She was at one of her favourite parts of the story: the bit where, with Marianne's life hanging in the balance, Colonel Brandon sets off on horseback in search of her mother. It occurred to Bea that Colonel Brandon really was one of the most overlooked romantic heroes; he deserved far more credit than he got. Give her a Colonel Brandon over a Willoughby any day of the week.

Bea was yet to find her real-life Colonel Brandon. She'd split from Rory, the guy she'd been dating in London, four months ago. She'd thought things had been going well, so it was a shock when he'd ended their relationship, telling her things 'weren't that deep' between them.

There was a pattern to Bea's dating history, she realized: she'd meet someone, they'd *seem* perfect, she'd fall head over heels, but it never lasted for long.

It was all very ... *disappointing* when she thought about it.

She wasn't sure she'd ever really been in love. Not properly. Not in the way she read about in her favourite romance novels. The closest she'd ever come was with Nathan, although she wasn't sure that really counted. She was just a teenager when they'd dated and what she'd *thought* was love back then was more likely just a high-school crush. She wasn't giving up, though. She knew her Colonel Brandon was out there somewhere, she just had to find him . . .

The journey back to Rye passed all too quickly, the way time always did when Bea's nose was buried in a book, and just as Mrs Dashwood arrived safely at the Palmer's estate in Somerset, Bea was almost home.

As she reached out her hand to ding the stop button, it occurred to her that Austen's words rang true: 'It isn't what we say or think that defines us, but what we do'.

Bea was certainly doing something now and, as she walked the short distance home with a spring in her step, the clouds finally parted and she could feel the heat from the sun's rays warming her back.

'Bea? Is that you?' her mum, Carol, called from the kitchen. 'Dinner's ready!'

'Okay,' she said, bending down to fuss the family dog, an exuberant Cavalier King Charles Spaniel, who was rushing towards her. 'How's your morning been, Wordsworth?' she said, stroking his long ears fondly.

'Bea! Dinner!' Carol called again.

'Yep. Coming!' she called back, following the scent of sausages that was wafting through from the kitchen, Wordsworth trotting along beside her.

'It's toad in the hole,' said Carol, spooning out a generous helping. 'Can you grab the gravy boat?'

'Sure,' replied Bea, taking it from the dresser.

'This is a treat,' said Gordon, her dad, stealing a roast

potato from one of the plates and shoving it into his mouth. 'Ow, that's hot,' he moaned.

'That'll teach you,' teased Carol. 'So, where have you been all day?' she asked Bea, placing a steaming plate of food in front of her husband.

'Let's eat, first,' said Bea, her voice jangling with nerves.

'Oh, why? What's happened?' Carol asked, concern etched on her face.

'Well, I've got some news,' said Bea, pulling out the chair next to her dad, who was already busy tucking into his supper. 'Shall I get some wine?' she asked, grabbing a bottle of red and pouring out three glasses.

'Wine? We don't usually—' said Carol.

'Let's make an exception,' interrupted Bea. 'Like I said, I've got news.'

'Don't mind if I do,' said Gordon, taking a swig from his glass.

'Well,' said Bea, inhaling deeply. 'It's about my job—'

'You've found something else, finally? That's great news, love. I know how much you hate it there,' said Carol.

'Yeah, I did hate it,' said Bea. This was it . . . time to come clean.

'Hang on. Did you say *did*?' Carol asked. 'Past tense? You haven't quit before finding something else, have you?' said Carol, putting down her knife and fork.

'Well . . . sort of,' said Bea, screwing up her face.

'What do you mean *sort of*? You've either quit or you haven't?' said Gordon.

'I've quit,' said Bea. 'I had to, Brendan was—' said Bea.

'A bully?' said Carol 'From everything you've told us, that's how I'd describe him.'

'Yes,' said Bea, hanging her head.

'And you didn't feel like you could stick with it? Until you'd found something else at least?' asked Gordon.

'No,' said Bea, shaking her head determinedly. 'Not after the way he spoke to me yesterday.'

'Well, I hope you told him where to shove his job, he sounds like an awful little man. You'll find something else soon enough,' said Carol.

'Good on you for standing up for yourself, love. Even if it does mean you're unemployed!' said Gordon, patting her hand.

'Well . . .' said Bea slowly. 'I've kinda got a plan.'

'How exciting!' said Carol. 'What is it?'

'I'm going to open a mobile bookshop in a horsebox,' Bea blurted out in one breath.

'A mobile what?' said Gordon.

'Bookshop,' said Bea.

'In a horsebox?' said Carol.

'I know it sounds mad, but,' Bea paused, her beaded bracelets rattling on her wrist, 'one was up for sale in Blossom Heath, someone Jess knows, and it was too good an opportunity to miss. I really think I can make a go of it; I want to try to, at least . . .' Bea paused, studying her parents' expressions to try to gauge their reactions.

'Well,' said Gordon, pushing his plate away. 'I wasn't expecting that.'

'Me neither,' Carol agreed, taking a large sip of wine. 'I know you love books, but your own business . . . it's a big risk.'

'I know it seems like this has come out of nowhere, believe me I get it, I'm as shocked as you are. But I've been trying to figure out what I'm meant to do for so long. All those failed interviews, trying to get into publishing . . . I never managed it, but I think, well, maybe this is it?' said Bea. 'I don't think I've ever felt quite so excited about anything, ever.'

They sat in silence for a few minutes.

'Well,' said Carol, after a long pause. 'It's your life, love, you've got to do what feels right.'

'If it's what you really want, Bea . . .' said Gordon.

'Seriously? You're not annoyed?' said Bea, relief coursing through her.

'Annoyed? Why would we be? You're not a child anymore, Beatrice. You're old enough to make your own decisions,' said Carol.

'And that means taking responsibility for them, even the bad ones. If it doesn't work out, you'll need to think about what you're doing to do,' said Gordon.

'Oh, I will. And I don't want you to worry about money either. I've got the temp agency as a back-up, so I can still keep paying rent,' said Bea.

'Pleased to hear it,' said Gordon, the lines creasing his forehead softening.

'Well, I propose a toast. To Bea and her bookshop!' said Carol, raising her glass.

'To Bea's horsebox,' said Gordon, clinking his glass against hers.

'To Bea's Book Wagon,' said Bea, finally, relief washing over her.

Although her parents had reacted to her news far better than she'd expected, Bea couldn't get her dad's words out of her head: she needed to take responsibility for her own decisions, *even the bad ones.* She just hoped that her decision to open a mobile bookshop wasn't going to be something she'd live to regret.

CHAPTER 4

Bea had arranged to meet Tori from the Cosy Cat Café for a drink at the Apple Tree on Monday evening. She'd spent the weekend researching business costs, running numbers and trying to come up with some kind of plan. Finance wasn't her thing, but she'd put her heart and soul into formulating options that would make Bea's Book Wagon a reality. She hoped Tori could help hone her ideas, one female entrepreneur supporting another.

'Bea, hi!' said Tori, as she approached the bar.

'Tori, hi! Can I get you a drink?' Bea asked, pulling her purse out of her bag.

'A negroni would be great, thanks.'

'Delicious! Can you make that two, please, Pete?'

'Sure,' said Pete, the landlord, taking two glasses and mixing their drinks.

'Thanks so much for doing this, I really appreciate it,' said Bea warmly.

'No problem,' replied Tori, waving a hand, 'I'm intrigued to hear all about this business proposal of yours. I'm no expert, but if I can help, I will.'

'I just want to pick your brain, really,' said Bea, paying for their drinks and heading for one of the window tables.

'Pick away,' said Tori, pulling up a chair opposite her.

'I love the Cosy Cat Café, you've done such a great job with it,' said Bea, taking a sip of her cocktail. 'All the cats are up for adoption, aren't they?'

'Yeah, we work with Izzy at New Beginnings Rescue Centre to try to find them their forever homes, and Grace at Brook House Vets helps with all the medical stuff.'

'I love that!'

'Thanks, it works well. We've rehomed over forty cats since we opened last year.'

'That's amazing,' said Bea.

'We do our best, but enough about that – fill me in on this business idea of yours. I'm dying to know all about it!' said Tori, leaning in.

'It's all been a bit of a bolt out of the blue really,' said Bea, quickly, 'I'm not sure I've thought it through properly, if I'm honest. There's so much to think about: budgets, logistics, insurance . . . I don't really know what I'm doing—'

'Bea,' said Tori, softly.

'Yes?'

'Why don't you take a breath and start at the beginning?'

'Sorry, yes, I'm rambling . . .' said Bea, flushing.

'Not at all, just take your time and tell me everything,' said Tori, encouragingly.

Bea explained the events of the past few days, from quitting her job to buying the horsebox. She showed Tori some screenshots of other mobile bookshops she'd found online and explained her vision for making Bea's Book Wagon a success.

'Looks like you've put a lot of thought into this, given the time you've had,' said Tori, scanning the images on Bea's phone. 'These look great!'

'I know, right? I'm hoping to create something similar, but there's so much to consider and I don't really know where to start. I know it's not the same thing – a bookshop and a cat café – but I thought you might be able to tell me about some of the basics of running a small business?'

'It can all feel a bit overwhelming when you're just getting started, can't it?'

'Yes, exactly!' Bea nodded. 'Jess mentioned that you've got a business degree, too, so that must've been helpful?'

'It was and it wasn't,' Tori laughed, taking a sip of her cocktail. 'I knew where to start when it came to putting together a business plan, but the animal welfare regulations were a lot to get my head around, and then I had to get Izzy at the rescue on board with the idea, too, not to mention the rest of the village. Not everyone was keen on the idea of a cat café at first . . .'

'Gosh, that's an awful lot to sort out,' said Bea. 'I hadn't really thought about that.'

'Well, of course we already had Mum's premises and an established café business, but I've got a business plan template I can email to you – that'll be a good starting point.'

'That would be great, thank you.'

'Considering you only came up with the idea on Friday, I'd say the fact you're already starting to get organized is pretty good going.'

'Really?' said Bea, eyes wide. 'I wasn't sure if it was a total madcap idea and I was wasting my—'

'Bea?'

'Yes?'

'Would you take a compliment?'

'Sorry,' Bea replied with a shy smile.

'And Bea?'

'Yes?'

'Stop apologizing.'

'Ah, right, yes . . . sorry. Oh, I mean—'

'Don't worry,' Tori smiled. 'It's fine. And as for it being a madcap idea . . .'

'Yes?' Bea whispered.

'You're talking to someone who opened a cat café, remember? I'm not sure it gets much more madcap than that,' Tori laughed.

'I suppose I'm in good company, then,' Bea chuckled.

She liked Tori. There was something about her that made Bea feel instantly calmer, her initial nerves about sharing her plans completely evaporating. Tori reached over to peer at Bea's phone again.

'Can I see the photos again?' Tori asked.

'I've got so many ideas. I love this one here,' Bea said, holding the screen up. 'It's got artificial flowers around the door – and look at the bunting they've used in this one,' she said, swiping through the gallery of images she'd curated. 'They've really inspired me,' she paused.

'I can see that,' said Tori, 'these all look pretty special.'

'Right? I've been thinking about my life a lot recently. I don't have a job, a mortgage, boyfriend, kids . . . any real responsibilities. I know buying the horsebox was an impulse, but I feel like this is it – my moment, I suppose – and if it doesn't work out, what's the worst that can happen? I get another job and I'm back where I started. I've got nothing to lose.'

'You should be proud of yourself,' said Tori, raising her glass. 'You're doing your own thing, not answering to anybody, escaping the nine-to-five for something you're obviously passionate about. How many people can say that?'

'I suppose so,' Bea agreed, clinking her glass against Tori's. 'To taking risks!'

'It's not going to be easy, though,' said Tori, her voice softening. 'Running a business is tough, and starting from scratch on your own is even tougher. It was bad enough for me and I had Mum's help; I wasn't alone.'

'Ah, yes, I see.'

'I'm sorry if that sounds harsh, Bea, but it can be pretty brutal at times.'

'No, I get it, I appreciate the honesty. That's why I wanted to talk to you.'

'Would you be up for getting another temp job, to tide you over financially in the short term?'

'Yes, absolutely. I'm going to need to. I'm planning to work on the horsebox in my evenings and weekends at first, so I'll need another income for a while. I was going to speak to the agency next week to see if they can find me something else.'

'Well, I could do with another pair of hands at the café. Mum's been wanting to take things more slowly recently; start easing herself into retirement. We were thinking about finding some cover so she could scale back her hours, so perhaps we could help each other out? Temporarily, at least.'

'Wow! I don't know what to say, Tori, that would be amazing!'

'It might not be a permanent thing, but we're always super busy in the summer, so how does thirty hours a week sound?'

'It sounds fantastic! Honestly, Tori, I don't know how to thank you.'

'It's my pleasure, you're helping us out. Mum's been wanting to work less hours for ages.'

'I'd better phone Charlotte and tell her I'll be taking the horsebox, then.'

'No time like the present,' said Tori. 'You make the call, and I'll get us another round,' she said. 'Same again?'

'Ooh, yes, please! Although two's my limit tonight – who knows what else I'll buy on eBay if I have one too many.'

'Ha! Good one!' laughed Tori as she headed for the bar.

As Bea swigged down the last of her negroni, she felt

happier than she had in months. Between buying the horsebox and landing a job at the Cosy Cat, she was going to be doing something with her life, finally. And she knew, deep down in the pit of her stomach, that after all the failed interviews and dreadful temp jobs, she was going to make it work – and that was *huge.*

'You're kidding,' said Jess, when Bea called her that evening. 'I can't believe you're going to be working at the Cosy Cat. Oh, Bea, I'm so happy for you!'

'I'm so thankful you hooked me up with Tori in the first place. I hoped she'd give me some advice, but I never expected to get a job out of it!'

'I'm just so pleased she can give you a bit of a helping hand. It's perfect and it gives you loads of time to work on the horsebox.'

'I spoke to Charlotte as soon as I left Tori's and confirmed the transaction. Nate's going to take me over there tomorrow to pick it up.'

'It's really happening!'

'I know, I can't quite believe it!'

'Are you excited?'

'Excited, terrified, overwhelmed . . . I've got all the feels.'

'I bet. It's all good though, Bea. And if you need me to lend a hand with a paintbrush, just shout.'

'Thanks, I will! I'm planning to make a start at the weekend after my shift at the library. My mind's literally buzzing with to-do lists and ideas.'

'Mobile bookshop owner, barista, librarian – I'm so proud of you, Bea!'

'Thank you!'

'Have you told Archie about it yet? What does he make of it all? I'm assuming he knows you've quit your job?'

'I don't think so. He's coming over tomorrow as well, so I'll fill him in then. I'm hoping I can rope him and his mates in to help if I need it—'

'Ooooh, tell him to bring Seb along, he's hot.'

'Jess!'

'What? He is!'

'Honestly!'

'Well, it sounds like everything's coming together nicely.'

'I just hope I haven't missed something fundamental that could ruin it all . . .'

'Course not, everything's going to be great!' said Jess, reassuringly. 'You're bound to feel a bit nervous, it's only natural.'

'You're right,' said Bea, nodding in agreement. 'I'm just overthinking things, that's all. It's going to be wonderful.' And, as the words left her mouth, Bea knew that she really did believe them.

CHAPTER 5

Bea walked up the steps to the library on Saturday morning, ready for her monthly shift with a smile on her face. She really did love this place. She could hear the chatter of excited voices coming from the children's section; the toddler Rhymetime class was underway and the kids were singing along to 'Hickory Dickory Dock'.

'Bea, hi!' said Matt, the manager, spotting her as she walked through the doors. He was the nicest boss to work for. *Nothing like Brendan . . .*

'Hiya,' said Bea brightly, stashing her handbag under the counter.

'How's things?'

'Good, thanks. It's been a hectic week.'

'So I've heard. Carol's been telling me all about your plans for a mobile bookshop – I think it's a wonderful idea!'

'You do?'

'Oh, absolutely. The mobile library barely meets demand, and we don't even have a bookshop around here. I can't wait to see it! You'll have to let me know when you've booked your first event – I'll be there!'

'Thanks, Matt.'

'I've got some paperwork to catch up with,' said Matt, 'so just shout if you need me. I'll be in my office.'

'Will do.'

'Hang on, looks like you've got a customer,' said Matt, pausing, then nodding towards an elderly gentleman wearing an immaculate tweed jacket, heading for the desk. 'I'll just get these returns back on the shelves while you see to him,' he said, picking up the nearest stack of books and heading for the non-fiction section.

'Can I help?' Bea asked the man as he approached.

'Please. I'm trying to find a book, but for the life of me I can't remember the title,' he explained. 'I thought I'd written it down, but I'll be damned if I can find the piece of paper,' he said, patting down his pockets.

'No problem, do you know the author?'

'Erm . . .' he said, shaking his head. 'Afraid not. Goodness, what must you think of me? I'm not usually so disorganized.'

'Don't worry, we'll figure it out. Can you remember what it's about?'

'Ah! That I can do,' said the man brightly. 'It's a crime novel, been on television, not the regular channels, one of those other things . . .'

'Streaming channels? Netflix? Amazon Prime?'

'Prime, that's the one!' he said, clicking his fingers. 'I saw a bit of it at my son's, and thought I'd try the book. I've always preferred books to TV.'

'Me too,' Bea agreed, feeling a strong affinity with the man. 'Do you remember any of the actors or characters?'

'Erm . . . now you're asking,' he said, shaking his head. 'Big fella . . . huge,' he said, arms outstretched. 'I remember my son saying he looked like a wrestler?'

'Ah, I think I know who you mean,' said Bea. She pulled out her phone and tapped away. 'Is this him?' she asked, holding up a picture of Alan Ritchson as Jack Reacher.

'That's the chap!' the man replied, delightedly.

'You're in luck,' said Bea, beaming at him. 'It's a series by Lee Child. There are twenty-eight books in all, so you're spoilt for choice.'

'Twenty-eight!' replied the man, eyes wide. 'Goodness, I'm not sure I can commit to that many!'

'Why don't you start with book one and take it from there?'

'It's as good a place as any.'

'Take a seat,' said Bea, aware he was leaning more heavily on his walking cane, 'I'll find it for you.'

'Thank you, my dear,' he said, lowering himself into the chair by the desk. 'And call me Arthur,' he continued, handing her his library card.

'Nice to meet you, Arthur, I'm Beatrice, but everyone calls me Bea,' she said, warmly. 'I'm one of the volunteers here.

'Back in a jiffy,' she said, heading towards the crime fiction section.

She quickly found the book she was searching for: *Killing Floor.*

'Here we are,' she said, making her way back to Arthur. 'Book number one.'

'Excellent,' said Arthur, heaving himself up from his seat.

'Now, let me just check this out for you,' said Bea, scanning his library card into the system. 'There, all done,' she said, passing the book across the desk.

'Thank you, Bea,' said Arthur, tucking it into his shopping bag. 'One down, twenty-seven to go, eh?'

'Exactly,' Bea chuckled. 'I hope you enjoy it.'

'Oh, I'm sure I will. And thank you for your help.'

'It's my pleasure,' said Bea.

'Next time, I'll be sure to know what I'm looking for before I arrive.'

'Don't worry, that's what I'm here for.'

'See you next time, Bea,' said Arthur, making his way towards the door.

'I'll have book two ready and waiting,' she called after him as he threw her a wave of thanks. And, as Bea picked up a stack of books to return to the shelves, she knew her talent for finding exactly the right book, with very little to go on, was a skill she could put to good use in the bookshop.

Bea spent the afternoon after her shift back at home, going through the boxes of books she had accumulated over the years. She was short of space in her parents' box room, and most of her books were either packed away or stacked up in corners, which was such a shame as she had limited editions she'd love to have out on display.

'Bea!' Carol called up the stairs. 'Archie's here!'

'Okay, I'll be down in a sec,' she shouted, putting a rather well-thumbed copy of *The Time Traveller's Wife* back in the nearest box.

'Hiya, Sis,' said Archie, 'off out tonight?' he said, eyeing her faded denim dungarees.

'Not in these,' Bea laughed.

'I'm meeting Freddie and Josh at The George in a bit if you fancy it?' he said, dunking a biscuit into his tea.

'Not tonight, Arch, I'm going through some books, seeing what I've got—'

'You could do with a clear out, you've got hundreds stashed away up there,' said Carol.

'Who said anything about a clear out? I'm doing a stock take, that's all,' said Bea, defensively.

'Mum's been telling me about your horsebox idea. Sounds pretty cool,' he said, slurping his tea.

'I'm glad you think so, as I'm hoping I can borrow your car to tow it?' Bea asked. 'Just until I get myself sorted,' she added quickly.

'Sure,' Archie agreed.

'Cheers, Arch. What's been going on with you, anyway? It's been a while,' Bea asked.

'I'm having a bit of a nightmare, actually, I was just telling

Mum. Seb's moving out, so I need to find a new tenant asap as I can't afford the mortgage on my own.'

'He never was very reliable, that one,' said Carol.

'I know, I know, and thanks again for bailing me out all those times. I can't have the room empty, though, and I don't know anyone who wants to move in with a stranger,' said Archie.

'What about Josh or Freddie?' asked Carol.

'They'd be awful to live with. Josh is so untidy and Freddie's constantly hungover. Honestly, Arch, it would be carnage,' said Bea, shaking her head.

'True. I'll have to put an ad on Rightmove or something,' said Archie.

'What about me?' suggested Bea suddenly, her mind whirring.

'What about you?' asked Archie, looking confused.

'How would you feel about me moving in?' asked Bea.

'You?' Archie blinked. 'Move in with me? In Blossom Heath?'

'Why not?' said Bea, shrugging.

'Erm, you don't have a job, for one thing. How are you gonna pay the rent?' asked Archie.

'Tori's offered me a job at the Cosy Cat,' said Bea. 'Just while I'm getting the business up and running.'

'Has she?' said Archie, surprised.

'Yes, and I'll be able to afford the same rent I pay to Mum and Dad, which can go towards your mortgage. I need to start getting myself sorted, Arch. Be a grown up. And moving out again would be a step in the right direction.'

'Us? Live together, though?' said Archie, blowing out a breath. 'I don't know, wouldn't it be weird?'

'Why? We've lived together most of our lives and at least you know I'm tidier than Josh, even with my boxes of books everywhere,' said Bea grinning at him.

'True,' said Archie, thoughtfully.

'You'd have more space than you've got here too,' said Carol, 'Archie's spare room is twice the size of our box room.'

'Are you trying to get rid of me?' said Bea in faux outrage.

'No, of course not,' said Carol. 'But I know you want your independence again.'

'I'll miss your cooking, though, Mum,' said Bea, turning to look at Archie. 'What do you reckon, then? Can I move in?'

'As long as you can meet the rent. I can't afford to sub you, Bea,' said Archie, seriously.

'I will,' said Bea, solemnly. 'And I'll give you my staff discount at the Cosy Cat.'

'Go on, then,' said Archie, grinning. 'You're on!'

'Yes! I promise you won't regret it,' said Bea, throwing her arms around him. 'Oooh, I'll be walking distance from Jess.'

'And Nathan,' said Carol, pointedly. 'You'll be able to see more of him, too.'

'He's helping me with the refurb of the horsebox actually—'

'You know I always hoped the two of you might get back together one day,' Carol cut in, her eyebrows flicking upwards.

'We dated at school, Mum, we were just kids,' said Bea, shaking her head.

'He's such a lovely boy, though—'

'Mum! We're just friends, that's all,' said Bea, folding her arms.

'Yeah, Bea,' said Archie with a sly smile, 'it'd be great if you two—'

'You can pack that in,' said Bea, sharply, 'unless you want to start discussing your love life . . . who was it Jess saw you out with last weekend?'

'Point taken,' said Archie, clearing his throat.

'Anyway, when's Seb moving out?' asked Bea, keen to change the subject.

'Friday,' said Archie.

'So, I could move in next weekend?' said Bea.

'If you like,' said Archie, noncommittally.

'How wonderful! This calls for a celebration,' squealed Carol, turning to the fridge. 'I'm sure I've got some fizz in here somewhere.'

'Looks like I've got a new housemate, then,' said Archie with a smile.

'Looks like you have,' Bea agreed. 'Who'd have thought?'

'Now, Bea,' said Carol, popping the cork on a bottle of Cava, her eyes glinting mischievously, 'why don't you tell me who Jess saw Archie with . . .'

CHAPTER 6

Bea couldn't quite believe it. Within the space of a few days, she'd got a job at the Cosy Cat, was about to start her own business *and* she had a new place to live. And the best thing about all of it was that *she'd* made it happen. Admittedly, her decision to buy the horsebox had been fuelled by alcohol, but she was finally creating a future that excited her – what did it matter how she got there?

Charlotte Bronte's words in *Jane Eyre* felt pretty apt right now: 'And your will shall decide your destiny.'

Jess had been over the moon when Bea had told her about her move to Blossom Heath, and Nathan had offered to help on moving day.

'Surely that must be the last box?' Gordon shouted from the hallway, as Bea made her way downstairs.

'Erm . . . I think there's a couple more on the landing,' she said, sheepishly.

'I don't understand how all this has come out of that tiny room?' said Gordon, scratching his head. 'It's like a Tardis.'

'Ha! I wish,' said Bea, setting her suitcase down by the front door.

'It's all books,' said Carol, peering over the top of the box she was carrying.

'Wordsworth, will you get out of the way?' Gordon grabbed the little Cavalier's collar as he made to dart between Carol's legs. 'The last thing we need this morning is to trip over *you*.'

'Oh, that might be Nathan,' said Bea, as a horn sounded in the street outside.

'About time,' Gordon huffed. 'We could have done with his muscles half an hour ago.'

'All right, love,' said Carol, testily, 'he's doing Bea a favour.'

'Exactly, Dad. He didn't have to give up his Sunday morning to come and help,' said Bea.

'Thank God he did, we'd never get this lot in the back of the Fiat,' said Carol, eyeing the boxes.

'Nathan, hi!' said Bea, swinging open the front door. 'Thanks so much for helping!' She hugged him tightly.

'Steady on, I haven't done anything yet!' said Nathan, grinning widely at her. 'Wow! Is this all yours?' he asked, looking at the stack of boxes surrounding him.

'Erm . . . yeah,' said Bea. 'Sorry, I've got tons of stuff. If there's not enough room—'

'Oh, we'll get this lot in, no problem,' said Nathan,

bending down to fuss Wordsworth, who was jumping around giddily at his feet.

'Would you like a cuppa, Nathan?' offered Carol.

'Best not, Mrs Miller, I've got to get back for milking,' said Nathan.

'Oh, call me Carol. I'm putting the kettle on anyway, love, are you sure you don't want one?'

'Mum, if Nathan's busy then—'

'It's fine,' said Nathan, 'I can squeeze a quick cuppa in.'

Carol's 'quick cuppa' turned out to be closer to an hour, and Bea practically had to drag Nathan out the front door to escape.

'I'm so sorry about Mum,' Bea groaned, as they finally drove away from her parents' house. 'Honestly, you didn't have to answer all her questions, she's so nosy.'

'She'd fit right in in Blossom Heath; everyone knows everybody's business there,' Nathan chuckled.

'And I thought Rye was bad for gossip.'

'It's just village life, you'll get used to it.'

'I'm sure I will,' said Bea. 'I've not got any exciting secrets to uncover anyway . . .'

'I still can't believe it, you know,' said Nathan, glancing sideways to smile at her.

'Believe what?'

'You. Moving to Blossom Heath.'

'I know!' said Bea, returning his smile. 'I can't believe I'm moving in with Archie . . . we might kill each other by the end of the first week.'

'Ha! If you've survived living with both your parents these past few months, living with Archie will be a breeze.'

'True. Speaking of parents, how's your dad? Is his knee any better?'

'It's improving, but it's still slowing him down a bit. He's much less hands on at the farm these days.'

'Is it his seventieth soon?'

'Next year, yeah,' Nathan nodded.

'Ooooh, I meant to tell you,' she said. 'I saw your cheese in that posh deli in Rye. Mum won't buy anything else now.'

Nathan had started producing cheese a few years earlier to help boost the dwindling income from the dairy herd, and ever since business had been booming. His Blossom Heath Blue was a local favourite.

'Pleased to hear it. I never imagined it would take off so well, if I'm honest,' he said. 'We're stocked by some local restaurants and cafés now, too; I've got a regular order from the Cosy Cat.'

'Oooh, that's great! I guess I'll see you next time you deliver.'

'Of course! Jess told me you're going to be working there.'

'Tori's been a lifesaver, I couldn't have gone ahead with the book wagon without some regular cash coming in each month.'

'No, I get that. Tori's great. She's been really supportive of the cheese business. I can't believe how much she manages to sell!'

'I'm so proud of you, Nate,' said Bea.

'Of me?'

'Yes, you! What you're doing at the farm is amazing, and you love it, don't you? I can tell.'

'Of course, I wouldn't do it if I didn't.'

'I'll have to pick your brains about business stuff, too, Tori's given me some pointers, but you must know loads, what with the farm and the cheese business.'

'A bit,' he replied. 'I make most of it up as I go along, to be honest, but you can always ask.'

'Thanks. You know, I've always envied you a bit,' said Bea, sheepishly.

'Why?'

'Well, we're both twenty-seven and you've always known exactly what you were going to do with your life. And there was me, clueless, bouncing from one dead-end temp job to another.'

'That's different, though, Bea. I grew up on the farm, I always knew I'd take it on one day, there wasn't really anything to figure out.'

'Even so I—'

'And look at what you're doing today? Moving out again . . . that's a big step.'

'Technically, I'm moving out of my mum's to live at my brother's,' said Bea, with a half-smile.

'I'm still living with my parents, remember? You're one step ahead of me.'

'But—'

'And you're about to start your own business – that takes

courage. I should know, I started the cheese business from scratch.'

'But that's different—'

'Things are looking up for you, Bea, *trust me*,' said Nathan, nodding.

'Well, when you put it like that,' conceded Bea, 'who am I to argue?'

Bea spotted Jess as soon as she entered the pub on Tuesday evening. The Mermaid was one of her favourite places in Rye. Situated in the citadel, the six-hundred-year-old inn was full of so much history you could almost feel it pouring out of the walls. The landlord's tales of the ghosts that walked the hallways always sent shivers down her spine. Although many of the pub's overnight guests claimed to have encountered the Grey Lady or the twelfth-century monk that was supposed to pace the rooms, Bea had never seen or felt anything herself, which left her a little sceptical.

'Bea!' called Jess from one of the corner booths. 'I've got you a rum and coke.'

'Ah, lovely, thank you!' said Bea, pulling her friend into a hug.

'Thanks for coming into town. I had a meeting with a new client this afternoon and we've not been out in Rye for ages!'

'Don't be daft, I love The Mermaid. How's freelance life going?'

'Yeah, good, I think. I've been designing a few logos

and some corporate branding. My clients seem happy, so I'm hoping they'll recommend me to some other local businesses.'

'That's great, Jess. You're such a talented artist; I loved that logo you did for the Cosy Cat Café. The mural on the wall is stunning.'

'Thanks,' said Jess, blushing slightly. 'It's still early days, so I'm still working in the shop most of the time, in lieu of paying Mum any rent,' she laughed. 'How's things with you?' she asked, taking a sip of her drink. 'It's great your parents took the news about the wagon better than you expected.'

'I know, I can't believe it. They've been wonderful. I think Mum's quite excited about it to be honest.'

'Well, she is a librarian, so I'm not surprised,' said Jess.

'I hadn't really thought about it like that.'

'Have you heard anything from Rory?'

'Nope, nothing. My life in London feels like forever ago, really. We were so well-suited, I just don't get it,' Bea said, shaking her head.

'Well, you'd only known him a few months.'

'We were together for nearly six, actually!' Bea protested.

'That's *no* time. You think every guy you meet is your perfect romantic hero and fall head over heels in a hot minute.'

'I do not!'

'Oh, come on, Bea, you fall in love at the drop of a hat.'

'That's not true!'

'What about Dillon?'

'Well, Dillon was different,' said Bea, casting her mind back to the semi-pro footballer she'd dated last year. 'Things got really intense really quickly, that's all.'

'And Max?'

'That was different, too,' Bea insisted, 'I mean, we met on Valentine's Day, that had to be a sign.'

'It's a lot of pressure . . .'

'What is?'

'To live up to your high expectations. Not everyone can be a character from a romance novel. It's just not real life.'

'Who said I—'

'Come on, Bea.'

'Okay, you *may* have a point,' Bea conceded. 'I guess I'm just looking for my happy-ever-after; there's nothing wrong with that.'

'No, of course there isn't. You know what you want. Whereas I expect every man I meet to be a let-down,' Jess laughed.

'You're going to have to let your guard down one of these days.'

'Who says?'

'The universe? The law of attraction, I don't know. But one day, you're going to fall head over heels; it's bound to happen.'

'Not if I can help it,' said Jess, determinedly. 'Anyway, how's living with Archie again?' she asked, keen to change the subject.

'Good, I think. We haven't killed each other yet.'

'He's earning mega bucks, isn't he? What does he do again?'

'Don't ask me,' laughed Bea, 'software developer, I think. I know it's got something to do with coding, but I haven't got a clue, really.'

'You and me both,' agreed Jess.

'Well, we can't all be good at the same things, can we?' laughed Bea, 'Archie's the IT specialist and I'm the ...'

'Literature legend?'

'I was going to say flaky one, but literature legend sounds much better.'

'You are, though! I mean, the book wagon idea is so creative and really leans into your skills.'

'What do you mean?' asked Bea.

'Well, look at all the books you've persuaded me to read over the years. It's a real talent to convince people to try reading outside of their comfort zone. You even got Dad into that Ann Cleeves series, and I don't think I'd seen him read a book in years. He's totally hooked now.'

'Oh, I'm so pleased!' said Bea, her face illuminated with a smile. 'I'm glad he's enjoying them.'

'He absolutely is. Mum's loving it, too; she said she's never had so much peace and quiet. She's thinking of getting him a Kindle for his birthday.'

'You know,' said Bea, her drink held in mid-air, 'there might be something in that ...'

'In what?'

'Recommending books – like a dating service, only for your perfect *read* rather than your perfect *partner*.'

'Great idea! I'd prefer a date with Seb, if I'm honest, but I'd give a book a go, too.'

'It could be totally personalized – you tell me about your favourite reads, hobbies, movies, TV programmes, stuff like that, then I'd recommend a reading list to choose from, or send a surprise each month, or something, like a subscription service.'

'See? Totally creative! That sounds brilliant,' said Jess, raising her glass.

'It does, doesn't it?' said Bea, a smile edging onto her lips as she added the idea to the long list of points already on her business plan.

CHAPTER 7

When Bea and Nathan pulled into the lane leading to Three Acre Farm, the horsebox tethered behind them, rain was lashing down against the windscreen and Bea was struggling to see out of the jeep's windows.

'God, this weather is horrendous!' said Nathan, flicking the wipers up to full speed.

'I know, it's proper end-of-days weather!' Bea agreed, leaning back against the headrest.

'Good thing we picked her up today, the forecast's even worse tomorrow and that lane up from the stables always floods.'

'Not more rain, surely? It's been raining all week.'

'There's an amber flood warning out for the whole county.'

'Seriously?'

'Uh-huh.'

'I know it's not quite April but I thought it was supposed to be April *showers* not April *monsoons*.'

'Ha!'

'Well, luckily I don't have much planned for tomorrow. I'm looking after Wordsworth for Mum and Dad, so as long as I can get out for a walk at some point, I can spend the rest of the day finishing off my business plan.'

'Here we are,' said Nathan, pulling into the yard. 'I'll reverse into the barn and then we can get her unhooked.'

'Her?' said Bea, tipping her head to one side as she clocked his use of the word for the second time.

'Bea's Book Wagon, right? Has to be a her, surely?'

'I guess so,' Bea laughed. 'I don't think I've ever named a vehicle before.'

'Oh, all of mine have names,' said Nathan, tapping the jeep's steering wheel affectionately. 'This is Gertie.'

'You're joking,' said Bea, stifling a giggle. 'Gertie?'

'Don't ask me why,' said Nathan, 'she's just Gertie, aren't you, old girl?'

'You're such a softie, Nate,' said Bea. 'Do you remember giving me your lunch on our first day at school?' Nathan shook his head. 'Mum had made me tuna sandwiches and you swapped them for your corned beef and pickle. Don't you remember?'

'Er, no,' said Nathan, scratching his head.

'Well, I do,' said Bea, fondly. 'I knew right away you were different from all the other boys.'

'You weren't so bad yourself,' said Nathan. 'You punched Oscar Halliday for calling me a loser when he beat me at cross country.'

'I'd forgotten about that,' said Bea, smiling.

'It was a proper punch, too; knocked him out cold. I was impressed.'

'He deserved it,' said Bea, proudly. 'He was such a bully. I got detention for a week, though, and Mum was fuming.'

'He got so much stick for it,' said Nathan, his mouth twitching in amusement. 'His reputation as a hard man was seriously dented after that.'

'Karma's a bitch,' said Bea, unable to suppress a grin. 'Right, I'll get out and direct you back, shall I?'

'Good idea.'

Bea pulled up her hood, climbed out of the jeep and swung open the barn doors. Being out in the rain for just a few seconds was enough to have her soaked to the skin, and even with both doors open, it was a tight fit getting the trailer inside. But, eventually, after some impressive manoeuvring from Nathan that wouldn't have been out of place on an episode of *Top Gear*, the horsebox was finally in the dry.

'Here she is,' said Bea, resting a hand on the wagon's cracked and peeling paintwork.

'Safe and sound.'

'Thanks, Nate. I couldn't have done this without your help.'

'No worries, it'll be easier to fix up being indoors, anyway. Even if the weather's bad, we can still crack on.'

'Let's have a look inside,' said Bea, excitedly. Nathan dropped the trailer's ramp with a gentle thud and they both peered in. 'God, it's a bit whiffy. What is that smell? Is it . . . *wee*?' she asked, pulling a face.

'Probably,' he said, laughing.

'Yuck!' said Bea, holding her nose.

'It's rotted the floor, but that's easy enough to replace,' said Nathan, 'I'll put down marine ply – that won't warp – and vinyl over the top. Job done.'

'Wow,' whispered Bea, 'I still can't believe it's mine.'

'Well, it is, and it's going to be great, Bea.'

'I've got loads of ideas for what I want to do inside.'

'Go on . . .' replied Nathan.

'I want to take this divider out, for starters,' she said, sliding it out of position and laying it carefully against the back wall. 'God, it looks huge without it!'

'Almost like it's doubled in size,' he teased.

'So, I want,' said Bea, pretending not to hear him, 'shelving along the walls . . . here and . . . here,' she said, tracing a hand along the sides. 'And then bookcases . . . here. Could you add stud walls? I want to paint them white to make it feel really spacious, and could we add a window at the back here?' she asked, drawing a square with her hands in the air.

'Uh-huh, that all sounds totally doable,' said Nathan, nodding.

'I can picture it already. I think I'll have to get the bookcases custom-made, though, I don't think standard IKEA Billys will fit . . .'

'Oh, that's easy enough.'

'Easy?' laughed Bea. 'The last time I picked up a saw was at school, and you remember how that turned out?'

'A three-hour wait in A&E and stitches, if I remember rightly?' said Nathan.

'I still have the scar, see?' said Bea, holding out her hand. He took it in his and brought it closer to his face.

'There's nothing there,' he said, looking up at her sceptically.

'Look! Right there,' she said, jabbing a finger into her outstretched palm.

'Hmmmmm . . .' He traced the faint line with the gentlest of touches. Bea's skin tingled at the contact, and she felt a flicker of surprise as her heart began to race and she sensed something unexpected, yet familiar.

A jolt of realization hit her, a surge of feelings reigniting, feelings she thought were long forgotten . . .

'Anyway, I was saying,' he blustered, dropping her hand. 'Sorry, what was I saying? I can't actually remember . . .' he trailed off, shaking his head.

'Bookcases?' Bea whispered.

'Oh, right, yeah,' he babbled. 'Well, we've got loads of wood lying around, I'm pretty sure I can build you some bookcases.' He turned away, running a hand through his unruly mop of hair.

'Seriously, Nate? I mean, that would be amazing . . . but I don't want you to feel like you *have* to, though.'

'Hey, it's no problem. I'd enjoy it actually, it's been ages since I've been able to get my chisels out,' he said, laughing.

'Well, if you're sure . . . thank you. I've had some other ideas, too,' said Bea, her imagination unleashed. 'I was thinking about adding an awning to the front so I could have beanbags, or even deckchairs to make a little outdoor reading area. I want to put an arch of flowers around the door here,' she explained, tracing it in the air, 'and fairy lights *everywhere*. It's going to look magical.'

'A car battery could power those; easy to install, and cheap, too.'

'Really? That sounds perfect.'

'Why don't you come in for a cuppa and you can tell me about some of your other ideas? You can catch up with Mum and Dad, too. Mum was baking when I left.'

'Oooh, go on then. I'd kill for one of your mum's scones, I'm starving.'

'Come on, then,' said Nathan, closing the wagon door and securing the bolt.

The weather outside had worsened, storm clouds had gathered and the rain had turned to hail. As Bea pulled up her hood, ready to dash towards the farmhouse, her mind was firmly fixed on the spark she had felt when Nathan took her hand.

Where the hell had that come from?

It had caught her completely off guard. She hadn't thought of Nathan as anything more than a friend in years, but were emotions she thought long-buried awakening once more?

'Wordsworth, stop, please!' Bea groaned from underneath the duvet the following morning. 'It's too early.' The little spaniel let out an ear-piercing bark. 'Come here for a cuddle,' she said, patting the pillow next to her. He hopped up on the bed and licked her face. 'Oh, for God's sake!' she said, throwing back the covers. 'Okay, okay, I'm getting up.'

Yesterday's rain had finally stopped and the sun was peering through the clouds at last. 'Looks like we can go for a walk after all,' she said, and the dog began bouncing around her heels excitedly. 'All right, all right, let me get dressed first.'

They hadn't even made it halfway along the footpath by the river but Bea had already skidded in the mud and landed flat on her back. The rain had turned the ground into a mudslide and she had totally misjudged her footwear.

'This was a terrible idea. Here, boy!' she called. Wordsworth, who was usually really obedient, darted off in the opposite direction, barking excitedly.

'Wordsworth!' Bea bellowed at the top of her lungs. 'Come!' He ignored her, sniffing and pawing at a patch of grass that was clearly more interesting. 'That's it,' she huffed, jogging towards him as best she could in her flipflops. 'Stop messing about.' But, as she reached for his collar, he ran off again, this time directly towards the river.

Splash!

By the time Bea reached the bank, Wordsworth had swum to the opposite side of the river and was sat panting, looking pleased with himself. If he could talk, Bea was pretty sure he'd be saying, 'I bet you didn't know I could do that, did you?'

'Come on, time to go home,' she said, waving her arms

and shaking his lead in the air. The dog didn't budge. 'Wordsworth, here boy!' she called, her patience waning. 'You got yourself over there, you can make it back,' she said encouragingly, pulling a packet of treats out of her pocket and shaking them. 'Wordsworth! Come!'

'Are you okay?' a voice called. Bea spun around to see a man further down the footpath jogging towards her.

'It's my dog,' she said, pointing towards Wordsworth. 'He's swum across the river and is refusing to come back.'

'Ah, I see.'

'I think I might have to wade across and get him.'

'Really? In those?' he asked, pointing to her feet. 'It's not that deep. I can get him for you if you like?' he offered.

'Oh no, I couldn't ask you to do that, it's too much—'

But the stranger didn't hesitate; he pulled off his wellies and jacket and skidded down the bank straight into the water, wading across with ease. Scooping Wordsworth up into his arms, he shouted, 'Got him!' and then made his way back across the river, which was swirling around his waist. 'Here, take him,' said the man, passing Wordsworth up to her.

Bea clipped the dog's lead back on – there was no way she was going to risk him running off again – and began patting him dry with her jacket.

'Thank you so much. Are you okay?' she asked, as the man attempted to clamber back up the steep bank. She reached out a hand to help him, just as he lost his footing in the mud and slipped all the way back down into the water.

'It's okay, I'm fine!' he said, spluttering.

His white T-shirt was soaked through to his skin, and Bea couldn't help noticing the way it was clinging to his well-defined abs. He was in good shape ... *really* good shape. She swallowed hard, suddenly aware of just how handsome he was.

'Are you sure?' said Bea, taking his arm successfully this time and helping him out of the river.

'I'm good, yeah,' he said, tousling his mop of dark, wet hair.

'I don't know what I would have done if you hadn't come along,' said Bea. 'I can't thank you enough.'

'You're welcome,' he said.

'Here, take this,' she said, picking his jacket up off the ground and handing it to him. 'You need to get warm.' As he took the coat from her, his hand brushed hers and butterflies surged in her stomach.

Who is this guy?

'Sorry, I'm Bea,' she said, quickly, 'and this troublemaker is Wordsworth,' she said, jangling the dog's lead. 'I don't know what's got into him today, he's usually so well behaved. He never goes in the river.'

'I guess there's a first time for everything.'

'Yeah, I suppose there is.'

'I'm Lochlan,' said the man, 'good to meet you,' he said, bending down to ruffle Wordsworth's fur. The dog licked his hand appreciatively.

'Lochlan,' Bea repeated under her breath, *God, even his name is exotic.*

'Do you live around here?'

'I've only just moved here; a couple of weeks ago actually,' she said, unable to take her eyes off him.

'Ah that explains it, I'm sure I'd have remembered if I'd seen you around before . . .'

Was he *flirting* with her?

'You live nearby?' she asked.

'Yes, near the village. I try to get out for a walk down here a couple of times a week, it's normally pretty quiet,' he laughed.

'And then we came along . . .' said Bea. 'Sorry to cause you all this trouble, you're soaked through,' she said, her eyes flicking back to those well-defined abs.

'It's just a bit of water, no harm done.'

'Even so—'

'Honestly, I'm glad I could help,' said Lochlan, sitting down on the bank to pull his wellies back on.

'Can I at least get your clothes dry-cleaned to say thank you?'

'How about a drink instead?' he said, his dark eyes glinting. 'Saturday night?'

'Oh,' said Bea, suddenly self-conscious. *A drink? Did he mean a date?* 'That would be lovely.'

'Good,' said Lochlan, flashing her a perfect smile. *Wow, those teeth really were sparkling.* 'Meet you at the Apple Tree at seven?'

'Perfect,' she said, beaming at him. 'See you then.'

Then she watched him walk away, her heart pounding.

*

'But, Jess, this was different, *nothing* like Rory or Dillon,' said Bea. 'It was literally the perfect meet-cute. He didn't think twice, just jumped right in the river. When he climbed out, his T-shirt was soaking wet, just like Colin Firth in *Pride and Prejudice*. Exactly the same. He was giving off total Darcy vibes. It's got to be a sign—'

'Bea, you always say this and it's never a sign. Real life just isn't like that; you don't even know this guy, he could be a total—'

'He isn't.'

'How do you *know*?'

'I just do. He's tall, dark *and* handsome. He's an actual real-life hero and how often do you meet one of those?'

'Well, just take it slowly this time, for God's sake!'

'Of course I will.'

'But you always say that and then by date number two you're head over heels obsessed.'

'This time it's different, Lochlan's different. I've just got a *feeling* about him.'

'I hope you're right, Bea, but just be careful, okay?'

'Promise.'

As Bea hung up the phone, she couldn't stop thinking about how she had met Lochlan. It really was like something from one of the romance novels she loved so much, and if that wasn't a sign, she didn't know what was.

CHAPTER 8

Bea arrived at the Apple Tree on Saturday at seven on the dot. She spotted Lochlan at the bar and her shoulders relaxed a little. They hadn't swapped numbers, and a tiny part of her thought he might not show up.

'Hiya,' said Lochlan, his face splitting into a grin. 'What can I get you?' he asked.

'Let me get them,' she said, quickly.

'Don't be daft, what do you fancy?' he said, pulling his wallet out of his jeans pocket.

'If you're sure? A rum and coke, please,' said Bea, slipping off her jacket and flicking her hair off her shoulders.

'You turned up then,' he said, tapping his card to pay.

'Of course! Did you think I might stand you up?' she asked, surprised.

'I'd be lying if I said it hadn't crossed my mind. I forgot to get your number.'

'Yeah, I know,' said Bea, 'I thought the same.'

'I'm glad it wasn't just me,' he said, clearly relieved.

'It wasn't,' she smiled.

'Shall we grab a table?'

'Sure,' said Bea, heading for a corner booth and sliding along the bench.

'How's your dog after his swim?'

'Oh, he's fine,' she laughed. 'I still can't believe you did that . . .'

'The water wasn't deep. I'm just glad he's okay.'

'Thanks to you, he is,' said Bea, smiling.

'And I got to meet you, which was an added bonus,' he said, flashing another perfect smile at her.

God he's gorgeous.

'So, what brings you to Blossom Heath? You said you'd just moved here?'

'That's right. I've moved in with my brother. He's got a house on the Meadowgate Mead estate.'

'And you like it there?'

'Yeah. It's got a cosy feel to it, even though it's new; not like some of those other new builds you see. You know, kind of soulless?' She noticed Lochlan's smile widening. 'What?'

'It's just that . . . well, I worked on that development.'

'Gosh! Did you? Well, it's lovely.'

'Thanks. I'm pretty proud of it.'

'So, you're a builder then?' she asked.

'No, I'm a property developer,' he said, taking a sip of his pint.

'Wow. And what does that mean exactly?'

'I look for parcels of land – old properties, sites that can be built on, redeveloped, that kind of thing – negotiate the deals, and help plan the developments. It's pretty lucrative.'

'I bet!' said Bea, impressed.

'What about you? What do you do?' Lochlan asked.

'Well,' Bea hesitated, she wasn't sure how Bea's Book Wagon compared to Lochlan's impressive resume. 'I'm at a crossroads at the moment. I've just left my job to set up my own business.'

'Doing what?' he asked.

'I'm converting an old horsebox, turning it into a mobile bookshop, well, *trying* to, at least. It's early days,' she said.

'How brilliant!' he said, enthusiastically. 'So, you're a bookseller then?'

'Hoping to be, yes,' she said, sipping her drink. 'I'm going to be working at the Cosy Cat for a bit, too, just while I get the business up and running.'

'I love that place!' said Lochlan, 'They do the best macchiatos.'

'I haven't started yet,' said Bea quickly, 'Monday's my first day.'

'I'll try to pop by.'

'Thanks,' said Bea, 'I've never worked as a barista before, I'm just hoping I don't screw up.'

'You'll be fine.'

'I hope so,' said Bea, feeling a bubble of nerves in her stomach at the prospect of her first day. 'So, what else do you get up to, when you're not saving dogs or building houses?'

'Ha! All the usual stuff, I guess: playing footie, eating out, catching up with my mates, dating.'

'Dating?' Bea wasn't sure this counted as date. Perhaps Lochlan was just being friendly? She swallowed hard before asking, 'So . . . is *this* a date?'

'Erm, I hope so?' he said, fixing his dark eyes on her.

God those eyes were intense.

'In fact,' he said, clearing his throat, 'I was hoping you might agree to a second? How about Thursday? There's somewhere I'd like to take you.'

'Uh-huh,' Bea nodded. All she could do right now was stare into his beautiful, big eyes.

'Pass me your phone,' said Lochlan, reaching out his hand. 'Let me give you my number.'

'You came back!' said Bea, beaming as Arthur made his way towards the enquiry desk at the library on Sunday.

'Had to, my dear. I whizzed through the book you found me in no time. I'm here for another one,' he said.

'I'm pleased you enjoyed it,' she beamed, placing *The Killing Floor* on the returns pile.

'I loved it,' said Arthur, his eyes sparkling. 'That Lee Child fellow is a very talented writer.'

'He really is,' Bea agreed.

'Much better than the television series, I think, but then again, I always prefer the book.'

'Oh, me too. It's always a bit of a let-down when they adapt something I love into a movie; it's never as good. I'll go grab you the next one in the series,' she said, hurrying off to the crime section.

When Bea returned to the desk, Arthur was flicking through the library's *What's On* pamphlet.

'See anything you fancy?' she asked.

'I was thinking about joining a book club. I don't suppose you run one here?'

'We don't, I'm afraid,' said Bea, shaking her head, 'but I'll ask around. I'm sure there must be one locally.'

'I've got so much time on my hands these days,' said Arthur, his voice cracking a little. 'When you get to my age, the hours just seem to stretch out in front of you, and most of my friends . . . well, they're no longer with us.'

'Oh, Arthur, I'm so sorry to hear that,' said Bea, kindly. 'You're welcome here any time, you know. If you just want to sit and read or have a browse. I'm here at the weekends and I'll always stick the kettle on for you.'

'Thank you, my dear. That's very kind.'

'I've brought you the next *two* books in the Reacher series, that should keep you busy for a while,' said Bea, scanning them out, 'and number three is an absolute corker, you're going to love it!'

'Excellent! Thank you,' said Arthur, putting the books in his shopping bag and turning to leave.

'Arthur?' Bea called after him. 'Fancy a cuppa before you go?'

'Now? Aren't you busy?'

'Busy?' said Bea, looking around her, 'you're the only other person here.'

'In that case, my dear, I take milk and two sugars,' he replied, his face breaking into a smile.

'Wow, Nate, this looks amazing! I didn't expect you to have made a start without me,' said Bea, surveying the brand-new floor he'd installed in the horsebox. 'I was going to start prepping this afternoon.'

'I had some free time, so thought I may as well crack on. How was the library?'

'Great. It was quiet, but there's this lovely old man called Arthur who came in today. I made him some tea and we had a bit of a natter. I think he's a bit lonely, to be honest.'

'Well, I'm sure you lifted his spirits. That was good of you, Bea, to take the time. But that's you all over . . .'

'What is?'

'You're kind. It's probably my favourite thing about you.'

'Stop, you're going to make me blush!' said Bea, her cheeks turning rosy anyway.

'Okay,' said Nathan, suppressing his laughter. 'Anyway, I can stick around, give you a hand?'

'Only if you've got time?'

'I have,' he said, rolling up the sleeves of his shirt to reveal his tattoos.

Bea's eyes rested on his forearms for a moment. Clearing her throat, she asked, 'Shall I start washing everything first?

Then we can both sand away the rust and grime and prep the surfaces for painting.'

'Oh, so glamourous,' sniggered Nathan.

'I've bought buckets and rubber gloves, they're by the door.'

'And I brought these,' said Nathan, throwing her a pair of ugly, brown overalls.

'Really?' said Bea, frowning. 'I'm not sure brown's my colour?'

'Unless you want that sweatshirt ruined?'

'I absolutely don't,' said Bea, shaking her head.

'Overalls it is, then.'

'Who knew you were so bossy?' said Bea, almost toppling over as she stepped into her overalls.

'Woah!' said Nathan, grabbing her arm to steady her.

'Thanks,' she said, gripping him tightly. She could feel his biceps through his shirt.

Wow, he was . . . strong.

For reasons she didn't want to acknowledge, she didn't want to let go. 'Right,' she said, finally turning away. 'Let's make a start then, shall we?'

CHAPTER 9

'Mum! What are you doing here?' asked Bea, halfway through her first shift at the Cosy Cat.

'How's it going?' asked Carol.

'Good, I think. I'm still getting the hang of the coffee machine, it's so complicated.'

'She's doing great,' said Tori, wiping her hands on her apron.

'Mum, this is Tori,' said Bea, 'Tori, this is my mum, Carol.'

'Good to meet you,' said Carol, shaking Tori's hand. 'Thanks for giving Bea the job, I know she really appreciates it.'

'Oh, it's no problem. She's very capable, and if it helps her out while she's doing up the horsebox, I'm happy to help,' said Tori. 'I'm excited to see the book wagon when it's finished.'

'You and me both,' said Carol, beaming. 'I wasn't sure about it when she first told me. Quitting her job like that, I was . . .'

'Horrified?' said Bea, arching an eyebrow.

'I was just . . . *surprised*, that's all,' said Carol. 'But now I've had time to get used to the idea, I can see the potential.'

'Me too,' said Tori, enthusiastically. 'And anything I can do to help, I will.'

'Tori's got a business degree, she's been helping with my business plan,' Bea explained.

'That's kind of you,' said Carol.

'Grab a table, Mum, and I'll come and take your order?' suggested Bea.

'I can't stop, I'm off to see Maggie. Can I get two skinny lattes to go?' said Carol.

'Absolutely,' said Bea, 'coming right up,' she said, filling the portafilter with coffee beans.

'Hey, you!' said a familiar voice. Bea turned to see Lochlan standing at the counter. He was wearing a navy suit with a crisp white shirt.

He looked jaw-droppingly gorgeous.

'Oh, Lochlan, hi!' Bea stuttered. Why did she suddenly feel all fingers and thumbs?

'How's your first day going?' he asked.

'Aren't you going to introduce us, sweetheart?' said Carol, pointedly.

'Oh, yeah,' Bea mumbled. 'This is Lochlan. Lochlan, this is my mum, Carol.'

'Lovely to meet you, Carol,' said Lochlan.

'You too,' Carol replied. 'So, how do you know Bea?'

'We met on the footpath by the river. She was in a spot of trouble with her dog,' said Lochlan, leaning against the counter.

'What trouble?' said Carol, turning to Bea. 'What happened?'

'Oh, it was nothing,' said Bea. 'He just got tangled in his lead, Lochlan helped me sort it out,' she continued, flashing him a look.

'Er, yes, that's right,' he said, catching on. 'We laughed about it at the pub afterwards,' added Lochlan.

Bea threw him a look to say *please stop talking.*

'You went for a drink?' asked Carol, excitedly.

'Oh, yeah,' said Lochlan, grinning. He immediately realized from the look on Bea's face that he'd said the wrong thing. 'We bumped into each other at the pub and got chatting,' he backtracked.

Lochlan mouthed '*Sorry*' to Bea over Carol's shoulder.

'Anyway, here are those lattes, Mum,' said Bea, passing them across the counter. 'You don't want to keep Maggie waiting.'

'No, I suppose not,' said Carol. 'Lovely to meet you, Lochlan.'

'You too,' said Lochlan.

'Bye, Mum. Thanks for popping in,' said Bea, watching her walk out the door. 'Thank God for that,' she said, slumping on the counter as soon as Carol was out of sight.

'Sorry, I dropped you in it, didn't I?' said Lochlan, wincing.

'Don't worry about it. I'd not told her what happened with Wordsworth, that's all.'

'And the pub thing? Embarrassed to be seen with me, eh?' he teased.

'God, no!' said Bea, mortified. 'I'd just literally never hear the end of it, you know?'

'I get it. My mum's the same.'

'You mean you *don't* want to introduce me to her already?' said Bea, in mock horror.

'No!' he replied, looking stricken. 'It's not that—'

'Relax, I'm only joking,' Bea laughed. 'Anyway, what can I get you?' she asked, flashing him her best smile.

'Flat white to go, please.'

'Coming up,' she said, grabbing another takeaway cup from the stack on the counter.

'Are you still good for Thursday?'

'Yes, I'm looking forward to it. Where is it we're going, again?'

'It's a surprise, but I think you're going to love it,' he said, pulling out his wallet. 'I'll pick you up at eight, if that works?'

'Great. I'll ping you my address.'

'See you Thursday, then,' he said, his hand lingering on hers as she passed him his coffee.

'Can't wait,' she murmured, watching him leave.

'Have you thought about a colour scheme yet?' Jess asked, as they sat on the sofa at Archie's place.

'What do you think about baby blue for the outside? And then the lettering in pale pink along the side?'

'Pastels are lovely, but they do get dirty quickly. Maybe go for slightly darker shades?' suggested Jess, unfurling her legs from under her.

'Good idea! I'm ordering the paint online, it's a fair bit cheaper than in store. And I'm painting the panelling inside in white to help it feel more spacious. I could add a bit more colour with rugs and cushions, though.'

'How are you doing for money?'

'I've got a few hundred left in my account, and Nathan reckons that should be enough to get everything else done. He's sorted the wood for me – he had loads left over from other jobs on the farm – and that's saved me hundreds.'

'Result!'

'Yeah, I know. He's been such a help; I wouldn't have been able to get it done without him.'

'Do you two fancy a takeaway tonight? My treat,' said Archie, planting himself on the sofa next to Jess.

'Er . . . *yes*!' said Bea.

'Like you even have to ask,' said Jess.

'Pizza?' suggested Archie, scrolling through the options on his phone

'Great,' said Bea and Jess in unison.

'Pepperoni okay?' he asked. Bea and Jess nodded. How's all this going?' he said, pointing towards the laptop.

'Good,' Bea nodded. 'There's still a long way to go, but I'm getting there.'

'We're painting at the weekend, if you fancy helping?' said Jess.

'I'm around, so sure, I'll help,' said Archie, tapping away on his phone

'Thanks, Arch,' said Bea.

'Food's on its way,' he said, shoving his phone back in his pocket.

'Excellent!' said Bea.

'I've got some work to finish. Can you listen out for the door?' he asked.

'Sure,' said Bea, as Archie headed back upstairs. 'That was weird. Offering to help with the painting? If I didn't know any better, I'd think he was up to something . . .'

'Like what?'

'I'm not sure exactly,' said Bea, eyes narrowed.

'How's it going, the two of you living together?'

'To be fair, we've not seen that much of each other, we've both been so busy. He finally seems to have figured out how to load a dishwasher, though, so that's a bonus.'

'That must be a relief,'

'Yeah, it is.'

'Anyway, what I *really* want to know is, how was the date with Lochlan?' Jess asked.

'Good, I think. It always feels a bit strange at first, doesn't it? Small talk, awkward silences—'

'There were awkward silences?' Jess asked, looking concerned.

'Well, no, not really. We both seemed pretty comfortable with each other.'

'*Comfortable?* Bea, is that what you want from a first date?'

'Well, not really, I suppose.'

'Was there any chemistry?'

'I think so. He's gorgeous, he makes me nervous—'

'And?' said Jess, leaning forward.

'When he climbed out of the river, wet T-shirt clinging to his chest . . . it was like something out of a Diet Coke ad.'

'Well,' said Jess, 'that sounds sexy.'

'It was,' Bea sighed, picturing the moment.

'Just make sure you're not rushing in, though,' Jess warned. 'I get that he's good looking, and right now he probably seems perfect but—'

'I *am* taking it slow, but I can still get caught up in the moment, can't I?'

'Of course,' said Jess, a smile escaping her lips.

'He came into the café today all suited and booted. He looked . . . *hot*. Mum popped in as well, so I had to introduce them and—'

'Hang on, your *mum's* met him?'

'I know,' said Bea, grimacing, 'It wasn't planned, believe me.'

'God, I bet!'

'She was on her way to see your mum, actually.'

'So, what did you do?' Jess laughed.

'Well, Lochlan kind of dropped me in it by saying we'd been out for a drink, so I had to pretend we'd just bumped into each other. I'm not sure Mum bought it, to be honest.'

'You're a terrible liar, there's no way she doesn't think that was a date.'

'You're probably right,' Bea sighed. 'It's not like it's some big secret, but you know what Mum's like. She'll insist I bring him over for dinner so she can grill him and, well, it's still early days.'

'Hey, I get it, my mum's exactly the same,' Jess agreed. 'So, are you seeing him again?'

'Yeah, Thursday.'

'Where are you going?'

'I'm not sure,' said Bea, shrugging, 'it's a surprise, apparently.'

'Ooooh, I wonder where he's taking you?' said Jess.

'I don't know, but I can't wait to find out!'

Bea was really struggling to concentrate on anything other than her date with Lochlan. She'd gone to Three Acre Farm to work on the horsebox, hoping it would take her mind off it.

It didn't.

If anything, she was clock-watching more than ever. By mid-afternoon, her shoulders were aching and her back was sore from all the sanding and scrubbing.

'How's it going?' said Nathan, walking into the barn with a plate of biscuits. 'These are from Mum,' he said.

'Ah, brilliant, I'm starving,' said Bea, biting into one. 'Mmmm . . . delicious.'

'Looks like all the prep is pretty much done,' said Nathan, inspecting the horsebox. 'Sorry I've not been able to help much, it's been hectic—'

'Don't be silly. I don't expect you to drop everything to help me all the time, you know.'

'I know, but if I could, I would.'

'Well, that's very sweet of you,' said Bea, smiling broadly. 'I think I'll be able to start painting on Saturday. Archie and Jess are going to help.'

'I've not seen Archie in ages, it'll be good to see him.'

'Don't stop working, though, I know how much you've got to do here. If you can help then great, but honestly, it'll be fine if you can't.'

'Okay, well I'll see how I get on,' said Nathan, grabbing a cookie from the plate and shoving it into his mouth whole.

'God, is that the time?' said Bea, glancing down at her watch. 'I'd best be off, I've got a, erm . . . a date tonight.'

'A date?' asked Nathan, looking taken aback. 'Who with?'

'Someone called Lochlan. He lives around here, maybe you know him?'

'Lochlan,' said Nathan, shaking his head. 'Don't think so. Well, have fun.'

'Thanks, Nate,' said Bea, planting a kiss on his cheek. 'See you Saturday, then!'

'Yep, see you Saturday.'

Nathan was surprised to hear that Bea was dating. He knew she'd split from Rory when she'd left London, but she hadn't said anything about seeing anyone new, although why would she?

It's just that they'd been spending a lot more time together recently, and he'd often wondered if there might still be something between them. Okay, it was nearly ten years since they'd been together, but it was purely circumstance that had caused them to break up: Bea was heading off to university and he was staying right here in Blossom Heath. If she hadn't left, who knows where it could have led?

Lochlan? Nathan definitely couldn't place the name, despite everyone knowing everyone around here, and a name like Lochlan wasn't easy to forget.

Anyway, it was only a date, it wasn't like Bea was planning to marry the guy. Nathan was just curious, he supposed; curious as to who Lochlan was and why Bea seeing him seemed to bother him quite so much.

CHAPTER 10

'Bloody hell, Bea! Who is this guy?' said Archie, peering out the window as Lochlan's bright red convertible pulled up outside. 'It's a Maserati. He's must have some serious cash; that thing's worth over £100k!'

'£100k? For a *car*? That's crazy!'

'What did you say he does?'

'He's a property developer. Anyway, I'll see you later, don't wait up.'

Bea didn't know much about cars, but as Lochlan jumped out and opened the passenger door for her, she couldn't help but be a little impressed.

'Wow, Bea. You look gorgeous,' he said, kissing her on the cheek.

God he smelled good.

Bea was wearing an emerald-green wrap dress with a low neckline, ridiculously high heels and bright red lipstick. It wasn't the kind of look she usually went for, but she had to admit she felt sexy as hell.

'I like the car,' she said, as Lochlan sped away from the kerb.

'I know, right? She's my pride and joy.'

'She? Don't tell me you name your cars too. My friend does that,' she said, her mind turning to Nathan. She wondered what he was up to this evening.

'Really?'

'Uh-huh. So, where are we off to? The suspense is killing me.'

'You'll have to wait a bit longer, I'm afraid. I hope you're hungry, though?'

'Always,' Bea laughed.

'Good. The seafood at this place is out of this world.'

'Ah, so we're going for dinner?'

'Not just any dinner, and not just any restaurant . . .'

'Well, we're not going into Hastings or Rye,' she said, as Lochlan turned the car in the opposite direction to both. 'So, where?'

'Brighton!'

'*Brighton*?' she repeated. That was over an hour's drive away, at least.

'It's worth it, this place is amazing. All the celebs go there, it's called Canteen 64.'

'Wasn't Tom Holland seen there the other week? I'm sure I saw something about it on the *Spotted in Sussex* Instagram feed.'

'Probably. It's the only restaurant I go to, nowadays, unless I'm in London. Rye's not up to much.'

'Oh? I've always quite liked it . . .'

'Wait until you've eaten here. I promise it'll blow your mind.'

'Well, it sounds great. I can't wait,' she replied, getting comfy in her seat, trying to ignore the niggle in the back of her mind that Lochlan's dismissive attitude to the local restaurants had lodged there.

The journey to Brighton passed quickly, and in no time at all they'd arrived at a stunning glass-fronted building at the end of a long, private driveway, illuminated by flaming torches. Valets in green velvet jackets were waiting to welcome guests at the entrance, swiftly taking Lochlan's car keys and directing them inside. It felt like something out of a movie.

'Mr Thompson, so lovely to see you again,' said a beautiful hostess waiting to greet them. 'Your usual table?'

'Please, Daniella,' Lochlan nodded.

Bea took in the stunning design as she followed Lochlan and the hostess into the restaurant. Everything screamed elegance, from the gilt-edged furniture to the lavish green, velvet décor. There was even a mermaid ice-sculpture next to the bar, where a pair of immaculately dressed barmen were throwing cocktail shakers in the air. Bea had never been anywhere like it before and, if she was honest, it made her feel a little self-conscious.

'Don't look now, but Cate Blanchett's here,' Lochlan

whispered, leaning in towards Bea as they sat down. Bea chanced a sideways glance and spotted the movie star a few tables away.

'Bloody hell, you're right,' she muttered.

'Can I get you some drinks to start with?' Daniella asked, not taking her eyes off Lochlan.

'Vodka martini, please,' said Lochlan, handing Bea the drinks menu.

'Oh, sorry. I'll just have a look,' said Bea, scanning it frantically.

'Take your time,' said Daniella, through a thin-lipped smile.

'I'll have an espresso martini, please,' said Bea.

'Excellent choice, Madam,' said Daniella, looking at her with disdain. Bea noticed that she seemed to float rather than walk, as she moved through the restaurant.

'Wow, this place is amazing,' said Bea.

'Told you you'd love it,' said Lochlan.

'I can't believe Cate Blanchett is here. I don't think I've ever seen a celeb in real life before, unless you count that guy from *The One Show,* and I'm not sure I do.'

'Last time I was here, the paparazzi were outside trying to get a shot of Paul McCartney before he left.'

'Wow, that's proper A-list,' said Bea, impressed.

'I'm glad you like it,' said Lochlan, a smile lighting up his face. Bea felt her stomach do a little flip.

'Your drinks,' said Daniella, placing the martinis in front of them. 'Are you ready to order?'

'Sorry, I haven't had chance to look,' said Bea, reaching for the menu.

'Why don't I order for both of us?' said Lochlan, taking it from her and closing it shut.

'Erm ... okay. I'm a bit of a fussy eater though, so maybe—'

'We'll take the oysters to start, and then sea bass for both of us.'

'Oh, I'm not sure I like oysters—'

'You'll love them,' said Lochlan, handing the menus back to Daniella, who sashayed away. 'They're divine.'

'Okay, well, if you're sure ...' said Bea, taking a sip of espresso martini. 'God, that's delicious.'

'To us,' said Lochlan, raising his glass.

'Erm, yes, to us,' she replied, clinking her glass against his.

'So, how are you getting on with the horsebox? Still doing it up?' he asked.

'Yep, although it doesn't look all that different yet. I'm getting started on the painting at the weekend, so hopefully that should transform it.'

'When are you planning on opening?'

'By the first May bank holiday, if I can get everything ready in time. It's the village fête that weekend, so it would be the perfect time to launch,' she said. 'There's still lots to do and I need to start sourcing more stock, work out pricing; there's a lot to think about,' she explained, feeling slightly overwhelmed by the enormity of the task ahead.

'I'm sure you'll get it ready in time.'

'I hope you're right,' said Bea, her stomach churning. 'I've got a call with a wholesaler tomorrow, so that's a start.'

'So, books are pretty important to you?' he asked.

'Well, I'm opening a mobile bookshop, so I guess you could say that,' Bea laughed.

'You light up when you talk about it, you know? It's good to have things in life you're passionate about, Bea,' he said, fixing his eyes on her.

'What about you? Do you read?'

'I try to, but I never seem to get the time these days,' he said.

'That's a shame.'

'I'm really busy with work, and when I do get any free time I tend to go for a run or hit the gym; do something physical, after being stuck at a desk all day.'

'Have you tried audiobooks? You can plug in when you're running, in the car—'

'That's a great idea!' Lochlan said with enthusiasm. 'I don't know why I've never thought of it.'

'Try Audible, or the library has a great app, too,' she said, pulling out her phone to show him her current read, the latest romcom by Marian Keyes. 'What kind of books do you like?' she asked, scrolling through some suggestions on her phone.

'Well—'

'No, don't tell me,' she said, holding up a hand, 'let me guess.' she continued, scanning his face. 'Hmmmm . . . I don't think you're a thriller guy,' she said, drumming her fingers on the tabletop, 'but fiction, definitely fiction.'

'Keep going,' said Lochlan, grinning.

'Sci-fi!' she said, after a lengthy pause. 'Terry Pratchett?'

'Wow, impressive,' said Lochlan, leaning back in his chair. 'You're spot on. *The Colour of Magic* is brilliant.'

'I know, right?' Bea agreed, taking another sip of her drink. 'Have you read *The Light Fantastic*?'

'Not yet,' he said, shaking his head. 'Like I said, I don't have a great deal of time.'

'Well, we can definitely fix that,' said Bea, beaming at him. 'Come into the library next time I'm working, I can help you join and set you up on BorrowBox. You'll be hooked on audiobooks in no time.'

'Your oysters,' said a waiter, placing a giant platter on the table in front of them. They looked . . . *disgusting.*

'So, what you do,' said Lochlan, picking one up, 'is loosen it from the shell with your fork, like this,' he continued, giving it a wiggle, 'then slurp it, but don't forget to chew. Like this,' he said, throwing back his head and chewing several times before swallowing. 'Delicious.'

'Okay,' said Bea, plucking an oyster from the platter, trying not to retch at the smell.

Why did it look like a giant bogey?

'That's it,' Lochlan said, encouragingly. 'Now just chew and swallow.'

'Right, yes,' said Bea, sucking in a deep breath.

Three, two, one . . . she threw back her head and in it went. *Why was it so damn chewy?*

It tasted *disgusting*, unimaginably disgusting. She was going to bring it straight back up, she knew it. She reached for her martini, downing the remainder of it in one.

'And? Aren't they delicious?' Lochlan asked, keenly.

'Delicious, yeah,' she lied. 'Very . . . *fresh*.'

'I knew you'd love them,' said Lochlan, beaming at her from across the table.

'I just need to go and powder my nose,' said Bea, grabbing her clutch bag. There was no way on earth she could eat another one.

'I'll save you some.'

'I don't want to spoil my main,' she said, almost too quickly. 'Honestly, you finish them.'

'If you're sure?'

'Oh, I am,' she said, standing up.

As she made her way through to the back of the restaurant, Bea realized that, no matter how hot Lochlan looked, she'd happily stay in the bathroom all night if it meant she didn't have to eat another oyster.

CHAPTER 11

The Apple Tree was packed when Bea, Jess, Archie and Nathan arrived after a hard day working on the wagon. Bea had to force her way through the crowds to get served at the bar.

'Three pints of cider and a double whisky, please, Beth,' said Bea, pulling out her purse when it was finally her turn.

'Coming right up,' said Beth, pulling the first pint. 'So, how are you? Settling in?'

'Yeah, good, thanks. I really like it here, everyone's been so welcoming.'

'That's Blossom Heath for you. I've been hearing all about your book wagon; it's the talk of the village, you know.'

'It is?' said Bea, her eyes wide in amazement.

'Yeah, Maggie's been filling us in. A mobile bookshop? What a treat! I'd much rather buy from an actual person than online.'

'Oh, me too! What do you usually read?'

'I'm a true crime fan, the grislier the better. Can't get enough of the stuff.'

'Really?' said Bea, surprised. 'I'm not sure I'd have guessed that, and I'm usually good at figuring out—'

'Oh, I love everything, really. Give me a good romance, too.'

'Ah,' said Bea, nodding. 'You strike me as someone who believes in happy-ever-afters.'

'You have to, don't you? What sort of a world would it be otherwise?' said Beth, lining Bea's drinks up along the bar.

'A pretty sad one,' Bea agreed.

'Speaking of happy-ever-afters,' said Beth, leaning in across the bar. 'Did I spot you in here with that Lochlan the other night?'

'Oh, yeah,' Bea nodded, bashfully.

'He's a looker, that's for sure. Nice guy too, by all accounts,' said Beth, approvingly.

'Well, we've only been on two dates, but so far he seems nice,' Bea gushed. 'We met when he jumped into the river to rescue my dog.'

'Did he?' said Beth, clearly impressed. 'How romantic.'

'I know,' Bea nodded. 'I've got a good feeling about him. Sorry, I'm getting carried away. I just like him, that's all.'

'You get carried away all you like, love. I hope it works out.'

'Me too. Do you know what? I'm going to see if he's free. What have I got to lose?' she said, pulling out her phone and sending Lochlan a text. It beeped instantly with a reply: *Be there as soon as I can xx*

Bea couldn't help clock-watching as she waited nervously for Lochlan to arrive at the pub.

'What's up with you?' asked Nathan, nudging her. 'You haven't stopped looking at the door since you sat down. Not boring you, are we?' he teased.

'No, course not,' Bea replied, 'I'm waiting for Lochlan, that's all,' she said, bouncing her foot up and down under the table.

'Lochlan? The guy you went on a date with?'

'That's the one.'

'And he's on his way here?'

'Yeah,' said Bea, smiling. 'He took me to this amazing restaurant in Brighton, Nate. Cate Blanchett was there . . . *actual* Cate Blanchett, can you believe it?'

'Blimey,' said Nathan, taking a swig of his pint.

'I know. You should have seen this place, it was uber fancy . . . I've never been anywhere like it before. We had oysters—'

'Oysters? But you hate oysters!' Nathan cut in. 'You used to call them sea bogeys?'

'Oh, they were totally disgusting, but he ordered for us both . . .'

'He ordered for you?' Nathan scowled, shaking his head. 'Bea, isn't that—'

'He was being *romantic*,' Bea insisted. 'Aren't oysters

supposed to be the food of love, or something? I couldn't exactly not eat them.'

'I'm pretty sure you wouldn't have eaten them if I'd turned up with a plate of oysters.'

'Yeah, but that's different, Nate, it's . . . well, *you.*'

'Right,' said Nathan, his face falling a little.

'Oh, he's here,' Bea said, grabbing Nathan by the arm. 'Right, you lot, play nice, okay?'

'Ooooh, the famous Lochlan,' said Jess, her eyes scanning the room, trying to catch sight of him. 'Bloody hell, Bea, is that him?'

Bea nodded as Lochlan made his way over, wearing a pair of skin-tight jeans and what looked like a designer shirt. Bea felt her pulse surge at the sight of him.

'I know you said he was hot, but he's *gorgeous,*' whispered Jess.

'You should see his car, mate,' said Archie, turning to Nathan. 'He's got a bloody Maserati!'

'Has he?' said Nathan, coolly.

'Hiya,' said Bea, leaping up from her seat and kissing Lochlan on the cheek.

'Hello, you,' said Lochlan, his dark eyes fixed on hers.

She could stare into those eyes all day long . . .

'Erm,' said Jess, subtly clearing her throat, 'Aren't you going to introduce us?'

'Oh, yes, sorry,' said Bea, flustered. 'Lochlan, these are my friends, Jess and Nathan, and this is my brother, Archie.'

'Good to meet you all,' said Lochlan, shaking Archie by the hand. 'Can I get another round?'

'Mine's a cider, cheers, mate,' said Archie, downing the dregs of his pint.

'I'll take a G&T, thanks,' said Jess.

'I'm good with this,' said Nathan, holding up his half-full glass.

'You sure?' said Lochlan.

'Yep, I'm good,' Nathan repeated. Was Bea imagining it or was Nathan being frosty?

'I'll give you a hand,' said Bea, following Lochlan towards the bar. 'I'm glad you could come tonight, I know it was short notice . . .'

'I can't think of a better way to spend my Saturday night,' said Lochlan, lacing his fingers through hers as they stood together at the bar.

'Me neither,' said Bea, staring up into his big, dark eyes.

All she could think about right now was kissing him, but the packed bar of the pub definitely wasn't the time *or* the place for their first kiss. She wished they were alone . . .

'Bea?' said Lochlan, snapping her back to reality.

'Sorry?' she said, aware that she hadn't been listening to anything he might have said in the past few minutes.

'I was saying you were right, that's all.'

'About what?'

'BorrowBox. I'm already halfway through listening to *The Light Fantastic*!'

'Are you enjoying it?' she asked.

'It's brilliant,' he said, tipping his head to one side. 'Thanks for the recommendation.'

'I'm thinking of organizing an event, actually, like speed-dating, but for books.'

'Well, aren't you full of good ideas this evening?' he said, leaning down to plant a kiss on her cheek. 'I always get my best ideas in the shower. I have to get out and type them into my phone's notes app before I forget, though, which is tricky when you're soaped up and naked,' he said, waggling his eyebrows.

'True,' she replied, picturing a lathered-up Lochlan. She swallowed hard.

'Are you okay to grab those?' he asked, nodding towards the two pints on the bar.

'Oh, yeah, sure,' she said, clearing her throat.

'Cheers for these,' said Archie, raising his glass, as they returned to the table.

'Yeah, thanks, Lochlan,' said Jess, taking a sip of her drink.

'So, what have you been up to today?' Lochlan asked, taking Bea's hand under the table.

'Working on the wagon at Nate's,' said Bea, smiling.

'Ah, that's right,' said Lochlan, 'you're at Three Acre Farm, aren't you?'

'That's me,' said Nathan.

'It's good of you to help Bea out like this,' said Lochlan. 'She told me how great you've been.'

'You're welcome to grab a paintbrush and lend a hand,' said Nathan.

'Me? Oh, no, I'm not very handy. I'm more of an ideas guy,' said Lochlan, setting down his pint. 'Anyway, I'm snowed under with work, there's no way I could get away, I'm afraid.'

'Lochlan's got his own property development firm,' Bea explained.

'Oh, yeah, Bea mentioned you'd been involved with building Meadowgate Mead,' said Archie.

'That's right. You know, we're always looking for more land to develop,' said Lochlan, pulling out his business card and turning to Nathan, 'if you're looking to make some extra cash, it's very lucrative. I know times are hard in farming at the—'

'I manage just fine, thanks,' said Nathan, folding his arms. 'I'm not looking to sell off my land.'

'Nate runs a cheese business, too,' Bea said, quickly. 'It's doing amazingly well.'

'We stock it in the shop, it's one of our bestsellers,' said Jess.

'The shop?' said Lochlan.

'Yeah, my parents run Harrison's,' Jess explained.

'Ah, I see,' said Lochlan.

'I don't think I've seen you in there before?' said Jess.

'I order all my groceries online,' said Lochlan.

'That explains it. Our customers can't get enough of Nate's Blossom Heath Blue or his goat's cheese; it's local, artisan stuff. You're branching out to some of the restaurants in Rye too, aren't you, Nate?' said Jess.

'Yep,' said Nathan.

'Nate supplies the Cosy Cat, too,' said Bea.

'Well, if you ever change your mind about the land—' said Lochlan.

'I won't,' replied Nathan.

'Either way, here's my card,' said Lochlan, sliding it across the table. Nathan didn't pick it up.

'Sorry, guys, I'm going to duck out,' said Archie, glancing at his phone. 'Seb and Josh are out in Rye and I'm going to go meet them. Anyone fancy it?'

'Nah, I need a long soak in the bath and an early night,' said Jess, yawning.

'Nate?' said Archie. 'You in? Why don't we leave these two to it,' he said, nodding towards Bea and Lochlan.

'I don't know, mate, I've got an early start tomorrow,' said Nathan, glancing at his watch.

'Oh, come on,' said Archie. 'You haven't been out with the lads in ages.'

'Go on then,' said Nathan, finishing his drink in one swift gulp.

'Yes! I'll get us an Uber,' said Archie, tapping on his phone. 'Let's wait outside.'

'Have fun, guys,' Jess called after them.

'And thanks for your help today,' Bea shouted to them.

'And then there were three,' Jess laughed. 'I'm going to make a move.'

'Actually, I'm pretty exhausted, too. Why don't we walk you home, Jess? Lochlan, do you want to come to mine? I reckon Archie will be out for a while . . .' said Bea.

'Good idea,' said Lochan, his eyes flashing.

'Right, let's go,' said Jess, taking a final sip of her drink.

*

Bea shivered as she stepped into the cool, night air.

'Wow, it's chilly out here,' she said, pulling her jacket tightly around her.

'Seriously, you don't need to walk me home, I can literally see the shop from here,' Jess laughed.

'Fine, but I'm not leaving till I see you go through the front door,' said Bea.

'It's Blossom Heath, not London, I'll be fine,' said Jess, rolling her eyes and striding off across the green.

'Do you mind if we—' Bea paused.

'Wait for her to go inside?' said Lochlan, slipping his fingers through hers.

'Uh-huh.'

'Course not,' he said, raising her hand to his lips and kissing it.

They stood in silence for a couple of minutes until they saw Jess wave at them from her front door. Bea waved back.

'Let's go,' said Bea, turning to face Lochlan. The air between them thickened.

Without speaking, Lochlan wrapped his arms around Bea's waist and pulled her in close. Every nerve in her body flickered into life. Her heart was pounding so hard she thought it might literally explode.

'Bea?' he whispered.

'Yes?' she murmured, a shiver of anticipation running down her spine.

'I don't think I can wait any longer . . .'

'Me neither,' she replied, leaning in towards him.

And as their lips touched, their first kiss was everything she hoped it would be: *utterly perfect*.

CHAPTER 12

'So, how's the to-do list looking?' Tori asked the following morning, setting a flat white and a slice of carrot cake down on the table, snapping Bea back to reality.

Things had got pretty heated pretty quickly when Bea and Lochlan had arrived back at her place last night. They'd practically ripped each other's clothes off as soon as they'd made it through the front door. By the time they'd reached the bedroom, a trail of clothes left scattered in their wake, she was groaning in pleasure as he covered her collarbone in tiny kisses. The sex had been mind-blowingly hot. Lochlan had known exactly what she wanted, his hands caressing her body in all the right places as waves of ecstasy coursed through her. She couldn't stop thinking about him.

'Sorry?' said Bea, looking up.

'You okay?' asked Tori.

'Yeah,' said Bea. 'Just a bit tired.' She really hoped Tori couldn't tell what she'd just been daydreaming about. Her cheeks reddened at the thought.

'I was asking how the to-do list was coming along?' Tori repeated, gesturing at the notepad on the table.

'Good,' replied Bea, reaching for her drink. 'Are you sure you don't mind me working on this while I'm here?'

'It's dead this afternoon, we should make the most of it. Anything I can help with?' said Tori, pulling up a chair,

'Erm . . . I don't think so. I've placed my first order with the wholesalers, I've bought a card reader, all my social media is up and running—'

'What about the boring stuff? Tax? Insurance?'

'I've registered for self-assessment and I've got quotes for public liability insurance. I think I'm all set.'

'Sounds like it. I reckon you'll be ready in time for the fair; there's still a fortnight to go.'

'I really hope so. Nate's been building the bookcases, they look amazing. I never knew he was such a good carpenter.'

'Ah, he's full of hidden talents is Nate. Can you keep a secret?'

'Me? Absolutely,' Bea nodded.

'I know you're close to Nate, but you have to promise me you won't say anything to him.'

'My lips are sealed,' said Bea, while gesturing zipping her mouth shut.

'Well, I've nominated his cheese line for a local business award.'

'Seriously?'

'Yes! They're announcing the shortlist in a few weeks, I'm hoping he'll be on it.'

'Wow, Tori, that's amazing, that would be great publicity for him.'

'That's what I thought. It's a quality product, so he deserves the recognition.'

'Fingers crossed, then,' said Bea.

'And remember, don't say a word. Until the shortlist's announced anyway. If he's on it, I'll have to tell him,' Tori laughed.

'Oh, yeah,' Bea sniggered, 'good point.'

'Anyway, you carry on,' said Tori, pointing towards Bea's to-do list. 'I might close up early if things don't pick up, I've got to take Ellie to the vets in a bit anyway, she's got a checkup booked in with Grace—'

'You were saying,' said Bea, looking up at the sound of the doorbell. 'Arthur, hello!' Bea called, as Tori let him inside.

'Bea!' said Arthur, warmly.

'I didn't know you lived in Blossom Heath?' said Bea. 'Tori, this is Arthur, we met at the library.'

'Pleased to meet you, Tori,' said Arthur. 'My daughter-in-law has been telling me about the cat café, so I thought I'd come and have a look for myself.'

'How lovely! Does she live in the village?' Tori asked.

'Yes, just on the outskirts,' Arthur explained. 'I'm in Rye, myself.'

'Why don't you join me for a cuppa?' said Bea. 'I was just about to take a break – if that's still okay, Tori?'

Tori nodded, enthusiastically.

'If you're sure I'm not imposing? You look like you're in the middle of something important,' said Arthur, gesturing towards the papers strewn all over the tabletop.

'Bea's working on plans for her new business,' said Tori. 'I'm sure she'd love to tell you all about it. What can I get you? Tea? Coffee?'

'A pot of tea would be just the ticket,' said Arthur, slipping off his jacket.

'And you have to try some of the carrot cake, Arthur. Tori's mum makes it, and it's just delicious,' said Bea.

'I do have a sweet tooth,' said Arthur. 'My doctor said I should be watching my cholesterol, but that does look good. I'll take a slice.'

'Coming right up,' said Tori, from behind the counter.

'Sit down, Arthur, I'll clear some room,' said Bea, gathering her paperwork up into a neat pile.

'So, what is it you're working on?' asked Arthur, easing himself gently into the seat opposite Bea.

'I'm just about to launch my own business,' said Bea. 'But I've never done anything like this before, so I've got a lot to learn.'

'What kind of business is it?'

'Well, I've bought a second-hand horsebox and I'm turning it into a mobile bookshop.'

'A mobile bookshop!' said Arthur. 'What a novel idea!'

'Thank you. It's all happened quite quickly, so it's been a bit overwhelming to be honest.'

'Well, that's the thing with running your own business, you have to be a jack of all trades: retailer, accountant, marketer, designer . . . you get the idea.'

'You're not wrong,' said Bea, leaning back in her chair. 'It's a big learning curve and I still don't understand half this stuff.'

'You'll get there. If I can do it, anyone can.'

'What was it you did exactly, Arthur? Did you have your own business, too?'

'I did, yes. I used to have a little antique shop by the quay in Rye.'

'Wow, did you? I love it down there, I bet you had some incredible finds!'

'Oh, I did well enough over the years. I learnt on the job, really, but you start to develop an eye. There was one item that stands out though . . .' he chuckled. 'I'll never forget it.'

'What was it?'

'I was doing a house clearance for a widow whose husband was a big stamp collector. He had a vast collection, so I catalogued them all, gave the lady a fair price . . .'

'And what happened?' Bea asked, her curiosity piqued.

'Well, when I was listing them ready for auction, a sealed

envelope fell out of one of the albums, and when I opened it there was a Penny Red inside!'

'And that's good? Valuable, I mean?'

'Not necessarily,' said Arthur, shaking a finger, 'they're old, but most are fairly common.'

'Oh,' said Bea, feeling slightly disappointed.

'Ah, I said *most* Penny Reds are fairly common,' said Arthur, his eyes glinting excitedly.

'And this one wasn't?'

'No, it wasn't. It was a Plate 77, which is *incredibly* rare. You can count the ones left in existence on one hand.'

'Wow! So, it was worth a lot then?'

'If you call £250,000 a lot?' Arthur shrugged.

'Sorry, *a quarter of a million pounds*?' said Bea, her mouth hanging open. 'For a *stamp*?'

'For a stamp,' Arthur nodded.

'But that's crazy.'

'That's antiques for you, Beatrice.'

'It must have set you up for life?'

'Oh, I didn't keep the money,' said Arthur, shaking his head.

'Why not?'

'It would have felt dishonest. I gave that widow what I thought was a fair price for her husband's collection; neither of us knew the Penny Red was there. I wasn't going to fiddle her out of what was rightfully hers. It would have been wrong.'

'Oh, Arthur,' said Bea, blowing out through her lips.

'That was so kind of you, I'm not sure other dealers would have done the same.'

'That may be true, but I wouldn't have slept a wink if I'd kept that stamp for myself.'

'You're a good person, Arthur,' said Bea, her heart swelling with admiration for the elderly gentleman sat with her.

'The widow did give me twenty-five thousand as a thank you, so I still did well out of the deal.'

'Here we go, Arthur, tea and cake,' said Tori, setting down a tray. 'I couldn't help overhearing your story and, well, *wow*.'

'I know, it was so exciting to find it,' said Arthur, beaming. 'Now, how much do I owe you?' he asked, pulling out his wallet.

'These are on the house,' said Tori, 'on one condition.'

'Oh?' replied Arthur.

'You have to come back again. I'd love to hear about the other treasures you've discovered,' said Tori.

'Of course!' laughed Arthur. 'It would be my pleasure.'

'I'm serious, Nate, I can't believe how amazing these look!' said Bea, running a hand along the handmade shelves he was carefully screwing to the internal walls of the wagon.

'They'll look even better when they're painted and full of books,' said Nathan.

'It's unrecognizable,' said Bea, 'I still can't believe we've finished it.'

'We haven't,' said Nathan, 'there's still a bit to do—'

'I got a few days free before my next shift at the Cosy Cat and I plan to spend it painting and shopping for soft furnishings and accessories.'

'You're on your own, there. Cushions are not my thing, I'm afraid,' said Nathan.

'I thought I might take Mum along,' said Bea. 'She's been really supportive with this whole crazy idea,' she said, gesturing towards the horsebox.

'She might foot the bill, too, if you take her?' said Nathan, wiggling his eyebrows.

'You never know,' Bea laughed.

'It's looking bloody good though, Bea,' he continued. 'I love the logo Jess designed, it's actually starting to look like . . . well, a—'

'Bookshop?'

'Exactly. You've done a great job.'

'No, *we've* done a great job, Nate,' she said, taking a step towards him. 'None of this would have happened without you, you know that, right?'

'Ah, don't be silly,' he replied, waving a hand dismissively.

'Seriously, if you hadn't been there that day at Charlotte's encouraging me, I don't think I'd have gone through with buying it.'

'You had Jess, too; she'd have talked you round.'

'It was *you*, Nate. Once you told me I could do it, I just . . . *believed* you, I guess,' she shrugged. 'Does that sound weird?'

'A little bit . . .' he said, shaking his head. 'Maybe?'

'I guess it's always been like that though, ever since school, I—'

'Nate!' called his mum, Sue, poking her head around the barn doors. 'I'm ready now if you want to go and get those deliveries done?'

'It's fine, you go, I need to crack on with the painting anyway,' said Bea, prising opening a tin of paint with a screwdriver.

'Okay, I'll see you later, though?' asked Nathan.

'Sure, I'm going to be here for the next few hours at least.' Bea laughed.

'Yeah, course,' said Nathan, heading towards the door.

'Right then,' said Bea, taking a deep breath, 'these bookcases aren't going to paint themselves,' she whispered, picking up a wide brush and dipping it into the thick, white paint. It was time to get started.

Nathan was struggling to concentrate on the road as he drove towards the Cosy Cat. Sue was chatting away animatedly, but he wasn't taking in a single word she was saying. He couldn't get his mind off Bea.

She'd said he was the reason she'd had the confidence to take on the bookshop project.

He was confused as to why his opinion mattered so much to her.

Why was it any different to Jess's, or Archie's, or Carol's? What had she been about to say to him before his mum had walked into the barn.

'It's always been like that though, ever since school, I—'

What was she going to say? Was she talking about their friendship? Or something else?

He shook his head. Whatever Bea had been about to tell him, she didn't get the chance to say it, and perhaps now he'd never know.

CHAPTER 13

'Bloody hell, Sis!' said Archie, surveying the pile of boxes stacked up in the garage. 'You'll never fit all these books in the horsebox.'

'Not all at once, I know, but hopefully I'll need lots of stock over the summer, so it made sense to bulk-order to see me through.'

'Even so, I think you might have overdone it,' said Archie, scratching his head.

'Hmmmm ... ' said Bea, looking around her, 'I might have got a little carried away.'

'A *little*?'

'Okay, okay, a lot. Oh, God. I'm going to be stuck with this lot when the book wagon turns out to be an epic failure, aren't I?' said Bea, chewing her lower lip.

'Hey, it's not going to fail,' said Archie, stepping towards her. 'It's going to be great, and it's better to be prepared.'

'God, I hope you're right, Arch. Now the fête is getting closer, it all feels a bit . . .'

'Stressful?'

'Yep,' said Bea, morosely.

'There's a fine line between excitement and fear,' said Archie encouragingly. 'That's what they say, isn't it? They're basically the same emotion.'

'Are they? Because I have to say, the fear thing feels a whole lot worse,' Bea said, mustering a weak smile.

'It's going to be great; you've got nothing to worry about, okay?'

'Okay,' Bea nodded, opening up one of the boxes and breathing in that familiar bookish smell.

'Are you sniffing them?' Archie asked, perplexed.

'Absolutely,' Bea nodded, 'I love the scent of new books,' she said, holding one under his nose.

'You're weird,' he laughed, batting her hand away. 'Are you seeing Mum today?'

'Yep. We're going shopping. I need to grab a shower first, though, I still reek of paint,' said Bea, holding out a strand of hair and sniffing it.

'I can't smell anything,' said Archie.

'I'm not sure you're the best judge, to be fair. Seb's room stank, and you couldn't smell that either.'

'Fair point,' said Archie. 'Have fun with Mum.'

Bea pulled up outside her parents' house just as her dad was taking Wordsworth for a walk.

'Bea!' said Gordon, pulling her into a hug. 'Your mum's really looking forward to this shopping trip, you know.'

'Me too,' said Bea, reaching down to fuss Wordsworth, who was giddy with excitement at seeing her.

'Have fun!' Gordon laughed, striding off in the direction of the nature reserve, dragging a reluctant Wordsworth behind him.

'Bea? Is that you?' said Carol, appearing in the doorway.

'Sure is, are you ready?'

'Before we go, I've got something for you, darling.'

'What is it?' said Bea, stepping inside the door.

'Just a little something for the wagon,' she said, reaching inside her shopping bag. 'Here,' she said, handing Bea a small package wrapped up in pink tissue paper. 'I hope you like it, I made it myself.' Bea carefully unwrapped the package to reveal a string of intricate, hand-crafted bunting in pretty, pastel colours.

'It's beautiful, Mum!' said Bea. 'Thank you!'

'Jess gave me the measurements,' Carol said, 'so you should have just the right amount to hang along the walls.'

'Thanks, Mum. Honestly, I love it, it'll look gorgeous.'

'Good, I'm glad,' said Carol, smiling at her brightly. 'I can't wait to see it all finished.'

'Me too,' Bea laughed. 'That's why today's quite important, I really want to get the décor right.'

'I'm so proud of you, sweetheart. It's brought me so much joy to see how happy books make you,' said Carol, her eyes misting with tears.

'Hey,' said Bea, taking her mum's hand. 'My love of

literature comes from you, and I'm so grateful for that, Mum, I really am.'

'Well, let's go and spend some of your dad's money, shall we? Whatever you want ... cushions, lighting, throws, it's on us, okay?'

'But, Mum, I—'

'No arguments,' said Carol, holding up a hand.

'Okay. And thanks, Mum, honestly, I really appreciate it,' said Bea, nodding.

'I know you do, darling. Now let's put this bunting away before Wordsworth gets back and rips it apart, shall we?'

'Good idea,' said Bea, wrapping it carefully back up in the tissue paper.

'Where do you fancy for lunch?' said Carol, picking up her handbag.

'Depends ...' said Bea, thoughtfully.

'On what?'

'On whether that's on you, too?'

'Okay, I *think* I'm ready now ...' said Bea, clutching her hands together tightly, as Nathan peered through a crack in the barn doors.

'You said that twenty minutes ago.'

'It's a big moment, I want to everything to be perfect,' said Bea, finally swinging the barn doors open.

'It will be,' said Nathan, grinning at her.

'You're the first person to see it finished, Nate. I want you to love it as much as I do.'

'I'm sure I will,' he nodded.

Bea had been shut away in the barn all day, sorting and filling the shelves of the wagon with books of every size, shape and colour. New books, old books, books for every kind of reader imaginable. Whatever you were looking for, Bea was sure you'd find a story to fall in love with somewhere on her shelves.

Once the bookcases had been arranged and organized, she'd carefully strung the bunting her mum had made alongside the fairy lights on the walls, plumped the beanbag and cushions in the tiny reading area, hung macramé planters filled with succulents from the ceiling and finally switched on the neon pink *Bookworm* lamp Nate had rigged up to a car battery.

This was it; she was finished. The wagon was finally ready, and it looked . . . *wonderful*. It was everything she'd imagined it would be and more. She'd put her heart and soul into this project. She felt . . . proud, but also apprehensive. Would everyone else love it as much as she did, and, crucially, love it enough to buy some books?

'So?' she asked, cautiously, as Nathan stepped inside. 'What do you think?'

'Bea! This is . . .'

'Good? Bad? Too much? What do you *think*?' she asked, her heart pounding in her chest.

'It's bloody brilliant!' he said, pulling her into a hug.

Without thinking, she threw her arms around his neck.

'Seriously? You like it?' she asked, tipping her head back to look up at him.

'I do,' he nodded. 'You're a genius, Bea.'

'And you're not just saying that because—'

'Because we've known each other a long time and you think I feel obliged to be nice?'

'Exactly,' said Bea, seriously. 'I'll know if you're lying, remember?'

'I'm not lying though, Bea. You've done an amazing job, you know that, right?'

'It wasn't just me. You, Jess, Archie – you all helped. I couldn't have done it without you lot.'

'Also true.'

'Thanks, Nate. For everything,' she said, realizing her arms were still around his neck. Why hadn't she let go?

'You'd do the same for me.'

'I would,' she whispered. They gazed into each other's eyes for a moment, then, suddenly self-conscious, Bea let her arms slip from around his neck.

'You know what we need to do next, though, don't you?' he said.

'No, what?'

'Get this little lady out on the road!'

CHAPTER 14

Bea looked up from the TV when she heard the distinctive purr of Lochlan's sports car outside her window that evening. She smiled as she swung open the front door.

'Got any dinner plans?' he called from the kerb, lowering the car window.

'No, but . . .'

'I've made us reservations.'

'Really? Give me five minutes to get changed—'

'You look fine,' said Lochlan, 'just get your keys and let's go.'

'Okay,' said Bea, grabbing her handbag from the banister and locking the door behind her. 'Where are we going?' she asked, climbing into the car.

'It's a surprise,' said Lochlan.

'So mysterious,' she laughed.

'I try,' he said, flashing her a smile that made her heart soar.

'Seriously, though, where are we going? I'm not dressed for anything fancy—'

'Like I said, you look fine,' he said, placing a warm hand over hers.

'Hmmmm ...'

'You might need these though ...' he said, pointing to a muddy pair of wellies in the footwell.

'Wellies? For a dinner date?'

'It's not your average dinner date,' said Lochlan, squeezing her hand.

'Obviously!' Bea laughed.

'How's your day been?'

'Good, well, *great* actually,' she replied. 'I've put all the finishing touches to the wagon, so I'm ready to open this weekend.'

'Wow, Bea, that's brilliant!' said Lochlan, turning to look at her. 'We can celebrate tonight. I'll get us some champagne.'

'Oh, you don't have to—'

'It's a moment, Bea, we should mark it.'

'Okay, thanks,' she said, smiling at him. 'That would be lovely.'

'So, you'll be launching at the village fête on Sunday, then?'

'Yep. I can't wait! Will you be able to make it?'

'Of course! I wouldn't miss it. I know how much it means to you.'

'Thanks, I'm really nervous. Just knowing you're going to be there helps.'

'Good, I'm glad,' he said, pulling on his sunglasses.

Bea took in the scenery as they passed through the villages of Appleton and Cherrydown towards Briarwood, and finally along a dirt track. 'Are you sure there's a restaurant down here?'

'Well, not exactly, no . . .'

'Where on earth are you taking me?' Bea asked. 'We're in the middle of nowhere.'

'Not quite nowhere,' Lochlan laughed, nodding towards a barn at the end of the track.

'Are those grapes?' Bea asked, pointing towards a field in the distance with rows of what looked like vines growing. 'Is this a vineyard?'

'Jackpot!' he laughed.

'Seriously? That's incredible, I had no idea this was here.'

'Me neither.'

'So, how did you find it?'

'I've got good contacts . . .'

'Like I said, *so* mysterious . . .'

'Let's just say it belongs to a friend of a friend. She's refurbished the barn, put in a kitchen, hired a chef. The plan is to open a pairing restaurant – you know? Different wines with each course.'

'Sounds great,' agreed Bea.

'Anyway, she's testing menus and was looking for some guinea pigs to try out the food, so I volunteered us,' he explained, pulling the car to a stop in front of the barn.

'It looks amazing,' said Bea, admiring the frosted glass doors embossed with the logo for Cherrydown Vineyard.

'Hello there, you must be Bea and Lochlan,' called a tall woman who was waiting to greet them. 'I'm Phoebe.'

'Lovely to meet you,' said Lochlan, shaking her hand.

'This place looks incredible,' said Bea.

'Thanks. Let me show you through, I've got some wines for you to try before dinner.'

Bea and Lochlan followed Phoebe through to the restaurant, which was fitted out with a beautiful low-lit bar area and comfy leather sofas.

'Wow, Phoebe, this is amazing,' said Bea, admiring the exposed beams and vaulted ceilings.

'Thank you. I must admit, I'm proud of it. I've poured some wine out for you at the bar, and we've got the private dining room ready. Chef's put together something really special for us today, so I hope you'll enjoy it.'

'I'm sure we will, thank you,' said Lochlan.

'I was hoping we could take a walk around the vineyard after dinner, if that's okay, Phoebe? Do a bit of stargazing?' he asked.

'Of course! It's still a bit muddy in places,' she replied. 'But it's a clear night, so you should have some great views. Zero light pollution.'

'Oh, that sounds wonderful,' Bea said, taking Lochlan's hand. 'So that's what the wellies were for?'

'Now, let's start with the rosé,' said Phoebe, handing Lochlan and Bea a glass each. 'Give it a swirl and a sniff first,' she said, demonstrating.

'That smells divine,' said Bea, inhaling, 'definitely fruity . . . maybe grapefruit or orange?'

'Very good,' said Phoebe, beaming at her, 'rosé wines generally have more fruit than traditional whites, so they're a lot less floral.'

'Now have a taste,' said Phoebe.

'We don't have to spit it out, do we?' asked Lochlan.

'No, absolutely not,' Phoebe laughed, 'that would be a terrible waste.'

Lochlan and Bea followed her instructions, taking a small sip and pausing briefly before swallowing.

'Absolutely delicious,' Lochlan murmured.

'I'm glad you like it,' said Phoebe.

'Oh, me too,' said Bea quickly, 'Could I buy some to take home, please?'

'We're not ready to retail just yet, but I'll put a box of whatever you'd like aside for you to take away,' said Phoebe.

'Oh, you don't have to—' said Bea.

'It'd be my pleasure,' said Phoebe, holding up a hand.

'That's really generous of you, thank you,' said Lochlan.

'Ah, it looks like we're ready for you now,' said Phoebe, as two black-and-white-uniformed waitresses appeared in the doorway. 'This is Rachel and Joanne, they'll be your servers today, I'll leave you in their very capable hands. And just let me know when you're ready to leave at the end of the evening and I'll drop you both home as we agreed.'

'Thanks, Phoebe,' said Lochlan, draining his glass.

'If you'd like to follow me,' said Rachel, leading the way to the private dining room.

'Wow,' said Bea, open-mouthed as they entered the

intimate space, lit with fairy lights and candles, soft music playing in the background. 'This is gorgeous,' she said, as Lochlan pulled out her chair.

'Chef's put together a special tasting menu for you this evening,' said Joanne, handing each of them a menu. 'We'll bring the first course through shortly.'

'Just look at this: guinea fowl, truffle, caviar,' whispered Bea.

'I know, right,' said Lochlan, raising his champagne flute. 'Here's to spending time together.'

'Thank you,' Bea said, leaning back in her chair as Rachel placed the first course in front of them. 'This looks great.'

'Mmmm,' said Lochlan, putting a forkful of truffle arancini into his mouth, 'Oh my God, Bea, you have to try this,' he said, holding up his fork.

'Ooooh,' she murmured, 'that's *so* good.'

'Right?'

'I could get used to this,' she said, taking another bite.

'Well, I'd have to learn to cook first,' laughed Lochlan. 'Beans on toast is more my level.'

'Oh, I'm not suggesting *you* cook, we should just come here every weekend,' she laughed.

'So, we're going to be spending our weekends together then?' asked Lochlan, reaching for her hand.

'Maybe . . .' she whispered.

'Hey, I'd like to spend more time with you,' he said. 'I really like you.'

'Good to know,' she said, blushing.

'The other night was pretty special,' he said, 'you know, back at yours . . .'

'Yeah, I know,' she said, her cheeks turning an even deeper shade of pink. She was very much hoping for a repeat performance later.

'Well, next time you fancy beans on toast at mine . . .'

'With grated cheese on top?'

'Absolutely,' he laughed.

'Then I'm in.'

After working their way through the six-course tasting menu, Marcel, the chef, came out of the kitchen to introduce himself.

'I hope you enjoyed the food this evening?' he asked, warmly.

'It was out of this world,' said Lochlan.

'It was the best meal I've ever had,' agreed Bea. 'This place is going to be a huge success.'

'You're very kind, thank you,' said Marcel, taking their plates. 'And now a stroll around the vineyard, yes?' he asked.

'Wow,' said Bea, as she and Lochlan walked slowly through the vines. 'Look at the stars,' she said, gazing upwards.

'I told you those wellies would come in handy,' he laughed, steadying her as she slipped in the mud.

'Whoops, nearly,' said Bea, holding on to him tightly. 'I think all that wine's gone to my head.'

'No problem,' said Lochlan, lacing his arm through hers.

'I think Phoebe said there's a viewing platform on top of that hill.'

'I can't believe how much clearer the skies are out here than in the village. I don't think I've ever seen them shine so bright.'

'Me neither,' Lochlan agreed.

'Whoooaa,' yelped Bea as she slid in another patch of mud.

'Gotcha!' said Lochlan, pulling her in close.

'Thanks,' she said, breathlessly, turning to face him.

'You're welcome,' he murmured.

'Good job you were here to catch me,' Bea whispered.

'I'll always catch you,' said Lochlan, kissing her softly on the mouth.

'Good to know,' Bea replied, sliding her arms around his neck and kissing him back.

In that moment, under a blanket of stars, Bea couldn't think of anywhere she'd rather be than right here, with Lochlan by her side.

'I can't believe tomorrow's the big day,' said Jess, sipping a glass of red wine.

'I know,' said Bea, taking another handful of popcorn from a big bowl on the coffee table.

'How are you feeling?'

'About as anxious as you'd expect for someone who used all their savings to buy a second-hand horsebox.'

'It might have been a bit impulsive, but you should be proud of yourself, Bea, you do know that, right?'

'I guess so, but there's so much that could go wrong. What if—'

'Hey, just try to relax, you've done everything you can to launch the business. It'll be great, I promise.'

'I hope so.'

'It *will*. The wagon looks amazing. Seriously, it's better than those ones we saw on Pinterest!'

'You think?'

'Absolutely. It's the little touches that make it feel really special. The lamp and all those framed prints on the walls are so cute,' said Jess, smiling. 'I love that one about magic . . . what does it say again?'

'Books are a uniquely portable magic.'

'Yes! Who said that?'

'Stephen King.'

'What? The horror guy?' said Jess, surprised.

'Uh-huh.'

'Who'd have thought?' Jess shrugged. 'And the tote bags, pin badges and bookmarks are brilliant. I love the "I'd rather be at book club" one, it's genius! They're going to sell really well.'

'Thank you, that means a lot, it really does,' said Bea, swallowing hard.

'You're welcome,' said Jess, squeezing her friend's hand.

'I just can't believe it's really happening.'

'I'll be honest, I wasn't sure how it was going to look when I first saw the state of the horsebox, but I didn't want to put a downner on the idea . . .'

'Jess! It was you who persuaded me to go for it!'

'The point is it's all finished, tomorrow's going to be brilliant, you're brilliant and I'm proud of you,' said Jess, with a decisive nod. 'Is Lochlan coming by the way?'

'Yes! He said he wouldn't miss it.'

'Dinner at the vineyard sounded amazing. As did the hot sex afterwards.'

'God, it was! He's really spoiling me and I'm loving every second of it!'

'Are you talking about the date or the sex?' Jess asked, waggling her eyebrows suggestively.

'Well, both, but the sex is . . .' Bea trailed off, biting her lower lip.

'Hot?'

'Well, yeah!' Bea laughed.

'But you're taking it slowly, yes?'

'Erm . . . kind of,' Bea stammered.

'Listen, I just want you to be careful, Bea. Don't rush in too hard too fast. You know what you're like. Just take it slow this time, okay?' Jess paused.

'But—' said Bea, keen to explain that, while things were moving quickly, it was Lochlan who was driving it.

'Seriously, Bea. I just don't want you to get hurt again. Take some time to get to know one another properly. You've only seen him, what, three times?'

'Well, four actually, if you include the day we met, but I get your point. I promise I will. I know you only want me to be happy.'

CHAPTER 15

Bea was wide awake well before her alarm went off the next morning, after a night spent tossing and turning, sleep evading her. But, no matter how tired she was, she couldn't contain her excitement at the thought of opening the doors of Bea's Book Wagon to customers for the first time.

'Archie? What are you doing up so early?' she said, as she padded downstairs to the kitchen.

'It's a big day, Sis. I thought you could do with a proper breakfast,' he replied, sliding some perfectly crispy bacon from the frying pan onto a stack of homemade pancakes.

'This looks delicious,' said Bea, her mouth watering.

'Turns out I'm actually quite good at this cooking lark, who knew?'

'Not me,' Bea laughed, taking a swig of orange juice and stuffing a rasher of bacon in her mouth. 'Mmmmmm, this is *so* good!'

'Well, don't go get getting any ideas, this is a one off, to celebrate your big day.'

'Thanks, Arch, I really appreciate it.'

'How are you feeling?'

'Like there's a bag of snakes wriggling around in my stomach,' said Bea. 'I don't think I've ever felt this nervous before.'

'Well, it's certainly not affecting your appetite,' said Archie, pointing towards her now half-empty plate.

'I'm stress-eating.'

'Today's going to be great. It's going to be sunny all day, so it should be really busy, and I'll be there to help out, so will Jess.'

'Thanks, Arch. Mum and Dad are bringing Wordsworth, and Matt said he'll be there too. He's been great, actually, telling everyone who comes into the library about it. He even put some flyers up for me.'

'Great. And Nate? He's coming, right?'

'Yep, he's got to work first, but he'll be there at some point. Lochlan's coming as well.'

'Cool, he seems like a nice guy.'

'Yeah, he is,' Bea said with a nod. 'Right, I'd better get ready, thanks for breakfast.'

'No problem. Do you need a hand getting the wagon hitched?'

'Nope, I'm good, I did it last night. Thanks for letting me leave it on the driveway, Arch. It's so much easier than going back and forth to the farm all the time. Now all the work's been done, there's no reason to keep it there, really.'

'I guess not.'

'Are you okay to tidy up?' asked Bea, turning to leave. 'I've got a grand opening to get ready for.'

Bea made the short drive to the village green alone. Archie had offered to ride along with her, but she wanted some time by herself to get her head straight. It was her opening day, and she was determined to make the business a success. When she arrived at the village green, she could see that lots of stallholders were already setting up.

She glanced at her watch. She was right on time – why were so many people early? She'd hoped to have plenty of room to reverse the wagon into place, but she could see that, wherever she was told to park, it was going to be a tight squeeze.

She followed the signs marked 'Exhibitors' and was met by a stern-looking woman in a tweed suit, wearing a fluorescent tabard.

'Name?' the woman barked.

'Oh, hi, I'm Bea Miller. Bea's Book Wagon,' said Bea, lowering the car window.

'Let me see,' said the woman, scanning the clipboard in her hands. 'Ah, yes. You're next to Tony's Tex Mex, over there on the right,' she said, pointing in the distance towards where a scruffy silver trailer was parked.

'Ah, yes. Got it,' said Bea.

'You need to turn left and follow the arrows,' said the woman, jerking her thumb furiously.

'Left? But I'll never be able to reverse in from that angle,' said Bea, panic rising in her chest. 'If I go right I can just back straight in.'

'That's impossible,' said the woman, haughtily. 'Health and safety – vehicles can only flow from one direction.'

'But I can't make that turn,' said Bea, 'look at what I'm towing!'

'Like I said, traffic must flow from one direction only, there's nothing I can do about it, it's all in the risk assessment,' the woman said, puffing out her chest.

'For God's sake,' Bea huffed, closing her window. If there was one thing she hated more than petty rules, it was the petty bureaucrats who enforced them.

As Bea circled around the green, which was far bumpier than she'd anticipated, she took some deep, calming breaths. It was going to be fine. Okay, it might be harder to reverse into her pitch from this angle, but she could totally deal with it, and she needed all the practice she could get.

At least that's what she *thought*. But after several attempts, Bea's arms were aching from heaving the steering wheel round, and sweat was starting to pour down her forehead.

'You want to get more swing on it, love,' the man at the next pitch – who she assumed was Tex Mex Tony – yelled.

'You don't say,' Bea muttered under her breath, while throwing him a half-hearted wave of thanks. If he thought it was so easy, he was welcome to give it a try himself.

'Turn your wheel hard-right,' another vendor piped up.

'You're never going to make it from that angle,' someone else shouted, helpfully.

Bea wasn't sure whether to laugh or cry. Having an audience was doing nothing for her confidence.

'Watch out, watch out!' yelled a woman, as a stocky yellow Labrador ran behind the trailer.

'Sorry,' Bea shouted. 'Maybe keep your dog on a lead when you see someone reversing,' she cursed under her breath.

'Bea?' said a strikingly good-looking man with dark, curly hair who was striding towards her. 'Tori sent me, she thought you could do with a hand.'

'No, I've got this, but thanks,' said Bea, determined not to give up. If she was going to be taking the wagon all over Sussex, she absolutely had to master parking it.

'Let me help?' he repeated.

'Okay, that would be great, thank you,' said Bea, gratefully. 'You must be Leo? Tori's boyfriend?'

'That's right,' he said, beaming at her. Bea had heard all about him from Jess, but this was the first time they'd met.

'Okay, straighten up and when I give you the signal, turn the steering wheel to the right as hard as you can,' he said.

'Got it,' she said, lining the wagon up for another attempt. As she kicked into reverse, Leo waved, and she turned the wheel full-lock to the right.

'That's it,' he shouted. 'Now just keep coming back,' he said, arms aloft. 'A little bit more, you've got loads of room. That's it, you're in!'

'Thank *God*!' said Bea, feeling triumphant, as she checked her mirrors and hopped out of the car. 'Thanks, Leo. I was getting in a right mess.'

'No worries. Are you okay unhitching?'

'Absolutely. It would have been easier coming in the other way, but the woman with the clipboard wouldn't let me. Apparently I'd be "breaking health and safety rules",' she scowled, putting air quotes around the words.

'Ah, that'll be Violet Davenport. She's a bit of a busybody.'

'You don't say?' Bea laughed. 'Thanks for the help, though.'

'Anytime. Tori said she'll be over soon. She's dying to see your book wagon. It looks ace by the way.'

'Thanks, Leo.'

Bea unhitched the wagon from the car and, when she went inside, she was pleased to see that all the books had remained on their shelves. She unpacked the crate with the lamps, plants and other knick-knacks she'd accumulated, and added the finishing touches, ready to open. As she switched on the fairy lights, she heard footsteps coming up the ramp behind her.

'Wow, Bea, this is awesome!' said Tori, looking around. 'I never expected it to be so . . .'

'Jaw-droppingly gorgeous?'

'Well, exactly,' Tori laughed. 'I can't believe it used to be a horsebox. Honestly, you'd never know, it feels like a *real* bookshop.'

'Really? You think so?'

'Yes! Smaller, obviously, but it's a bit of a Tardis, isn't it? There's way more space than you'd think. Oh, is that a reading nook? Cute!' said Tori, pointing towards the beanbag.

'Yes, there's only enough room for a few kids really, but I've got some deckchairs to put outside for grown-ups.'

'What a great idea! Ooooh, I love these bookmarks,' said Tori, picking up one decorated with cats. 'Obviously, I'm buying this immediately.'

'Thanks! That makes you my first customer!'

'I'm honoured!'

'It'll give me a chance to try out the card machine, too,' said Bea, grabbing it from the box. 'Okay, so that's £2.99,' she said, inputting the amount. Tori tapped her card and the transaction was complete.

'Listen, I'm going to have to run, I've left Mum and Leo to set up our stall, but I'll be back later for a proper browse. If you run into any bother, just give me a shout. We're at the other end of the field, next to the WI stall.'

'Great, thanks. Jess and Archie should be here in a bit, but I'm sure I'll be fine.'

'Good luck!'

'See you.'

As Bea headed outside with a deckchair under each arm, it looked as though all the other stallholders were in position. There wasn't a vacant pitch to be seen anywhere on the green.

'Bea!' cried Jess, jogging towards her.

'Ah, I'm so glad to see you,' said Bea, pulling her friend into a tight hug.

'The wagon looks great! You've got a fab spot here, too. Tony's always has a massive queue, so that'll draw people in. What can I help with?'

'I think I'm all set,' said Bea, pushing her sunglasses up her nose.

'I'll grab us a coffee from Tori then. Flat white?'

'Amazing, thank you!'

'What time's Lochlan getting here?'

'Erm . . . I'm not actually sure. He didn't say.'

'But he's definitely coming?'

'Yeah, I mean, he said he is.'

'Cool. Hang on, here's Archie. Coffee?' Jess shouted as Archie strolled towards them.

'Please. Cappuccino,' he replied. 'All right, Sis. Any customers yet?'

'Yeah, Tori bought a bookmark,' said Bea.

'Bless her. And the fête's not even open yet,' said Archie. 'What can I do?'

'Well, nothing actually, everything's ready. We might as well sit down,' said Bea, lowering herself into one of the deckchairs.

'How are the nerves?'

'Better now I'm here,' said Bea.

'Listen, before it gets busy, I just wanted to say . . .'

'Yes?'

'Well, I'm proud of you, Bea,' he blurted out. 'What you've done takes guts; quitting your job like that, taking a risk. Not everyone has it in them.'

'Wow, thanks,' Bea gulped. It wasn't like Archie to be so sentimental, and it meant a lot. 'You've been great, too, letting me move in, lowering the rent for me a bit, not freaking out—'

'In fairness, I did freak out a bit,' he cut in.

'A bit is totally allowed,' Bea laughed. 'What I mean is, you've really helped me out, Arch, and that means a lot. I might not always say it, but I'm lucky to have such a great brother.'

'Steady on, Bea. You'll have me reaching for the tissues in a minute.'

'If anyone's going to be crying today, it'll be me,' said Bea.

'Honestly, I leave you two alone for five minutes and you get all emosh! Here, get these down you,' said Jess, handing them both a cup. 'To Bea's Book Wagon!' she announced, raising her coffee aloft.

'Oh my god!' said Bea. 'Look! They're letting people in, this is it!'

CHAPTER 16

The morning was a whirlwind of activity. Bea's Book Wagon seemed to be one of the star attractions and it had seen a steady stream of customers all *ooohing* and *ahhhing* at the interior and commenting on the innovative use of the horsebox.

'Bea! I can't believe it! I just can't believe it,' said Charlotte, as she brought her two young daughters, Melody and Hazel, over to the makeshift desk – a clever pull-down square of wood on hinges Nathan had designed – to pay for the books they had chosen.

'Charlotte!' said Bea, her face breaking into a wide grin. 'You like it, then?'

'Like it? I don't even recognize it! You've done an amazing job.'

'Thanks. It was a team effort, though, Nathan and Jess helped out. I couldn't have done it without them,' said Bea.

'I'm just so glad it's all worked out, it's all I've heard people talking about all morning: "Have you seen the new bookshop?" You're the talk of the village.'

'Am I? Well, that's lovely to hear.'

'Now, girls, what books have you chosen?' Charlotte asked her daughters.

'*Room on the Broom*,' said Melody, handing Bea her book.

'Good choice,' said Bea, 'it's one of my favourites.'

Melody beamed at her.

'What about you, Hazel?' asked Charlotte.

'*Diary of a Wimpy Kid*,' said Hazel, holding her book up proudly.

'I love those books!' said Bea. 'They're so funny, aren't they?'

'Yes!' agreed Hazel. 'I've been reading them at school.'

'Have you?' asked Bea. 'Well, it'll be good to have your own copy at home, won't it?'

'Yes!' said Hazel, nodding.

'That's £14.98, please,' said Bea, holding up the card machine for Charlotte.

'Thanks, Bea,' said Charlotte, tapping her card. 'We'd best get on, I've promised the girls one of Tori's cupcakes,' said Charlotte.

'Oooh, how lovely. Enjoy!' said Bea.

'Excuse me? Is it okay to bring dogs inside?' asked a woman holding the lead of a very excitable black and white Border Collie, while peering into the wagon.

'Yes, of course,' said Bea. 'She's a total cutie, what's her name?'

'Scout,' she replied, as the dog held out a paw for Bea to shake. 'And I'm Rose. I'm a friend of Tori's—'

'Oh, of course! Tori's mentioned you. You live at Harper Farm with Jake, don't you?'

'That's right! I've been dying to see the book wagon. Tori's been telling me all about it.'

'She's been great, she's helped so much, I'm very lucky.'

'Tori's a star. I'm after a favour actually . . .'

'Oh, okay. Happy to help if I can.'

'I'm a teacher at Blossom Heath Primary, and I was wondering if you might bring the book wagon for a visit one day? The kids would love it and—'

'Yes, of course!'

'Excellent, that's great news! We don't have a bookshop or library here, and we've only got a limited supply of books at the school, so it'd be lovely for the kids to have a bit more choice and try something new. Perhaps if you came late one afternoon, the children could have a look around and then, if you hang on after school finishes, their parents could pay for any books they want when they come to collect them?'

'That sounds brilliant, I'd love to!'

'Maybe we could think about making it a regular thing, once a month or something?'

'Absolutely.'

'Thanks, Bea. I'll be in touch, get a date booked in?'

'Perfect.'

'While I'm here, have you got a copy of the new Paige Toon novel?'

'I do, let me grab it for you.'

'I've been dying to read it!'

'I know, it's on my TBR list, too. She's great, isn't she?'

'Oh, I love her, I've read all her books.'

'Me too,' said Bea, 'she's such a great storyteller. That's £8.99, please.'

Rose tapped her card on the machine, but the transaction didn't go through.

'That's weird,' said Bea, twitching her nose. 'Maybe you need to insert it?'

'Sure, I've probably just tapped too many times today,' Rose laughed, inserting her card into the reader and entering her PIN.

'Hmmmm, it still hasn't worked. I'm so sorry about this,' said Bea.

'Need a hand?' asked Nathan, strolling towards the book wagon.

'Nate! Am I glad to see you!' said Bea, 'the card machine's stopped working.'

'Hmmmmm . . . not really my area of expertise. You can take cash, though, right?'

'Erm . . . yeah.'

'I've got cash on me, Bea,' said Rose, handing over a ten-pound note. As Bea counted out her change and slipped a free bookmark in the paper bag before handing the parcel over, she spotted Beth out of the corner of her eye, staring intently at the framed quote posters on the wall.

'Hey, Beth,' said Bea. 'I'm so glad you popped in, I've got a favour to ask you.'

'Okay . . .'

'I've had this idea for a book speed-dating event, and I was wondering if I could host it at the pub?'

'Book speed-dating? What on earth's that when it's at home?' Beth asked, eyebrows raised.

'It's kind of like normal speed dating, but rather than matching people, I'll be trying to match readers to their perfect book.'

'Sounds interesting,' said Beth, 'You'd have to run it on a mid-week night, but it would be a good way to draw in more customers when we're quieter, anyway. I'll run it past Pete first, but you'll do all the organizing, yes?'

'Oh, yes, definitely,' said Bea, nodding vigorously. 'All you'll need to do is serve the drinks, I'll sort everything else out.'

'Sounds good, love. Let me check with Pete and we'll get a date in the diary.'

'Excellent! Thanks, Beth.'

Bea was taking cash and offering her bank details to anyone who was happy to pay via transfer, when Nathan jogged back to the wagon.

'Tony's sorted it!' he said.

'Seriously?' said Bea. 'What was wrong with it?'

'Your Bluetooth had disconnected. He said he'll show you

how to reconnect once his queue dies down,' said Nathan, 'in case it happens again.'

'God, Jess was right about him, his queue never gets any shorter, does it?'

'Ah, Tony's Tex Mex is legendary, I'll get you some later. You haven't lived until you've tried his chicken enchiladas.'

'Ooooh, sounds delish.'

The next time Bea glanced at her watch, it was almost two, and she couldn't quite believe how much stock she'd sold. Good job she still had boxes of books stacked up in Archie's garage; it looked like she'd be needing to use them all far faster than she'd anticipated.

'How's it going?' asked Nathan, stepping inside the wagon, the door swinging shut behind him with a bang.

'Can you open it?' asked Bea. 'I don't want people to think I'm closed.'

'Sure,' said Nathan, turning the handle. Nothing happened. The lever remained firmly in position. 'Shit,' he muttered.

'What's wrong?'

'The handle's stuck.'

'Here, let me try, it can be a bit temperamental,' said Bea, twisting and jiggling the lever. It still wouldn't budge. 'Damn! It's jammed.'

'Let me have another go,' said Nathan, as Bea stepped aside. He yanked the handle down with force, shouldering the door at the same time.

Nothing.

'No, no, no, no,' Bea wailed. 'This can't be happening.'

'It'll be okay. We'll call Archie, he can take the handle off from outside.'

'Good idea,' said Bea, grabbing her phone. 'I don't believe it,' she groaned. 'There's no signal. What about you?' she asked.

Nathan patted down his pockets.

'I think I've left mine in the truck. Sorry,' he said, grimacing.

'Great,' she huffed, banging hard on the door yelling, 'Hello? We're stuck in here! Hello?' in the hope that someone would hear her.

'Don't panic,' Nathan shrugged. 'Someone will come along in a minute and open it from the outside. It'll be fine.'

'You go to the gym, can't you just rip the handle off?' she suggested.

'I know I'm in good shape, but I'm not actually the *Incredible Hulk*,' he teased, flexing his biceps.

'Fair point,' she conceded. 'You're right, though, someone will be along soon. I might as well restock the shelves, there's more boxes in the corner.'

'Good idea,' said Nathan, heaving a box on to the makeshift desk and rummaging inside.

'I can't even remember what's in here, to be honest,' said Bea, reaching into the box, her hand brushing against his rough fingers.

Her heart thudded against her ribs. Nathan looked up

and something flashed in his eyes. Bea had seen that look a thousand times before, but not for years.

'Look, *Pride and Prejudice*!' she said, attempting to disperse the electricity that was crackling in the air around them.

'Austen. One of your favourites,' Nathan replied, his eyes crinkling at the sides as he smiled.

'Do you remember when I took you to see that film?' she laughed.

'Yes! *Pride and Prejudice and Zombies*!'

'Jeez, it was awful.'

'Hey, I thought it was okay, actually.'

'You were drooling over Lily James for most of it, I'm surprised you even—'

'Actually,' he interrupted. 'I spent most of the time trying to work up the courage to put my arm around you . . .'

'Oh,' said Bea, her eyes widening in surprise. 'Yeah, I remember, I think it was the first time we—'

'Kissed.'

She paused before replying,

'As first kisses go, it was pretty good,' she said, smiling at the memory.

'It was,' Nathan agreed, his eyes firmly fixed on hers.

'Well, you certainly took your time about it,' Bea said. 'I was waiting all night for you to make a move,' she continued, turning her attention back to the box of books. 'I thought I was going to have to take matters into my own hands.'

'Oh, really?' he said, tipping his head to one side.

'Absolutely! And then Duncan Jones from Year Twelve ruined it all by chucking a box of popcorn over us!'

'Bastard!' Nathan laughed.

'Total bastard!' she agreed. 'What else is in here?' she asked, turning a book over in her hands to show Nathan the cover.

'*Lady Chatterley's Lover.* Isn't this supposed to be a bit ... *spicy*?' he said, raising his eyebrows. 'Wasn't it banned?'

'Uh-huh. It's definitely a five chili rating. Super spicy.'

Bang! There was a thud on the wagon door.

'Bea? Are you okay in there?' Archie's voice called from outside.

'The door's stuck!' said Bea. 'The handle won't budge.' Archie rattled the lever from outside and the door miraculously swung open.

'You were saying?' said Archie, grinning widely.

'What the—' said Bea.

'Seems fine now,' said Archie, waggling the handle up and down. 'Are you sure you two just didn't want some alone time?' he teased.

'Don't be daft,' said Bea, her cheeks burning red.

Why was it suddenly so hot in here?

Putting the lock-in with Nathan out of her mind, Bea continued to welcome a steady stream of customers through the bookshop's doors for the remainder of the day.

'Are you okay there?' she asked a lady who had been browsing the shelves for a while.

'Oh, I'm just looking really ... you've got such a

marvellous collection, I don't know where to start. Is that a vintage edition of *Jane Eyre* over there?' she asked, her face obscured by a pair of huge sunglasses.

'Yes. I've tried to mix the old and the new, so there's something for everyone,' said Bea.

'I can see that. A mobile bookshop . . . such a wonderful idea! Do you mind if I take some photos?'

'No, of course not. Go ahead. I'll leave you to it, but do shout if you need my help with anything.'

'Thank you. I'll take the *Jane Eyre*, if you could put that aside for me?'

'Sure, no problem,' said Bea, with a smile.

'Are you on social media at all?' she asked.

'Yes, we're @beasbookwagon on Instagram.'

'Perfect, I'll look you up.'

'Mum, Dad, you made it!' said Bea, as Wordsworth made a beeline for her, tail wagging enthusiastically.

'Of course we did, we wouldn't miss your opening day,' said Carol, giving her daughter a hug.

'Bea, this looks incredible, I had no idea you could work such wonders with an old horsebox,' said Gordon.

'She's very talented, aren't you, darling? She takes after her mother,' said Carol.

'Hello!' called Matt from the doorway.

'Matt! I'm so glad you're here!' said Bea.

'We wouldn't miss it,' said Matt, warmly. 'Bea, this is my husband, Harry, I don't think you've met?'

'No, but I've heard all about you. Good to meet you, Harry,' said Bea.

'You too. Matt's not stopped talking about this, you know? He's been dying to see it finished and I can see why,' said Harry, 'it's so cute!'

'Thanks. I'm so glad you like it,' said Bea.

'It looks amazing, Bea,' said Matt.

'Thanks, Matt,' said Bea.

'Why don't we leave Bea to it?' said Carol, nodding towards a customer approaching the desk with a stack of books. 'We can come back once it's a bit quieter.'

'Thanks for popping by,' said Bea. 'I'll see you all later.'

'I'll take these,' said the woman in the sunglasses, handing the pile of books to Bea.

'Perfect. I'll bag them up for you. You've got a great selection here,' she said, glancing at the titles.

'I must confess to having a bit of an addiction . . .'

'Don't worry,' said Bea, whispering conspiratorially, 'You're in good company. You can't move at my house for books. You read a lot then, I assume?' Bea asked.

'Read, write . . .'

'Oh, you're a writer?'

'I try. Truth be told, I'm having a bit of a block at the moment, so I'm on a little mini break to try to recharge my batteries a bit.'

'You're staying in Blossom Heath?'

'Nearby, yes,' said the woman, tapping her card on the machine.

'Are you here for long?' asked Bea.

'Not sure, really, it depends how things go.'

'With the writing?'

'Partly.'

'Well, it's lovely here. I'm Bea by the way,' she said.

'Nice to meet you, Bea. I'm Katerina,' said the woman and, as she turned to leave, Bea couldn't shake the feeling that they'd met before; something about her turn of phrase sounded familiar but she couldn't put her finger on why.

'I think that might be your last customer of the day,' said Nathan, several hours and many purchases later.

'Yeah, it looks like things are starting to wind down,' said Bea, throwing herself into one of the deckchairs outside the wagon.

'How do you think it's gone?' he asked, sitting down next to her.

'Better than I expected, for sure. I mean, I've not totalled up the takings, but I've shifted a ton of stock, way more than I thought I would, so that's got to be a good thing?'

'Absolutely, and everyone's raving about it, too. Seriously, Bea, it's been a huge success. Shall I help you pack up, then you can take the trailer home and we can meet up at the pub later to celebrate?'

'Ah,' said Bea, checking her watch – it was nearly six, 'I'm not sure. Lochlan was supposed to be coming, but I've not seen him all day.' Bea pulled her phone out of her pocket and checked for messages.

Nothing.

She'd been so busy, she'd barely had time to notice that Lochlan hadn't made an appearance, but now she wondered why he hadn't shown up.

'No worries, I'll just help you pack up and then head off,' said Nathan.

'It's fine, Nate, the pub sounds good.'

'Okay, great. Archie's already there,' he said, 'he's meeting Jess there later.'

'Is it me or have they been spending a lot of time together recently? I'm not missing something am I?'

'Archie and Jess? Nah, I doubt it' said Nathan, pushing his sunglasses up his nose. 'Anyway, wouldn't Jess have told you if something was going on?'

'You're right, he's definitely not her type.'

'Hey, I've just remembered, didn't I promise you the best chicken enchiladas you'll ever taste?'

'Yes! You'd better be quick though, looks like Tony's packing up . . .'

'On it,' said Nathan, striding over to the stall.

Bea picked up her phone and sent a WhatsApp message to Lochlan: *Fête went well, sorry I didn't see you. Let me know if you're around later xx*

She sighed, confused by his absence and disappointed not to have seen him.

When she looked up, she saw Nathan walking towards her holding two chicken enchiladas, with a bottle of beer tucked under each arm, and she couldn't help but smile.

Here she was, sat in the late afternoon sun with one of her favourite people in the world. The first day had been a success, and she was about to enjoy a cold beer with what were allegedly the world's best enchiladas. Did it really matter that Lochlan had let her down?

CHAPTER 17

'So, have you heard from him yet?' asked Jess, over coffee at the Cosy Cat the next morning. 'I still can't believe he didn't show up!'

'Yeah, he sent a message late last night after I got back from the pub. He got caught up with work stuff in London. He couldn't get out of it, apparently,' Bea said, nonchalantly.

'He should have let you know, though.'

'He said he was in meetings all day.'

'On a bank holiday weekend?' said Jess, eyes narrowed.

'Uh-huh.'

'And you believe him?'

'It's not a big deal.'

'Hmmmmm . . . if you say so. Not quite Mr Perfect after all, though.'

'Oh, it's fine, Jess. Seriously, I've already forgotten it,' said

Bea. 'He couldn't make it, he's apologized, we're fine,' she said, arms folded.

'If a guy I was dating missed something that was as important to me as yesterday was to you, I'm not sure I'd feel the same way . . .'

'Well, thankfully you're not dating him, so we're good. By the way, did I tell you I got a few more bookings out of yesterday?' said Bea, keen to change the subject.

'No! That's great news.'

'I know. I'm visiting the primary school in a few weeks, and the WI have invited me to go to their next meeting to give a talk about the renovation and people can buy books afterwards.'

'Fantastic, how exciting!'

'I've reserved a pitch at a few other summer fairs as well, one in Cherrydown in July and another in Appleton in August. If I can get at least one booking a month over the summer, that gives me some financial security, then I can work out what to do longer term once the holidays are over.'

'Sounds like a good plan,' Jess agreed, equally glad to be off the subject of Lochlan.

'Arthur!' said Bea, leaping up from her chair as he pulled open the door.

'Hello there, my dear,' he said warmly.

'Arthur, this is my friend Jess. Would you like to join us?' Bea offered.

'Only if I'm not interrupting?' he said, taking off his hat.

'No, of course not,' said Bea. 'I'm not working today,

but grab a seat and I'll get you a coffee. Cream, two sugars, right?'

'You remembered!' said Arthur.

'Isn't this supposed to be your day off?' asked Joyce, who was busy at the coffee machine as Bea approached the counter.

'Yeah, but is it okay if I get Arthur a coffee?' asked Bea.

'I'll get it, love. What's he having?' asked Joyce.

'Flat white, cream and two sugars,' said Bea.

'You sit down, I'll bring it over,' said Joyce.

'Thanks,' replied Bea.

'And the next thing I knew, I'd signed up to join the Merchant Navy,' Arthur was saying, as Bea returned to the table.

'Coffee's on its way. What's that about the Navy?' asked Bea.

'He's been telling me all about how he got conscripted by accident,' said Jess, wiping tears of laughter from her cheek. 'Arthur's a hoot!'

'You're too kind,' said Arthur, handing her a handkerchief from his top pocket. 'I'm sorry I missed your big day yesterday, Beatrice,' he apologized. 'I had planned on coming to see the book wagon on opening day, but my arthritis had other ideas, I'm afraid.'

'Oh no, I'm sorry to hear that,' said Bea, her voice edged with concern.

'All part of getting old, I'm afraid, not something you young ones need to worry about yet,' he said, shaking his head. 'I do want to hear all about it, though.'

'Here we are. Coffee with cream and two sugars,' said Joyce, setting a mug down on the table.

'Thank you,' said Arthur, with a look of gratitude.

'Well, it was a total triumph,' Jess gushed.

'I knew it!' said Arthur, snapping his fingers.

'Bea's already got more bookings; she'll be busy all summer at this rate,' said Jess.

'I don't know about that,' said Bea, 'but yesterday went well, so it's a start.'

'And a start is all you need,' said Arthur, blowing on his coffee to cool it down a little.

'I meant to ask you, how's the search for a book club going? I've been asking around, but I've not found one yet,' said Bea.

'Me neither, I'm afraid. I'm on the waiting list for one in Rye called *Books & Prosecco,* but I'm not sure it's really for me, if I'm honest,' said Arthur.

'Hang on,' said Bea, her mind whirring. 'Why haven't I thought of this before?' she muttered, an idea forming in her head. 'I could start one in the wagon!'

'That does sound more my thing,' said Arthur animatedly.

'I could take it on the road and visit all the local villages. Once a month or something?' said Bea.

'Bea's Book Club! I love it!' squealed Jess.

'It does have a certain ring to it,' agreed Arthur.

'I could do food and drink as well. Maybe Nate could supply cheese . . . ooooh and we could have wine from the vineyard I went to with Lochlan,' said Bea excitedly.

'So, kinda like a supper club, but with books, too?' said Jess, mulling it over.

'Yes, exactly. Cheese, wine and books – they go together perfectly,' said Bea.

'Well, you can count me in if there's wine involved,' said Jess, leaning back in her chair.

'Me too,' said Arthur, 'It sounds like a lovely way to spend an evening. Good food, good wine, a good book and even better company.'

'Hmmmmm . . . the book wagon isn't big enough to hold it inside,' said Bea, pausing thoughtfully. 'I could ask people to bring their own seating, and it could be al fresco, on camping chairs or picnic blankets?'

'Brilliant!' said Jess.

'I'll probably need a permit or something, and maybe a booze licence to sell the wine, but I could talk to the parish council and ask?' said Bea.

'I guess the weather might be a problem, too. If it rains, you're screwed. And what would you do during the colder months?' said Jess.

'True,' said Bea, frowning. 'Maybe I could move it to the village hall if the weather's bad? I'll make some enquiries, but I reckon it could work.'

'I've got faith in you, my dear. If you can turn a horsebox into a bookshop in just a few weeks, I'm certain you can host a book club worthy of the Bard himself,' said Arthur. 'You just need to put your mind to it. Now where do I sign up?'

'Steady on, Arthur, I'll need to do some research first,' Bea laughed.

'Time is of the essence, my dear, otherwise I may be forced to join the ladies at *Books & Prosecco,* and I fear that could be more than I can bear,' said Arthur.

'Don't worry, Arthur,' giggled Jess. 'Once she puts her mind to something, she sees it through. Isn't that right, Bea?'

'Absolutely,' said Bea. 'I'll have Bea's Book Club up and running as soon as possible,' she said, patting his hand gently.

She just had to hope that Nathan and Phoebe would be happy to supply their produce at cost prices, otherwise the cheese and wine book club would be missing two out of its three vital components.

Bea had planned a quiet night in on the sofa, stuffing her face with chocolate. Archie was at football and she intended to make the most of having the television to herself by re-watching *Bridgerton.* She'd barely made it ten minutes into the first episode, when there was a knock on the front door.

Eurgh, she groaned. *Who could that be?*

She wasn't expecting anyone.

She scooped her hair back into a loose bun and padded towards the front door, opening it to see Lochlan holding a bunch of bright red roses.

'Oh, hello' she said, conscious of the fact she was wearing a pair of old sweatpants and no make-up.

'These are for you,' he said, handing her the bouquet, 'I

wanted to apologize in person for not making it to the fête. I know how important it was to you, and I should have been there.'

'There's no need,' she said, 'you've already explained. But the flowers are beautiful, thank you. Come in, I was just about to open a bottle of wine.'

'I can't stay too long, though, I've got an early meeting to prep for,' he said, stepping inside.

'No worries. Red?' she asked, putting the flowers in the sink and taking a corkscrew from the drawer.

'Yes, please.'

'Can you grab us some glasses?' she asked, pointing towards the cabinet above the microwave. 'Sorry, I wasn't expecting company,' she said, collecting empty chocolate wrappers off the sofa as they went through to the lounge.

'Ah, you're a *Bridgerton* fan,' he said, nodding towards the TV.

'Yeah. Have you seen it?'

'It's not really my thing,' he said, holding out the glasses for her to fill.

'No, I guess not,' she said, her heart sinking a little.

'Are you sure I'm not interrupting?' he said, taking a sip of wine. 'Maybe I should just go if you want to watch this?'

'No, it's fine, honestly.'

'You should see the state of my place on match days. Cheetos and beer cans everywhere.'

Bea let out a snort of laughter.

'Sorry,' she said. 'I can't imagine you in sweatpants, covered in Cheeto dust.'

'Have I shattered the illusion?' he asked. 'I'm not only suits and sunglasses you know.'

'Of course you're not. It's . . .'

'What?'

'Well, it means you're not *perfect,* and that's a good thing.'

'Is it?'

'Well, there's no such thing as perfect, really, is there?'

'No, I suppose not.'

'Sorry,' said Bea, as her phone vibrated on the coffee table. 'It's Jess. I won't be a minute. Jess. Hi, sorry, can I call you later? Lochlan's here—'

'Check your email, Bea! Right now!' said Jess, quickly.

'Why? What's happened?'

'K. L. Fletcher has posted pictures of the book wagon in her author newsletter! She must've been at the fête; she's featured you as her bookshop of the month!'

'What? As in *A Murder at Midnight*? That K. L. Fletcher?'

'Yes! *That* K. L. Fletcher.'

'The *Sunday Times*-bestselling, Nibbie-award-winning K. L. Fletcher?'

'Oh, for God's sake, Bea. *Yes*! Mum signed up to her newsletter after you recommended her latest book. You subscribe too, right? Just check your email, would you?' said Jess, exasperated.

'Hang on,' said Bea, swiping through her phone to pull up her email.

'What's going on?' asked Lochlan, puzzled.

'K. L. Fletcher has mentioned the wagon in her author newsletter—'

'Wow! That's amazing! *A Murder at Midnight* is brilliant,' said Lochlan, sitting up.

'You've read it?' asked Bea.

'Everyone's read it!' said Lochlan, leaning across to look at Bea's phone. 'Aren't they making it into a movie?'

'Bloody hell,' said Bea, her hand shaking. 'Jess is right! Look,' she said, tilting the screen towards him. There it was. Under the heading 'Bookshop of the Month', a photo of the wagon with text that read, 'First visit to Bea's Book Wagon and I loved it! How cute is this little mobile bookshop?! Every town should have one! And that's exactly why it's my bookshop of the month!'

Bea scrolled through the rest of the email, which she knew went out to thousands of readers. There were more photos of the inside of the bookshop, as well as a link to Bea's Instagram.

'You should get on Instagram and check your notifications,' said Lochlan, jabbing a finger at the screen.

'Wow,' said Bea, blowing out a long breath as she scrolled through to her account, which already had over a hundred new followers. 'I can't believe it. Bea's Book Wagon's Insta famous!'

'Hello?' said a voice at the other end of the line. 'Bea? Are you still there?' asked Jess.

'God, sorry, I forgot you were there,' said Bea, lifting the phone back up to her ear.

'I can't believe it! K. L. Fletcher visited my bookshop, and I didn't even know it,' said Bea.

'Well, no one knows what she looks like, do they?' said Jess. 'That's kind of her thing, isn't it? She's not on social media and doesn't do interviews or public events.'

'Oh. My. God. There *was* a woman,' said Bea, the cogs in her brain whirring. 'She was wearing dark glasses and didn't take them off, not even when she came inside. She asked if she could take some photos . . . what was her name . . .' she said, shaking her head, willing herself to remember. '*Katerina*! Yes, that was it!'

'That's *got* to be her. The K must stand for Katerina. God, Bea, I can't believe you were stood right next to her, that's mad!' said Jess. 'She's mega famous.'

'I know! I've read all her books!' said Bea.

'You surprise me,' Jess laughed.

'Listen, Jess, I'm going to have to go, Lochlan's here . . .' said Bea.

'Ah, I see,' said Jess.

Bea could hear the disapproval in Jess's tone.

'I'll give you a call tomorrow though, okay?' Bea promised.

'If you're working tomorrow, I can pop into the Cosy Cat,' said Jess.

'Great, I'll see you then. I start at 1pm,' said Bea, hanging up.

'I bet you're glad you took that call,' said Lochlan, smiling at her.

'I still can't believe it,' said Bea, breathlessly, 'K. L. Fletcher in my shop!'

'It's fantastic, Bea. You can't buy publicity like that and, believe me, I've tried.'

'Maybe she'll come back? Although she did buy loads of books, so maybe not . . .'

'Perhaps she lives near here and will become a regular customer?'

'No, she said she was just here on holiday, trying to write her next book.'

'You know, I heard Jennifer Lawrence has already been signed for the lead role in the film . . .'

'No way!'

'And Timothée Chalamet too . . .'

'How do you know all this?'

'Oh, I've just got good contacts,' said Lochlan, uncrossing his legs. 'I had dinner with Cate Blanchett the other night and she's got all the inside goss,' he teased, his eyes sparkling mischievously.

CHAPTER 18

Bea felt like she was walking on air. She was flying high from the success of her opening day, and her diary was filling up with bookings for the rest of the summer. Her social media presence had grown since K. L. Fletcher's newsletter had dropped, and she was thinking of launching her online store early for people who couldn't visit the book wagon in person, with monthly subscription boxes and gift vouchers too. It would be a lot of work, but she needed to plan for a revenue stream that lasted all year, not just over the summer months.

Things between her and Lochlan were going well, too, although he was going to be in London for a couple of weeks for work, but they planned to spend some time together once he was back. And, anyway, didn't absence make the heart grow fonder?

Bea spent the morning before her shift at the Cosy Cat browsing Rye's flea markets and charity shops hoping to find some bookish gems, and she wasn't disappointed. She picked up a beautiful selection of clothbound classics, including *Little Women* and *Emma*, an early edition of *Old Possum's Book of Practical Cats* by T. S. Eliot, which she earmarked for Tori, and a box set of vintage Roald Dahl's.

Her visit to the primary school was in a couple of weeks and she needed to stock more books to appeal to the children and ignite their joy of reading. She'd also bumped into Phoebe, giving Bea the perfect opportunity to tell her about her idea for the new cheese and wine book club. To her relief, Phoebe agreed to supply the wine with a hefty discount off the RRP, so now all she needed to do was ask Nathan about the cheese and speak to the council about permissions and licences.

When Bea arrived at the Cosy Cat for her shift, Tori was bubbling with excitement.

'What's going on?' asked Bea, 'you look like you've won the lottery.'

'No, nothing like that,' said Tori, quickly, 'Do you remember I told you I'd entered Nate for that local business award—'

'Yes!'

'Well, he's made the shortlist, he's down to the final four!'

'No way!' gasped Bea, 'that's amazing. I bet he's thrilled—'

'I haven't actually told him yet,' said Tori, sheepishly.

'Why not?' asked Bea, confused.

'What if he's annoyed that I entered him, you know, behind his back?'

'Annoyed?' said Bea, wrinkling her forehead. 'Why would he be annoyed? It's recognition for all his hard work, isn't it?'

'I hope you're right. There's a swanky awards ceremony in Brighton. Black tie, the works. I'm not sure if it's his scene, and if he wins he'll have to make a speech—'

'Oh, crikey!' said Bea, shaking her head, doubtful that Nathan even owned a pair of smart trousers, let alone a suit. 'Listen, I'm sure it'll be fine, he'll be over the moon.'

'Well,' said Tori, nodding towards the window where Nathan could be seen outside unloading his truck. 'He's here, so I hope you're right . . .'

'Hey, Nate,' said Bea, opening the door to help him with the boxes.

'Cheers,' he said gratefully. 'I'll just drop these, and I've got a few more in the truck, Tori.'

'Great, thanks, Nate,' Tori replied. 'I've got something to tell you,' she added, as Nathan hauled the heaviest box onto the counter.

'Oh yeah, what?' he asked.

'You've been shortlisted in the East Sussex Business awards: Best Local Food Supplier,' said Bea, with a little whoop of delight.

'How? I haven't entered any awards—'

'Ah, that's because I entered you . . .' said Tori with a shy smile.

'You *did*?' said Nathan.

'You've got such a great product, Nate, so I spoke to some of the other places you supply and a few of us got together and nominated you,' Tori explained.

'Well, I . . .' said Nathan.

'And now you've made the shortlist, isn't that amazing?' said Bea, giving him a hug.

'Yeah, I suppose it is. Thanks, Tori, that's really kind of you,' said Nathan, processing the news.

'There's only four finalists in your category,' Tori explained. 'And the winner will be announced at a dinner in Brighton at the Grand Hotel; you're going to get a letter with all the details apparently.'

'Yeah and it sounds pretty posh, too, black tie and everything—' Bea said.

'I won't have to make a speech, will I?' asked Nathan, looking horrified.

'Well, yeah, if you win—' said Tori.

'Oh, God,' cringed Nathan, screwing up his face, 'I'm terrible at that kind of stuff.'

'I can help you write it if you like? You'll be fine,' said Bea, reassuringly.

'That would be great, thanks,' said Nathan, visibly relieved.

'I'm assuming he gets to take a plus one?' Bea asked Tori.

'I'm not sure, to be honest, maybe you'll have to wait for the letter to come through, Nate.' said Tori.

'It's so exciting. I wonder if there's, like, a cash prize or a trophy or something?' Bea said.

'Hey, what are you both doing tonight?' Tori asked.

'Nothing,' Nathan shrugged.

'Me neither,' said Bea.

'Why don't we go out?' suggested Tori. 'Just the four of us? I'll text Leo and see if he can meet us at the pub after he finishes work,' said Tori, grabbing her phone.

'Love to!' said Bea. 'Count me in!'

'Perfect!' said Tori. 'Meet you there at seven?'

'Great,' said Nathan. 'Let me just grab the rest of the boxes.'

'Nate,' said Bea, catching his arm, 'Congratulations again, it's great news, you really deserve it.'

'Thanks, Bea,' he said.

And, as she watched him walk out the door, Bea's heart swelled with pride for everything Nathan had achieved. Diversifying to make the cheese at the farm had been a huge risk, and she knew he'd had to work hard and learn quickly to make it the success it was now. If Bea's Book Wagon had half the success of Three Acre Cheeses, she'd be a very happy bookseller indeed.

'Bea! Over here!' called Tori, as she walked towards the bar of the Apple Tree.

'Hiya,' said Bea, slipping off her jacket.

'Pete, can I get another glass, please?' asked Tori, holding a bottle of chilled prosecco.

'Is Nathan here?' Bea asked.

'No, not yet,' said Tori, shaking her head.

'Tori's just been telling me about this award he's up for,' said Pete.

'I know, it's great, isn't it?' said Bea.

'Speak of the devil,' said Tori, as Nathan entered the pub.

'Congratulations,' said Pete, 'what you having, lad? It's on the house.'

'I'll have a pint of bitter, thanks, Pete,' said Nathan.

'Actually, can you make that two? Leo's not much of a fan of fizz either,' said Tori.

'More for us then,' said Bea, taking a sip of her drink and wrinkling her nose as the bubbles fizzed in her mouth. 'Delicious.'

As they made their way through the pub towards Leo, who was sat at a table near the back, there were shouts of 'Congrats, Nate' and 'Well done, lad', and several of the locals raised a glass towards them.

'Crikey, news spreads fast around here,' said Bea, pulling up a chair opposite Leo.

'You can say that again,' Nathan laughed.

'I propose a toast . . .' said Tori, raising her glass. 'To Nate and his mouth-wateringly delicious cheeses.'

'To Nate,' chorused Bea and Leo, clinking their glasses together.

'Let's not forget Bea and her book wagon!' said Nathan.

'To Bea,' repeated Tori and Leo.

'It looked like you were really busy at the fête. My niece, Lara, can't stop talking about it; she said you're going to her school in a couple of weeks?' asked Leo.

'Ah, yeah! I'm looking forward to it,' said Bea, smiling. 'I don't want to jinx things,' she continued, crossing her fingers, 'but I sold way more than I expected, I've already had to order more stock. I'd have been happy just to break even after the pitch fee, but I actually made a profit,' said Bea.

'Tori said a famous author was there?' said Leo.

'Yeah, and she featured me in her newsletter too, which has definitely helped,' said Bea. 'There isn't room to stock everything I'd like to in the wagon,' Bea continued, 'so I'm hoping I can persuade Archie to build me an online store sooner rather than later.'

'You know . . .' said Tori, thoughtfully. 'You could always have some shelf space at the Cosy Cat if you've got any cat-themed books or gifts?'

'Ooooh, that would be amazing,' said Bea, excitedly. 'I've seen some gorgeous cat bookmarks and notebooks on one of the wholesaler websites, and there's loads of books I can think of. Not just fiction, but books about how to care for your cat.'

'Sounds perfect,' said Tori.

'And look at this,' said Bea, pulling out her phone to show Tori a picture of a tote bag with a cat sleeping on top of a stack of books underneath a slogan saying, 'Easily distracted by cats and books.'

'Oh my God, I *love* that,' said Tori, enthusiastically.

'I've been thinking about the subscription boxes too. I'm going to have a different theme each month and, if I can sort them out in time, subscribers will get a signed copy of the book, as well as goodies themed around that month's pick: bookmarks, chocolates, wax melts, that kind of thing. Everything you need to create the right mood to relax and enjoy a good book at home,' Bea explained.

'Great idea,' said Tori.

'And I was thinking I could do an online book club for subscribers over Zoom, perhaps even see if I can get the authors to join?' said Bea, her eyes shining with excitement.

'I'm sure you'll get loads of people joining if it's free,' said Tori.

'Hopefully, yes. I just need to cost it all out. Postage and packaging is the tricky bit – the heavier and bigger the parcel, the more it's going to cost – so I'll need to do some research. But I've seen loads of similar services, so it's definitely viable. I just need to work out what my USP will be,' said Bea.

'What's a USP?' asked Nathan.

'Unique selling point. You know, what's going to make my subscription boxes stand out from all the others,' Bea explained.

'Sounds like you've thought of everything,' said Leo, impressed.

'I'm trying to. Oooh, maybe I should talk to the owners

of that gift shop, the Pink Ribbon, is it? Perhaps they'd be up for collaborating with me?' said Bea.

'Yeah, Anya and Simon are lovely, they've always been really supportive of the café, I'm sure they'd be up for it,' said Tori.

'Good to know,' said Bea, topping up her prosecco glass.

'And what about your book club idea? Any more thoughts about that?' asked Tori.

'I bumped into Phoebe in Rye the other day and she's agreed to supply the wine at a really great price, so I just need to ask you actually, Nate, if I can buy some cheese?' Bea asked.

'Hang on, what's cheese got to do with a book club?' Nate asked, confusion etched on his face.

'Well, I want to run a book club with a difference, you know?' said Bea. 'Something that feels a little bit more like a proper night out. So, I thought it could be a cheese, wine *and* book thing,' she explained.

'Ah, that makes sense. Great idea, but isn't the wagon a bit small for that? You wouldn't get many people in it,' said Nathan.

'If it was just during the summer, when it's nice weather, we could sit outside with deckchairs and picnic blankets, though? Maybe on the village green? Or, if the weather's bad, and in the winter, in the village hall if it's free?' said Bea.

'And there's the problem,' said Tori.

'Why's that?' asked Leo, puzzled.

'Convincing the new head of the parish council to give Bea a permit to use either the green or the hall,' said Tori.

'Who is it, then?' asked Nathan.

'Violet Davenport,' said Tori with a sigh.

'Well, I think I might have come up with a plan to win her over,' said Bea, with a knowing look. 'If I play my cards right, I think getting the permit might be easier than you think.'

CHAPTER 19

Bea reversed the wagon into the village hall car park right on time on Monday evening, ready for the Women's Institute meeting.

'Bea!' said Jean, who was loitering at the entrance to greet her. 'Welcome to the Blossom Heath Belles.'

'Hi, Jean, thanks again for having me,' said Bea, climbing out of the car.

'Well, doesn't this look wonderful?' said Jean, stepping back to admire the wagon. 'I can't wait to hear all about how you transformed it from a horsebox to a bookshop.'

'Thanks. I'm actually a bit nervous,' said Bea, opening up the back doors to the horsebox. 'I've never given a talk before . . .'

'Oh, don't worry, we're a nice bunch, we're just grateful to have any special guests at all, really. In fact, I think we're going to have a few more than usual turn up tonight.'

'Do you know how many exactly?' Bea asked, swallowing hard.

'Well, we always get a few people drop out at the last minute, but there should be at least forty—'

'*Forty*?' Bea repeated, her mouth turning dry.

'Listen, you can't be any worse than the chap we had last month from the council, who talked about the new recycling scheme. He had the charisma of a plank. Terrible evening, and lots of people left halfway through,' said Jean, shaking her head.

'Oh God, did they?' said Bea, her nerves jangling. 'Well, I might start with this then,' she said, grabbing a crate from inside the book wagon.

'What's this?' asked Jean, peering into the box, which was full of brown paper packages tied up with string.

'It's called Blind Date with a Book,' said Bea. 'You choose a book from the box and there's a description of what it's about on the gift tag, but the title and author are a mystery . . .'

'Ooooh, what a lovely idea,' said Jean.

'This one,' said Bea, flipping its cardboard tag over, 'is an enemies-to-lovers romance, with strong community dynamics. Whereas this,' she continued, selecting another package, 'is a thriller, published in 2020, set in London, with dark humour.'

'These will go down a treat,' said Jean, her eyes glinting with excitement.

'I was thinking of pricing them at a pound each? They're all second-hand, so—'

'A pound!' said Jean, waving a hand, 'No, that's silly, I suggest you make it at least two pounds.'

'If you don't think that's too—'

'It's a bargain, dear, and such a novelty,' said Jean, confidently. 'In fact,' she continued, pressing two pound coins into Bea's hand, 'I'll take that thriller myself,' she said, 'before anyone else can get their mitts on it.'

'Okay, great,' said Bea, handing her the book. 'Thank you.'

'Oh, and you must make sure you get some of my Vicky sponge before you start, don't wait for the break. It won Best in Show at the fête, you know,' said Jean, turning to leave. 'I'll put a slice aside for you.'

'Thanks, Jean, that sounds lovely!'

With the wagon set up and ready for visitors, Bea took a deep breath and walked up the steps to the village hall. She'd been watching people steadily pouring inside for the last fifteen minutes, the queasy sensation in her stomach increasing, but as she opened the doors she was instantly met with a reassuring hum of conversation and laughter. The hall felt like it was literally buzzing with anticipation, and the cake table seemed to be the most popular place in the room, with scones, cupcakes and flapjacks being served alongside mugs of tea and cups of squash.

'Bea!' cried Maggie, who was sat in the front row next to Beth.

'Hiya,' said Bea, relieved to see a few familiar faces.

'It's packed in here tonight,' said Maggie, looking around the room. 'It's never usually this busy,'

'Really?' said Bea, the knot in her stomach tightening again. 'There's definitely more people than I expected ...'

'Oh, don't worry, love. You'll be great. And we're so excited to see the book wagon, aren't we, Beth?' said Maggie.

'Absolutely! There's a few things I want to add to my TBR list ...' said Beth, encouragingly.

'Thanks,' said Bea, forcing a smile.

'Here we go, Bea,' said Jean, handing her a paper plate with a huge slice of Victoria sponge. 'Take a seat just there,' she said, pointing to a chair at the side of the stage. 'We've got some WI business to get through first, so just relax and tuck into that.'

'Okay, great,' said Bea, taking a huge bite. Jam and cream oozed down her chin.

God, that was delicious.

She could see why Jean had won at the fête; the sponge was so light it could give the Cosy Cat a run for its money ...

Bea listened attentively as Jean explained the order of events for the evening. She even joined in with the chorus of *Jerusalem*, mumbling her way through the verses she didn't know, and, before she knew it, she heard Jean say, 'Please give Beatrice Miller a very warm, Blossom Heath Belles' welcome ...' Bea sucked in a breath and took centre stage.

The first person she spotted in the audience, sitting in the middle of the front row, was Violet Davenport. She hoped it wasn't a bad omen ...

*

Bea tried to get the audience on side early by promising to be more entertaining than the recycling man, and she distinctly heard laughter ringing around the hall. She talked about her lifelong love of literature, the hours she'd spent in the library with her mum as a child, the years she'd spent trying to get a job in publishing, and how she'd come up with the idea of opening a mobile bookshop after spotting a horsebox coffee shop in Rye market.

She'd left out the part about quitting her job on impulse and getting drunk as a lord before buying her wagon on eBay: there was only so much she had to share, surely?

The audience had been full of questions: did the wagon still smell of horses? Where did she get her design ideas? Had Nathan really built all the shelves by hand?

She finished the talk by giving the audience two book recommendations, *The Women Who Wouldn't Leave* by Victoria Scott, a heart-warming story about the power of sisterhood and community that she felt was perfect for WI members, and *A Force To Be Reckoned With: A History of the Women's Institute* by Jane Robinson, which showcased the movement's past as a force for change, from the suffragettes right through to its current campaigns. She remembered to let them know that both books were available to purchase from the bookshop.

As everyone gathered their bags, Jean took to the stage to remind them all that the wagon would be open for browsing for the next hour. Bea slipped out of the hall to turn on the fairy lights.

The bookshop looked magical; the dusky evening sunlight was the perfect backdrop.

'Oh, look at these totes,' said Joyce, putting one that declared, 'There is no such thing as too many books,' over her shoulder to show her friend, Clara.

'I'll take that!' said Clara, popping a selection of books inside. 'I'll take these, too, thanks, Bea. That should keep me going for a while.'

'Excellent,' said Bea, turning on the card machine. 'Don't forget the Blind Date with a Book boxes are inside the hall, you might want to check those out too.'

'Come on, Clara, let's see what we can find,' said Joyce.

'I'll take this,' said a booming voice. Bea looked up to see Violet Davenport standing by the door, waving a book over her head impatiently.

'Miss Davenport, lovely to see you again,' said Bea, as politely as possible.

'Have we met?' Violet asked.

'Yes. At the village fête, you were kind enough to help direct me when I was struggling to park.'

'Ah, that's right, you were going against the flow of traffic if I remember rightly?'

'Yep, that was me,' said Bea, nodding awkwardly. 'Actually, I'm glad I caught you. I took the liberty of putting a book aside for you . . .'

'For me?' asked Violet, clearly baffled.

'I've seen you in the café a few times; you've been reading the latest Kate Fisher book, right?'

'Yes, that's right.'

'It's great, isn't it?' said Bea. 'I loved it!'

'You've read it?'

'Of course! Kate's a brilliant writer. Have you read *The Forgotten Heart*?'

'It's her best, in my opinion,' said Violet. Was Bea mistaken or could she detect a slightly warmer tone in Violet's voice now?

'Oh, you're absolutely right. I assumed you'd want to read the next one, *The House by the Bay*.'

'Yes, but it's not out until—'

'Tomorrow?' said Bea, reaching to pull a copy of the book from a shelf marked 'Reserves' behind her.

'How have you managed—'

'*Technically* it's not publishing until tomorrow, but my stock has already arrived . . .' said Bea, glancing at her watch. 'As long as I don't put the transaction through the till until the morning, I can't see a problem if you're happy with that?'

'My lips are sealed,' nodded Violet in agreement.

'We're going to be reading this at our first book club, if you'd like to come?'

'A book club,' said Violet, 'what an interesting idea.'

'I'll add you to my list, I just need to confirm a venue first,' said Bea, flashing her best smile in Violet's direction. 'Actually, that might be something you can help me with. I think I heard you're on the parish council?'

'I'm the new chair,' said Violet, standing taller.

'It's just, I think I might need a permit to use the village green? Perhaps you might be able to—'

'I'm sure there's something I can do to help,' Violet whispered, conspiratorially.

'And, sorry, while I've got you, Miss Davenport,' Bea continued, pushing her luck. 'I wondered if I might be able to open a free library on the green as well? It would be the perfect location, and I'd put up the box and stock it with books, so it wouldn't cost the council a penny,' Bea explained, hoping she wasn't testing Violet's good will too much.

'I'll put it to the committee. We're always looking for new initiatives, and I'm sure a book swap would help foster some community spirit. Leave it with me, dear,' said Violet, patting Bea's hand.

Dear? Had Violet really just called her 'dear'? Miracles really could happen, Bea thought, as she carefully wrapped Violet's purchases with extra ribbon and an especially flouncy bow.

CHAPTER 20

Sure that the permit to use the green and, if needed, the hall, were safe in Violet's capable hands, Bea was keen to get the first book club event confirmed. She'd had fifteen sign-ups already, and had provisionally set the date for a week on Tuesday, so she was relieved when a letter on official Parish Council headed paper arrived just two days later to confirm that all permissions had been granted, even congratulating her on her innovation and wishing her luck.

Bea made a mental note to send Violet some flowers to say thank you and, of course, offer her a free ticket to the next book club meeting.

She had an hour to kill before her shift at the Cosy Cat, so decided to head into the village early and pay a visit to the Pink Ribbon to ask about collaborating on her subscription service, and hopefully to pick Simon or Anya's brains.

Bea was full of ideas, but there was so much choice online, she didn't really know where to start. She'd visited the shop a couple of times to buy greetings cards and candles, but she didn't know Simon and Anya at all, so she hoped they wouldn't think she was being cheeky by asking for their advice.

'Morning,' said a woman Bea hoped was Anya, looking up from a stunning silk scarf she was wrapping up.

'Hi, sorry, are you the owner?' Bea asked.

'I am, yes. Well, me and my partner, Simon. I'm Anya, how can I help you?' she asked.

'Well, I was hoping I could pick your brain, if that's okay? I've just opened a mobile bookshop and I want to get my online store and subscription service up and running soon. I'm selling book-themed gifts as well, and I was thinking . . .'

'Who better to ask than someone who runs a gift shop?'

'Well, yes, exactly,' Bea laughed.

'Happy to help,' said Anya, smiling broadly. 'What do you want to know?'

'There are so many things to choose from, it's hard to know where to start, really. Plus, I don't want to step on your toes and sell anything that you already stock here.'

'Well, that's really kind of you to even think about, so thank you. Not everyone would consider that,' said Anya, gratefully.

'So, do you sell anything bookish here?'

'Only the bookmarks,' said Anya, pointing to a carousel

by the door. 'But they're quite popular, particularly the animal ones.'

'These are cute!' said Bea, picking up one covered in kittens.

'And we've got some local interest books by the till, they're for tourists mainly. We've got a wholesaler we use who offers sale or return, so anything that doesn't sell can be sent back. I'll give you their details if you like?' said Anya.

'That would be great, thank you,' Bea replied.

'You're going to need to think about shipping costs and packaging for your subscription service, though, but that's not something we do here.'

'You don't have an online shop?'

'Nope, just the physical shop, and even that might not be open for much longer . . .' said Anya, her voice breaking a little.

'You're not shutting down, are you?' Bea asked.

'We're not sure at the moment. My mum's not been well, so we've been thinking about moving back to Scotland to be nearer to her.'

'And you'd have to give up the shop, I suppose, if you can't find someone to run it for you?'

'Yep,' Anya nodded. 'The lease is up soon, so in a way it's perfect timing. The landlord's lovely, so I'm sure he'd have let us renew, but . . .'

'Couldn't your mum move to Sussex instead so you could stay here?' Bea suggested.

'I wouldn't even ask her. She loves Scotland, and all her friends and memories are there. We lost my dad a few years ago, and I know it would break her heart to leave their home,' Anya explained, her eyes misty with tears.

'I'm so sorry,' said Bea, with genuine sympathy. 'That must be really tough.'

'Thanks. I appreciate that,' said Anya, keen to change the subject. 'If you need any more advice, my door's always open. Well, for now anyway.'

'Thank you, that's really kind of you. I hope everything works out. Oh, before I forget, would you mind putting up one of these posters for me? I'm running a book speed-dating night at the pub next week, in case you fancy it?'

'Sounds like fun, we'll try and make it.'

'Excellent! Sorry, I need to dash,' said Bea, glancing at her watch, 'I'm due at the Cosy Cat in a minute.'

'No problem. I might pop over for a slice of cake later to cheer myself up.'

'I'll put something aside for you,' said Bea, turning to leave.

'Thanks,' Anya replied. 'Oh, and Bea?'

'Yes?'

'Don't say anything to anyone, will you, about closing the shop? We haven't really decided one way or another yet, and I don't want anyone knowing until we have.'

'My lips are sealed,' Bea assured her.

*

As Bea rushed across the green towards the café, she couldn't help thinking about the tough decision that lay ahead for Anya. She was lucky her parents were both still in good health, but she knew that would change one day. She couldn't imagine her parents not being around for ever; the prospect was too awful to contemplate. Bea was so wrapped up in her thoughts that she didn't notice the woman walking towards her, carrying a coffee in a takeaway cup until it was almost too late.

'Oh god, sorry,' said Bea, side-stepping at the last minute to try to avoid bumping into her.

'Oh, shit,' said the woman, looking up from her phone a second too late and crashing straight into Bea, her cup lurching up in the air, covering them both in hot liquid. 'Oh no!' screamed the woman. 'Wow, that's hot, are you okay?' she asked, nudging her sunglasses down her nose to look at Bea. 'That was totally my fault, I wasn't paying attention to where I was going at all,' she apologized.

'It's fine,' said Bea, taking a tissue out of her bag and attempting to mop herself down.

'It's Bea, isn't it? From the bookshop?' the woman asked.

'And you're . . . Katerina, right? We met at the fête?' Bea asked, recognizing her immediately.

'Yeah, hello again,' Katerina sighed, shaking out the dregs from the cup. 'Pistachio latte, totally scrumptious, what a waste.'

'Let me get you another. It's from the Cosy Cat, right?' Bea asked.

'Oh, no. It was my fault, I should be getting you a coffee,' Katerina insisted.

'It's no trouble, I work there part time. I was just about to start a shift actually. Seriously, it's on the house, okay?'

'Okay, well, thank you,' said Katerina, pulling her sunglasses back down. 'I was just going to go and watch the ducks for a bit.'

'Well, you go and sit on the bench and I'll bring you another coffee in a minute.'

'If you're sure? That would be great. Thank you.'

Bea hurried towards the Cosy Cat. She couldn't quite believe her luck. Katerina, aka K. L. Fletcher, was back in Blossom Heath, and she was just about to get her a coffee. Should she confess to knowing who she was, or let her sit and have her coffee in peace? It must be exhausting being a celebrity, so Bea wasn't surprised that Katerina preferred to be incognito, covering her face with those huge sunglasses and using only her initials as her official author name.

No, she wouldn't say a thing, Katerina had told her she was here to write, to get some peace and quiet, and Bea wasn't going to spoil that for her.

She'd just get the replacement coffee and take it out to her. That was it.

Katerina was sat quietly by the duck pond, watching the world go by, when Bea returned with a fresh pistachio latte.

'Here you go,' said Bea, handing her the takeaway cup.

'Thanks,' Katerina replied, smiling up at her. 'Do you want to sit?' she asked, patting the vacant space next to her.

'Oh, okay, if you don't mind?' said Bea, sitting down.

'It's peaceful here, isn't it?' said Katerina, looking out over the pond as the ducks squabbled over stale breadcrumbs.

'Yeah, it is,' Bea agreed, pausing before adding bravely, 'how's the writing going?'

'Ah, yes, I'd forgotten I told you that,' Katerina admitted. 'Let's just say it's not right now. I'm under a lot of pressure, which is just stifling my creative flow to be honest.'

'I'm sorry to hear that,' said Bea. 'Your last book was so—'

Katerina froze, the cup paused halfway to her mouth. She turned to look at Bea and whispered, 'You know who I am, don't you?'

'I think I do, yes. You're K. L. Fletcher, aren't you?' Bea asked, cursing inwardly as she broke her promise to herself not to let on as to the author's real identity.

'Uh-huh,' Katerina replied in a flat, monotone voice.

'Don't worry,' Bea added quickly. 'I won't tell anyone, I promise.'

'I suppose it's my own fault, really,' Katerina sighed, 'I did include your wagon in my newsletter, and I told you I was a writer. It was silly of me, but I couldn't resist,' she continued, a smile lighting up her face, 'your bookshop is so pretty.'

'Thank you,' said Bea, feeling herself blush. 'That's lovely of you to say.'

'Well, it's true,' said Katerina, reaching out and patting Bea's hand.

'I mean it though,' said Bea, 'I really won't tell anyone you're here.'

'Thank you,' said Katerina, the relief clear in her voice. 'And thanks for the coffee, Bea. I'm sure I'll see you again,' said Katerina, standing to leave.

'I hope so,' Bea replied, smiling as she watched Katerina walk away.

CHAPTER 21

Lochlan was due back from his work trip on Friday and Bea couldn't wait to see him. They'd been messaging while he'd been away, but it wasn't the same, and she was looking forward to spending the day with him on Saturday.

She'd persuaded Archie to help her create a Shopify store, in exchange for doing his ironing for a month, and she'd ordered some stock from the wholesaler Anya had recommended to add to her product lines. She just needed to make a few final tweaks to the site before it was ready to launch.

She'd spent hours taking photos for the website and her Instagram grid, and bought some props for the shop: more fairy lights and candles. She'd found some cute vintage teacups at the market and brought home some leftover pastries from her shift at the café, too, just for decorative purposes, of course.

Bea had watched loads of 'how to take the perfect flat lay'

videos and scrolled through Bookstagram for inspiration, and she'd taken dozens of photos of book stacks, organized by size, colour, genre, author and title, incorporating every theme she could think of. She'd even bribed Wordsworth with treats to model next to a shelfie with *Marley and Me, Lily and the Octopus,* and a personal favourite, Erika Waller's *Dog Days.*

Concentrating on building a bank of images she could use helped pass the time quickly and, before she knew it, it was Saturday morning and she could get ready to meet Lochlan.

She'd told him to leave the planning of their day out to her – she wanted it to be a surprise – and she was looking forward to taking him to her favourite beach for a picnic, followed by a shopping trip to all her favourite spots in Rye. She pictured them walking hand in hand through the cobbled streets . . . *so romantic.*

Bea hadn't been to Lochlan's place before, so when she pulled up outside an exclusive gated development with just four houses, each of which could have fitted Archie's house inside it ten times over *at least,* she'd had to check her satnav to make sure she was in the right place.

Was this really where he lived?

When she pressed the buzzer and Lochlan's voice sounded through the speaker, she still couldn't quite believe it.

'Hey, babe, I'll buzz you through,' he said, and the wrought-iron gates in front of her swung open.

Before Bea had time to climb out of her car, Lochlan had already shut his front door behind him and was leaning down to kiss her on the cheek.

'I've missed you,' he murmured in her ear.

'You too,' said Bea, feeling a warm glow in the pit of her stomach. 'This place is ... wow,' she said, lost for words.

'Yeah, it's not bad, is it?' he replied, smiling.

God that smile.

'I'd invite you in, but the cleaner's just arrived,' he added.

'Oh, yeah, sure,' said Bea, hiding her disappointment. She'd have loved to have had a look around ... next time, hopefully.

'We can take my car if you like? I don't mind driving,' he said, eyeing Archie's Nissan Micra suspiciously.

'No, it's fine,' said Bea, 'we're going a bit off the beaten track, and I know the way.'

'Are you sure? We'd be more comfortable in mine—'

'Honestly, it's fine,' she said. 'Come on, jump in and we can get going!'

'So, where are we heading?' he asked, climbing into the passenger's seat, his aftershave wafting through the car.

'It's a surprise,' said Bea, 'but I think you're going to love it!'

'Are we going back to Canteen 64?' he asked, pulling on his seatbelt.

'Er ... afraid not,' she laughed. Was she imagining it, or did his face fall a little?

'But we are going for lunch, though?'

'Oh, absolutely,' said Bea, driving back through the metal gates slowly.

'Great, I'm starving,' said Lochlan, reaching out to squeeze her hand. She felt her stomach do a little flip. She'd almost forgotten how utterly gorgeous he was.

On their drive to the beach, Lochlan told her all about his time in London. He was working on a big new project with some foreign investors. If everything went through, the deal would be worth millions, apparently. He'd stayed in a luxurious boutique hotel in Mayfair – she'd have loved it, he told her. In fact, he said she should come up for the night the next time he had a client dinner, so she could see for herself.

'That sounds wonderful,' she said, excited by the prospect of a mini break in London with the hot guy sat next to her.

'We'll sort out a date,' said Lochlan.

'Definitely! Ah, we're here!' said Bea, as she pulled into a tiny car park at the top of Fairlight cliffs.

'Is that France?' asked Lochlan, climbing out of the car and walking towards the edge of the cliffs.

'Uh-huh,' Bea replied. 'On a clear day, you can see for miles.'

'What have you got there?' he asked, as Bea hauled a wicker hamper out of the boot.

'We're having a picnic on the beach!' Bea announced.

'On the beach?' said Lochlan, looking horrified.

'Yes . . .' Bea faltered.

'But we'll get covered in sand,' he replied. 'I thought we were going to a restaurant. You know, somewhere nice?'

'I thought this would be a bit different; something a bit more fun,' said Bea, feeling a little stung. 'It's a gorgeous day, we should make the most of it.' She'd thought her plan had been romantic, but from the look on Lochlan's face, he clearly thought it was anything but.

'I wish you'd said, I wouldn't have worn these shoes,' said Lochlan, looking down at what looked like a very expensive pair of leather loafers on his feet.

'Sorry,' said Bea, shaking her head. 'I didn't think.'

'Don't worry,' he said, more brightly, the clouds disappearing from his face as quickly as they had formed. 'I've got others. You're right, it is a gorgeous day.'

'Great!'

'Here, let me,' said Lochlan, taking the basket from her. 'How do we get down?'

'Over there,' she said, pointing to a set of wooden steps at the edge of the car park. 'It's steep, so be careful.'

'I will,' Lochlan called behind him, descending the steps at speed. Bea gripped the handrail tightly, she'd never had much of a head for heights.

'Phew,' said Bea, finally stepping onto the beach a few minutes after him. 'Good. There's no one else here,' she said, taking in the empty golden sand and clear blue water.

'I can see why you like it here,' said Lochlan, setting down the hamper and stopping to admire the view.

'Every time I'm here it's deserted, I love it. Everywhere gets so busy, especially in the summer.'

'Let's eat,' said Lochlan, impatiently, opening up the picnic basket and pulling out a tartan blanket.

Bea had carefully packed all her favourite picnic food:

sausage rolls, scotch eggs, a fancy quiche, salads, chips and dips and even some cupcakes from the café.

'Fizz!' said Lochlan, unpacking the bottle of champagne she'd snuck in at the last minute, cold from the fridge. 'Now this really is a decent spread,' he said, popping the cork with a bang.

'Here,' said Bea, 'we've got strawberries too,' she said, popping one into her mouth, followed by a glug of champagne.

'Hey, what about me?'

'Here you go,' she said, feeding him one in a way she hoped was seductive.

'Fancy a spot of skinny dipping?' he asked, waggling his eyebrows suggestively.

'Do you know how cold that water is?' Bea laughed.

'I'm sure we'd warm up pretty quickly—'

'Knowing my luck someone would steal our clothes.'

'But there's no one else here, Bea, it's just us two.'

'We haven't got any towels or anything.'

'Spoil sport,' he joked, before reaching for a sausage roll. 'God, these are spectacular,' he laughed.

'I got them from the café, Joyce is an excellent cook.'

'You're not wrong,' said Lochlan. 'So, what have you been up to? How's business?'

'Good,' said Bea, taking another sip of her champagne. 'I did an event at the WI, I'm starting a book club on the village green and my online store is nearly ready to launch. Oh, and I've got a book speed-dating event at the pub on Monday night.'

'Wow, you have been busy,' said Lochlan, through a mouthful of pastry.

'I've got a few more events booked in for the summer as well; you'll have to come along, see for yourself, you've not seen the wagon yet, I'd love to show you one—'

'I'm going to be pretty busy for the next few months, this deal in London is big, if I can pull it off—'

'You're going back to London?'

'Back and forth. Don't worry, I'll be around some weekends, we can still hang out.'

'Oh, okay . . .' said Bea. *Hang out?* Is that what they were doing? Admittedly they'd not had a conversation about whether this was going anywhere, but she'd thought, *hoped*, it was leading somewhere.

'So, have you made any plans for the rest of the day, if skinny dipping is definitely off the agenda?' he asked, his eyes sparkling mischievously.

'Yes, I thought we could head into Rye to look at—'

'Actually, I've booked a slot for us to visit Lamb House, up in the Citadel there. I'm sure you've been before, but I haven't, and I thought it might be nice to go together?'

'Oh, I'd love to!' said Bea, reaching over the remains of their picnic to squeeze his hand and pushing aside a flicker of annoyance that he'd gone ahead and booked something when she'd asked him to leave the plans for today to her. 'It's one of my favourite places.'

Tucked away in a narrow, cobbled street, Lamb House is a beautiful Georgian property with a strong literary history. Now a National Trust property, the house was once home to Henry James, as well as a string of other literary greats, including E. F. Benson and Rumer Godden. Bea had spent many hours wandering around the walled gardens and wood-panelled rooms, taking in the atmosphere. It was no wonder it had inspired so many writers to produce some of their greatest works there.

'I'm guessing we won't be needing a tour guide then?' Lochlan teased. 'Shall we make a move?' he said, starting to collect the empty Tupperware and plastic glasses. 'I've booked us in for two, so that should give us plenty of time to have a wander first.'

'There's a couple of great second-hand bookshops I'd love to show you, so the more time we have the better,' Bea replied, popping the last strawberry in her mouth.

'Oh, shit! Is that rain?' asked Lochlan, as a huge drop of water landed on his cheek.

'But it wasn't forecast,' said Bea, looking up at the sky just as the heavens opened. 'Quick, over there,' she said, throwing everything into the hamper and darting towards the cliffs.

'You're soaked,' said Lochlan, as she tried to shake out her dress where it was clinging to her legs.

'I really am,' she laughed, 'you can literally see *everything*.'

'Hey, I'm not complaining,' said Lochlan, pulling her towards him. She shivered as the rain trickled down her back. He wrapped her in his arms and leaned in to kiss her. The touch of his hands on her wet skin felt electric. She kissed him right back, running her hands through his hair.

Suddenly, she realized she didn't care whether they made it

to Rye or not. Being here with Lochlan was all the romance she needed.

Eventually the rain clouds cleared and, by the time they reached Rye, the May sunshine was beating down on them as they wandered the cobbled streets towards Lamb House hand in hand.

Lochlan had loved it just as much as she'd hoped he would – or at least he had when she could tear him away from his phone. He seemed to be fielding endless work calls and Bea couldn't help feeling a little irked. She'd cast apologetic glances at the National Trust guide who was leading their tour, every time his phone rang.

'I was thinking we could have a poke around the antique shops by the quay next?' said Bea, looping her arm through his as they left Lamb House. 'There's a really cute little tea-shop, they do the best spiced apple cake—'

'Really?' said Lochlan, finally shoving his mobile into his pocket. 'It's a bloody nightmare here, with everyone stopping to take photos. It's too touristy, don't you think?'

'Too touristy?' Bea repeated. She wasn't sure how to respond. She loved Rye and its quaint cobbled streets.

'Yeah, don't get me wrong, Lamb House was great, but once you've seen one sixteenth-century house full of beams, you've kinda seen them all, right?' he shrugged.

'We could go to The Mermaid? It's gorgeous, like stepping back in time,' said Bea, wistfully. 'There's secret passageways, smugglers songs on the walls, it's—'

'It'll be full of tourists.'

'Okay, well how about—'

'Oh, I know!' he interrupted. 'There's a new Scandi design place just opened in Ashford. I've been meaning to go there to look at some pieces for the London show homes; top of the range stuff apparently. One of our designers told me about it. We could go for cocktails after?'

'Erm . . . I guess we could, if you're not enjoying Rye?'

'Like I said . . . it's just not my vibe.'

'Maybe another time? When it's less busy?' Bea suggested.

'Yeah, maybe,' said Lochlan. 'Shall we make a move then?' he said, glancing at his watch. 'We should make it to the showroom before closing if we leave now,' he said, striding off in the direction of the car.

'Wow, would you look at this! I told you it was cool,' said Lochlan, as they walked into the trendy cocktail bar in Ashford later that day.

'Yeah, it looks nice,' said Bea, gazing around at the gold bar stools and stylish black leather booths dotted around the cocktail bar. If she was being honest, her afternoon with Lochlan had fallen a little flat. Yes, the kiss on the beach had been hot and she'd loved spending time with him at Lamb House, but the hours they'd spent looking at custom-made Norwegian furniture on an industrial estate in Ashford, didn't quite hit the mark.

'Why don't you grab a table and I'll get the drinks in? What do you fancy?' he asked.

'A mocktail, seeing as I'm driving.'

'Ah, yeah, sorry I forgot,' said Lochlan, picking up a drinks menu. 'Any preference?'

'Surprise me,' said Bea, heading for a booth at the back of the bar. Bea couldn't help noticing a redhead checking Lochlan out as he waited at the bar. She wasn't being very subtle about it but, as Lochlan made his way back with their drinks, his attention remained firmly fixed on Bea. A small smile escaped Bea's lips as she registered the look of disappointment on the redhead's face.

'Watermelon mojito,' said Lochlan, setting the pink drink decorated with mint leaves in front of her.

'Ooooh, this looks delicious,' said Bea, taking a sip. 'Mmmm . . . it is. What have you got?' she asked, eyeing the thick, green liquid in Lochlan's glass, which looked pretty disgusting.

'Midnight Mochi,' he said, taking a swig. 'It's like a matcha latte with a gin kick.'

'It looks a bit like pond slime,' she said, wrinkling her nose.

'Well, it tastes great,' he laughed. 'Here, try it,' he said, sliding the glass towards her.

Bea sniffed the contents suspiciously.

'It smells better than it looks,' she laughed, taking the tiniest of sips. 'Ooooh, I love it!' she said, surprised that something that looked so repugnant could taste so delicious.

'Told you!' Lochlan grinned. 'There's this amazing bar we take clients to in London, they've got a great mixologist.

We'll go when you come up. We can work our way through the menu. You'll love the hotel. Here, let me show you,' he said, pulling up their Instagram account on his phone and handing it to her.

'Wow! This looks gorgeous,' she said, scrolling through the photos on their grid. There was a swimming pool, a spa, a Michelin-starred restaurant, and it even had a 'secret' garden that reminded her of *Notting Hill*. She could just imagine sneaking in after hours, just like Hugh Grant and Julia Roberts had in the film.

'There are some great bookshops in London I'd love to check out while I'm there . . . Daunts in Marylebone High Street is a must, and Hatchards of course!'

'Of course,' Lochlan chuckled.

'Ooooh, and I've read about a canal barge bookshop too, Word on the Water. It looks amazing, it reminds me a bit of the wagon actually . . .'

'Okay, sure,' said Lochlan. 'But you have to promise me one thing, Bea?

'What?' she asked.

'That we won't spend the *entire* weekend looking at books. The hotel room's got a hot tub *and* an Emperor mattress,' he whispered, leaning in towards her.

'I think I can promise that,' Bea murmured, closing the distance between them and placing a soft, lingering kiss on his lips.

CHAPTER 22

Bea arrived at the Apple Tree on Monday evening, ready for the book speed-dating night. She'd posted it on her socials and was relieved to have eighteen tickets sold at five pounds each, which included a drink and a free bookmark.

'Bea!' said Beth, greeting her from behind the bar. 'I've reserved the back bar for you, so feel free to arrange the tables however you'd like.'

'Great, thank you,' said Bea, 'I'll go and set up now, if that's okay?'

'Of course,' Beth replied. 'Do you know how many are coming?'

'Eighteen, I hope. At least, that's how many tickets I've sold,' Bea explained. 'Archie's bringing a few mates along, Jess and Maggie are coming, but I'm not sure who else,' she continued.

'Brilliant! Do you fancy a drink?' Beth asked.

'Oooh, yes, please.'

Bea made her way to the back of the pub, rum and coke in hand, and began shifting the furniture around so her guests would be sat in pairs. She laid out some flyers for the book wagon, listing her upcoming events, and just as she was putting a couple of cute bookmarks on each table, her first guests arrived.

Archie had been true to his word and brought Seb, Josh and Freddie along. Jess was there with Maggie, Tori and Joyce. Bea didn't know the other ten ticket holders, but they seemed lovely, so she really hoped everyone would get on and have a good time.

As everyone took a seat, Bea took a deep breath.

'Hello, all!' she said, brightly. 'Thanks for coming to Bea's Book Wagon's first book speed-dating night!'

'Hang on?' called Freddie. '*Book* speed-dating?'

'That's right,' Bea nodded.

'Archie said it was speed-dating! He never mentioned anything about the book part,' Josh agreed.

'Didn't he? Oh dear, sorry about that,' said Bea, throwing Archie a thunderous glare.

'You don't think I would have got them here if they thought they were only coming to meet their perfect book, do you?' Archie chuckled, jerking a thumb towards his mates.

'Well, whatever brought you here, thank you for coming!' Bea continued. 'Let me explain how this works. I'll be pairing you up and you'll have three minutes to persuade your partner to read your favourite book. Explain to them what you loved about it, why it captured your heart and how it made you feel. I'm sure we'll all be adding some exciting new reads to our TBR lists by the end of the evening.'

'Our TB-what?' said Josh, looking confused.

'It stands for To Be Read,' whispered the gorgeous woman next to him. 'It's book code, don't worry, I'll help you,' she said, flashing him a smile.

Bea noticed Josh shift a little closer to the woman, grinning, all previous doubts about book speed-dating clearly forgotten.

'I'll go first, to help everyone get the idea,' suggested Bea.

'Yes, please,' said Tori.

'So, the book I'm recommending is Emily Bronte's *Wuthering Heights.* As love stories go, it's definitely not your standard romance,' Bea paused. 'It's wild and dark, brooding and cruel, but unbelievably poetic and romantic at the same time. The characters are complex and the author draws you in from the very first page. There's love, passion, betrayal and revenge, as well as supernatural elements. And, if that isn't enough, it's set on the Yorkshire Moors. If you love your romance on the darker side, with a fiery, brooding hero, who has some despicable qualities, then this is for you! So, the question is, will you swipe left or right?'

'Right, definitely right' called Joyce.

'Me too!' said Maggie. 'I love an antihero.'

'Heathcliff's definitely that,' agreed Bea.

'How do you even know about swiping right, Mum?' asked Jess, suspiciously.

'You're not both secretly on Tinder, are you?' added Tori.

'We're just up to speed on modern dating, aren't we, Mags?' said Joyce, with a cheeky wink.

'Well, I have *Wuthering Heights* in stock in the wagon, so if anyone fancies a trip to the wild Yorkshire Moors to meet Cathy and Heathcliff, let me know,' said Bea. Several hands shot into the air. 'Great, I'll put them aside for you.'

'Thanks, love,' said Joyce.

'So, now you know how it's done, I'll let you all figure out your starting pairs,' said Bea.

She saw Josh suggest to the woman next to him that they should pair up first.

'When your three minutes are up, I'll ring the bell,' she explained, playing the app on her phone, which was surprisingly realistic, 'and then you'll all move around clockwise. Any questions?' There was a collective shaking of heads. 'Right then. Three, two, one . . . go!'

The room was immediately buzzing with conversation, and Bea caught snippets as she wandered round. Archie was explaining the merits of Stephen King to Jess, who was having none of it. She was a laugh-out-loud romcom kind of girl, but she'd have an equally tough job trying to convince Archie to try a Marian Keyes.

Bea took the time to make sure everyone was having fun, popping to the bar to fetch drinks and helping out when people forgot author names or titles. When she finally called time on the last three-minute session, everyone started to clap saying how much fun they'd had and asking if they could sign up for the next one.

'I'll check with Beth, but I'm hoping it can be a regular thing. Maybe on the first Monday of every month?' said Bea.

'Great, thanks. I'm Claire, by the way,' the brunette Josh had been talking to said. 'I run Snippers, the salon on the green.'

'Oh, I thought I'd seen you before, I just wasn't quite sure where,' said Bea. 'Lovely to meet you, and thanks again for coming.'

'I've really enjoyed it,' said Claire, 'I'll definitely be back for the next one.'

'That's great!' said Bea, beaming at her. 'I'll see you soon, then, and don't forget, if you want to buy any of the books you've been recommended, just let me know. If I don't have them in stock, I can order them for you.'

'Actually, Josh and I are going to stick around for a drink,' said Claire, sheepishly. 'It turns out we're both big sci-fi geeks!'

'Ah, amazing! Josh is lovely,' said Bea, marvelling at the power of books bringing people together.

'I'm off now,' said Archie, 'I'm just going to walk Jess and Mags home first.'

'Okay,' Bea nodded, 'I want to talk to Beth first, see you later,' said Bea.

'All done, love?' Beth asked as Bea approached the bar.

'Yep, I'm just going to put the tables back—'

'Oh, don't worry about that, I'll get Pete to do it in the morning,' said Beth. 'How did it go?'

'Really well,' said Bea, smiling. 'I was hoping I could make it a regular event, if you're happy to let me host it here?'

'More than happy,' said Pete, appearing from the kitchen. 'We've doubled our takings for a normal Monday night, thanks to you.'

'Oh, that's great! Would the first Monday of every month be okay?' Bea suggested.

'Absolutely! I'll put it on our events page on the website, with a link to your Instagram account so people can contact you to book tickets,' said Beth.

'Brilliant, thanks, Beth,' said Bea, saying her goodbyes.

As she pulled on her jacket and started the short walk home, adrenaline was pumping through her veins. The event had been a success, with orders for all of the books recommended. It wouldn't earn her a fortune, but it was another income for the business and would definitely help keep her finances afloat.

CHAPTER 23

Bea arrived at Blossom Heath Primary School just after lunch the next day, ready to welcome the children into Bea's Book Wagon for the first time. She reversed into the car park with ease – she really was getting the hang of manoeuvring the horsebox now – and Rose was waiting to greet her at reception.

'Bea, hi! Thanks so much for coming,' said Rose, giving her a hug.

'Thanks for asking me. I've been looking forward to it,' Bea replied, glancing at the displays of art on the walls with interest. It had been a long time since she'd set foot in a school, and it was a somewhat odd experience. She was subconsciously waiting for a booming voice to yell, 'Beatrice Miller, stop doing that and come here!' A phrase she'd heard frequently while at secondary school. 'So, how shall we do this?' she asked.

'You'll be meeting the Key Stage One children today.

Each teacher will bring their class out to have a look inside, see which books they fancy reading, and then, when their parents pick them up, they can buy them if they want to, or we can order them for our school library, if that's okay? The head has been able to squeeze some budget out of the school governors, and she's put me in charge of spending it.'

'I've got my card machine at the ready,' Bea laughed, tapping her handbag. 'Remind me what age Key Stage One is?'

'Ages five to seven.'

'Perfect,' said Bea, 'I ordered a bunch of new books for that age group from the wholesaler I use, so hopefully there'll be plenty to go around.'

'Brilliant, and if we've got the time, there's a couple of our kids that I think might benefit from spending a bit longer in the bookshop with you, if that's okay? They're on our reluctant readers programme, so they read each week to the school dog—'

'Sorry? You have a school dog?' asked Bea, surprised.

'Oh, yeah, Bertie. He belongs to our headteacher.'

'And he listens to the kids read?'

'Yeah, I know! It sounds silly, but it really works. There's no judgement from him; he doesn't care if the kids stumble over words or make mistakes, he just sits and listens.'

'Aw, I love that,' said Bea, smiling.

'The children adore him, and weirdly he seems to enjoy it too – his tail never stops wagging.'

'I bet! I'd have loved to have had a dog to read to when I was at school.'

'Me too, to be honest,' said Rose, nodding. 'He's starting to slow down a bit now he's older, but he saw Grace last week and she gave him a clean bill of health.'

'That's reassuring. I can't wait to meet him! So, I'll just get set up and wait for you to come out, shall I?'

'Yep. I'll bring my class first, just give me five minutes. I need you to sign in, if that's okay? I know we've had your DBS check through, so we're good to go on that front.'

'Perfect. See you in a bit,' said Bea.

As Bea returned to the wagon, she could see some curious little faces peering out of the classroom windows nearest to the car park. Some children were waving at her, so she waved back, smiling. She arranged all the deckchairs and bean bags under the awning, and double-checked that all the children's books were displayed on the lowest shelves, ready for the pupils to start exploring. She'd brought a mix of titles to appeal to readers of all ages, so hopefully every child would find something they liked. She'd even ordered some book-character cuddly toys to help bring the stories to life, like the Gruffalo, the alien from *Aliens Love Underpants*, Peter Rabbit and Paddington.

As Bea switched on the fairy lights and plumped up the cushions, she could hear chattering voices approaching from across

the playground.

'Hummingbird Class, can we all say hello to Miss Miller?' said Rose.

'Hello, Miss Miller,' the children parroted back.

'Is your name, Bea?' one of the taller boys asked, pointing at the writing on the side of the wagon. 'It says Bea's Book Wagon. See?'

'Excellent detective skills, Ethan,' said Rose, leaning in towards Bea. 'You don't mind if they call you Bea, do you?' she whispered.

'No, it's fine,' said Bea, smiling.

'So, Bea is going to tell us about how she turned a horse-box into her beautiful book wagon,' Rose explained.

'What? Horses used to live in there? In the shop?' a doubtful-looking Ethan asked.

'Well, yes, they did, Ethan,' replied Bea. 'This absolutely used to be a horsebox before I turned it into a bookshop.'

'No way!' chorused the children in hushed whispers.

'Yes way!' said Bea, chuckling at their shocked faces. 'I bought it from Millcroft Stables, and my friends and I pretty much rebuilt it from the floor up. We put in new walls, a new ceiling, and all these shelves are handmade by Nathan who makes the cheese.'

'Wow!' said Ethan, amazed, 'that's so cool!'

'I think so too,' Bea agreed.

'We're all going to get the chance to go inside in small groups, as there's not enough room for all of us at once. Milton, Stacey, Percy, Hannah, Ethan and Sky – you six can go first, Rose explained.

Bea smiled as Ethan punched the air in delight.

'And the rest of us will wait outside quietly until you've finished, okay everyone?' said Rose in a no-nonsense tone.

'Yes, Miss,' the class chorused.

'Come on, you lot,' said Bea, to the six children who were lined up at the steps. 'Let's go!'

'Wow, this place is really cool,' said Ethan, as he ran his hands over the spines of Bea's Harry Potter collection.

'Look at these bookmarks,' said Stacey, 'they're from *Dork Diaries*! I love those books!'

'How much are these?' asked a little boy she thought might be Milton, picking up a pack of stickers on her makeshift desk.

'Oooh, stickers,' said Sky, '*cool*.'

'Actually, these are for you,' said Bea, opening up one of the packs she'd ordered in especially for the school visit. They read 'I've visited Bea's Book Wagon' in a variety of colours.

'Yesss!' said Ethan, 'Can we choose?' he asked, tugging Bea's sleeve.

'Go for it,' said Bea, with a nod, as the children huddled around the pack, pulling out a round sticker each and placing them on their shirts. In no time at all, all six children had selected a book to be put aside, ready for when their parents would collect them from school, and the next three groups were equally as chuffed with their stickers.

'Well, hello there,' said Bea, bending down to fuss Bertie as he walked up the steps with the last group of children. Bea looked up to see a scruffy-looking boy walking across the playground towards her. His shirt was untucked, his hands stuffed into his pockets, and he was kicking a pebble, scuffing his shoes with every attempt.

'I've been told I have to find a book,' he said, his head bowed. He couldn't have looked less enthusiastic if he'd tried. Bea wondered if he might be one of the reluctant readers Rose had mentioned.

'Why don't you come in and we'll see if we can find a book you like the look of?'

'I don't like books,' said the boy, confirming Bea's suspicion.

'Well, shall we have a look anyway?' she tried.

'Wow, it's epic in here, Miss,' he said, his eyes wide as he looked around. 'These lights are sick,' he said, pointing to the fairy lights Nathan had installed.

'Glad you like them,' said Bea, smiling. 'My friend Nate put them in. They're powered by a car battery,' she continued, 'because there's no electricity in the wagon.'

'No way! That's awesome,' the boy said.

'He made all the bookcases too.'

'He built all of this?' said the boy, reaching out to touch one of the shelves. 'I wish I could do woodwork. Mrs Connolly says I have to wait until I go to secondary school, and that's ages away.'

'How old are you now?'

'Nine,' he said, puffing out his chest.

'Wow, nine. Well, you'll go to secondary school at eleven, so not too long to wait.'

'It's two years, Miss,' he replied, incredulous. 'That's forever.'

'It might seem like that now, but it'll fly by.'

'It will not,' said the boy, kneeling down to fuss Bertie, who had settled himself in the corner and was happily snoring away.

'Is that Bertie snoring?' Bea asked.

'Yeah, he does it all the time, Miss,' the boy giggled. 'Mrs Connolly said it's because he's old and needs more sleep.'

'Why don't we let him get some rest, then, and I'll help you choose a book? What's your name by the way?' Bea asked, hoping he might be named after a character from a book she could recommend.

'I'm Billy, and I told you, I don't like reading,' said Billy, the confidence in his voice vanishing. 'It's boring.'

'Okay, so if you don't like reading, what do you like doing?' Bea asked.

'Well, I like horses and football, Miss. I'm in the school team. We're playing Rye Primary next week and I bet we'll thrash them,' he said, excitedly.

'Hmmm . . . horses and football. Have you heard of an author called Michael Morpurgo, Billy?'

'No, who's he?'

'He wrote a book I think you might actually like. It's called *Billy the Kid,* and it's about a football player called Billy who played for Chelsea. He also wrote a very famous book called *War Horse,* about a horse called Joey. It even got made into a film. I think you might like both of them. Here you go,' she said, scanning the shelves and finding a second-hand copy of *War Horse.*

'I like the cover,' said Billy, gazing at the black and white image of Joey's face above a line of soldiers. 'Can I take it home?'

'Yes! Of course.'

'Cool, thanks, Miss!'

As Billy jogged back across the playground to class, his book tucked safely under his arm, Bea couldn't help feeling a warm sense of pride. She hoped Billy would enjoy *War Horse*, even though it was very sad, and that it might change his mind that all books were boring.

By the time the school bell rang, signalling the end of the school day, Bea was exhausted. She didn't know how Rose managed it; answering questions from chatty children for just one afternoon had wiped her out. The busiest part of the day was, however, just about to start, if the queue of parents forming at the door was any indication. Bea just hoped they were all actually here to buy books, as she'd ended up giving away many more to other reluctant readers than she'd planned to. She spotted Mrs Connolly bustling through the crowd, Rose at her side.

'Lovely to meet you, Beatrice,' said the headteacher, shaking her hand. 'Thank you so much for coming to see us today. Rose tells me the children have loved it.'

'They really have,' Rose agreed.

'Now, it turns out your visit has been more popular with the parents than anticipated, as you can see,' Mrs Connolly said, pointing towards the queue, which was now snaking around the playground. 'So, Rose and I are going to be on the door, managing numbers – think of us as your *bouncers* if you will,' Mrs Connolly chuckled. 'No more than eight people in at any one time, if that works for you?'

'Perfect, thank you,' said Bea, gratefully.

'We'll try and get everyone through the door, but I was hoping that you might come back tomorrow? If you're free, that is?' Mrs Connolly added quickly, 'just in case.'

'Wow, yes, of course. I'd love to!' said Bea, her face splitting into a grin. She hadn't expected to be asked back so soon.

'Excellent! Rose, if you can feed that information down the line, for anyone who can't wait this afternoon?' Mrs Connolly instructed.

'On it,' said Rose, making her way across the playground to the back of the queue.

'And I think we could make this a regular visit, Bea, given the level of interest, don't you agree?'

Did she agree? *Erm . . . yes!*

'That would be amazing, Mrs Connolly, thank you!'

'I'll talk to some of the other local headteachers, I'm sure they'd want you to visit their schools too. Cherrydown and Appleton, for example. They only have tiny school libraries as well.'

'I'd really appreciate that, Mrs Connolly,' said Bea, her voice full of gratitude.

'Excellent! Right then,' Mrs Connolly said, smoothing down her dress. 'Let's get the first customers in, shall we?'

CHAPTER 24

'Hello!' said Nathan, as Bea pulled into the yard at Three Acre Farm later that evening. 'I wasn't expecting to see you today,' he said, walking towards her car.

'I thought I'd surprise you,' said Bea, switching off the engine. 'I'm not in the way here, am I?' she asked, jerking her thumb back towards the wagon.

'No, you're fine. Cuppa?'

'God, yes, please. You read my mind,' said Bea, climbing out of the car. 'It's been a hectic day.'

'Oh, yeah?'

'I've been at the school all afternoon, I'm shattered,' she said, following him through to the farmhouse kitchen. 'Oooh, that smells good,' she said, as the aroma of something sweet and spicy filled her nostrils.

'Cinnamon buns,' said Sue, appearing from the larder. 'Get them while they're hot,' she laughed, pulling off her apron.

'I'm heading down to the cowshed now to give your father a hand,' she explained to Nathan, 'but lovely to see you, Bea.'

'You too,' said Bea. 'Say hello to Martin for me, and thanks for the buns, they look amazing,' she said, glancing at the batch sat cooling on the counter. She could feel her mouth starting to water.

'So, to what do I owe the pleasure?' said Nathan, setting two steaming mugs of tea on the table and grabbing a bun from the cooling rack. 'Ouch, that's hot,' he said, blowing on his fingers.

'You were warned,' Bea laughed.

'I know, but they look too good to wait,' said Nathan. 'Want one?' he asked.

'I'll wait until they've cooled down a bit, I think,' said Bea.

'Okay,' Nathan shrugged, pulling up a chair. 'By the way, how did last night go? The book-dating thing? Archie said Josh bagged an actual date out of it, with Claire from the hairdressers.'

'Yeah, they seemed quite cosy at the pub when I left,' said Bea.

'Clearly.'

'It was a good crowd, lots of people I didn't know. Beth and Pete have said I can make it a monthly thing too, which is good.'

'Great! I'll try to make the next one, if I can. So, how was the school thing today?'

'Really good,' Bea nodded, '*amazing* actually,' she said. 'I can't believe how many books I sold. I reckon most of the parents bought at least one, and I'm going back tomorrow to open for a bunch of people who couldn't wait around today.'

'Bloody hell, Bea, that's fantastic,' said Nathan.

'I know, I can't quite believe it. I'm going to have to place an urgent hotline order this evening. I needed to do a proper stock-take anyway, and I sold out of cuddly toys as well. Who knew a stuffed Hungry Caterpillar would prove so popular?'

'Not me, that's for sure,' Nathan chuckled.

'I know! Anyway, I wanted to go over plans for the book club, if that's okay? I spoke to Phoebe yesterday and she's going to deliver the wine to me on Wednesday.'

'God, yeah, it's next week, right?'

'Thursday,' Bea nodded, 'so we've still got plenty of time.'

'How many people are coming?'

'Sixteen. Tickets are up on Eventbrite and include a copy of the book, as well as the cheese and wine, but people can purchase more from you and Phoebe on the night, if you wanted to bring some extra stock along?'

'Great. Sixteen's a good number.'

'Yeah, not too big, not too small.'

'I was going to do individual grazing platters, with a sample of all the cheeses, plus some crackers, chutney, apricots, and I've been experimenting with caramelized walnuts.'

'Sounds delicious.'

'Hang on,' he said, leaping up from his chair. 'I've got some from the batch I made yesterday, I'll get them,' he continued, heading towards the larder. 'Here,' he said, placing a sandwich bag full of nuts in front of her, 'give them a try.'

'God, they smell amazing,' Bea said, reaching her hand into the bag and grabbing a handful. 'Sweet and . . . sort of earthy,' she continued as she bit one in half. 'Bloody hell, Nate, these are gorgeous.'

'They're not bad, are they?' he said, smiling broadly as he took some for himself.

'Are you sure *you* made them? They taste like they're from one of those posh delis in Rye . . .' she said, her eyes narrowed suspiciously.

'Of course I made them,' he laughed. 'It's pretty simple really, just chuck them in the pan with butter and sugar and – voila,' he said, holding up the bag. 'They go great with the cheese.'

'I bet!' Bea agreed.

'Oh, I just remembered, there's something I wanted to ask you,' Nathan said, getting up again to rummage through a pile of papers on the dresser.

'What?' Bea asked, taking a sip of her tea.

'Those business awards, I've had the letter,' he said, passing an envelope to her. 'They're on the thirteenth of August and I get to bring a plus one. I wondered if you fancied coming with me?'

'I'd love to!' said Bea, scanning the letter. 'Ooooh, it's at The Grand in Brighton,' she said. 'Very posh, and Tori was right, it is black tie! That gives me the perfect excuse to buy a new dress.'

'Ah, yeah, that's the other thing, I don't own a tux,' he paused.

'Archie does! You're about the same size, I'm sure he won't mind you borrowing it.'

'You reckon?'

'Sure,' she said. 'Pop in next time you're passing and you can try it on.'

'Okay, I will,' said Nathan, grinning at her. 'Cheers, Bea.'

'So, are you excited?' she asked, leaning towards him.

'I haven't thought about it much, really,' he said, indifferently. 'But a night out in Brighton would be good. I don't think I'm going to win, anyway. Sizzling Hog, Manor Park Dairy and the East Sussex Brewery Company are on the shortlist too.'

'But that doesn't mean you won't win,' she said, reaching across the table and slotting her hand into his. 'You've got as good a product as they do.'

'It's fine,' Nathan said, smiling. 'Not expecting to win helps take the pressure off. At least I wouldn't have to make a speech. I mean, can you imagine?' he shuddered.

'You should probably prepare something in advance though—'

'Just in case?'

'No,' said Bea, shaking her head. 'For *when*, not *if*, you win. Now, pass me one of those cinnamon buns,' she said, decisively.

Bea slept through her alarm the following morning. She'd had her a nose buried in *The House by the Bay* until the early hours. She kept telling herself, *just one more chapter*, until she'd finally drifted off with her reading light still on.

Bea showered and dressed as quickly as she could, and arrived at the Cosy Cat just as Tori was flipping the sign on the door to open.

'Sorry,' said Bea, stashing her bag behind the counter.

'What for? You're not late,' said Tori, brightly.

'No, but I'm cutting it fine.'

'Late night?' Tori asked.

'You could say that—'

'Date with Lochlan?' asked Tori, one eyebrow raised.

'I wish! No, he's still in London. I was just up late reading for book club.'

'Oh my God, I'm loving that book,' said Tori with a gasp. 'It's *so* good.'

'I know! How far have you got?'

'I'm almost three quarters of the way through, and Damian is just about to reveal a secret . . .'

'Don't tell me, don't tell me!' said Bea, covering her ears. 'You're a bit ahead of me.'

'Don't worry,' Tori laughed, 'I won't drop any spoilers.'

'Oooh, before I forget, I've got something for you,' said Bea, grabbing her bag from behind the counter and pulling out a novel, *Summer at the Cat Café*. 'I saw it and thought of you.'

'Oh, thanks, Bea,' said Tori, reading out the blurb on the back. 'The purrrfect summer read.' How cute!'

'I thought we could add it to the other books here?' Bea suggested.

'Definitely, but I'm keeping this copy to read first! So, are you all set for book club?' Tori asked.

'I think so,' Bea nodded, scooping up a little grey tabby that was rubbing against her ankles. 'Hey, you're new?'

'Yep, that's Alfie,' said Tori, scratching the cat under his chin, as he purred contentedly.

'I'd love a cat, but Archie's allergic . . .'

'Ah, that's a shame,' Tori agreed.

'I know. Plus, we dog-sit Wordsworth all the time. Maybe one day, though,' Bea continued. 'For now, working here will have to do.'

'Well, if you ever change your mind, I'm sure Izzy and I can find you a hypoallergenic cat.'

The morning absolutely flew by; it was the busiest shift Bea had ever worked at the Cosy Cat. As quickly as she cleared a table, a new set of customers would arrive, and the lunchtime rush was only just getting started.

'I don't know what's got into everyone today,' whispered Tori, as Bea took another order through to the kitchen. 'It's not been this busy in ages.'

'Don't knock it,' said Bea, 'the till hasn't stopped ringing all morning.'

'Mum's arriving soon, so that should take some of the pressure off.' Tori replied.

'I can stay on a bit longer, if you need me?' said Bea, helpfully. 'But I'm back at the school this afternoon, so I'll have to leave by two at the latest.'

'Thanks, I might take you up on that.'

Joyce's arrival had helped get them through the lunchtime

rush, but by the time Bea was getting ready to leave, she was exhausted.

'Here,' said Tori, handing her a mug of coffee, 'take five minutes before you rush off.'

'Thanks,' said Bea, gratefully, rubbing her back, 'My feet are killing me.' Just then the door dinged to signal the arrival of more customers. 'Hey, Matt! Lovely to see you,' said Bea, smiling at the sight of her library boss and his husband.

'Making the most of my day off,' said Matt. 'Fancy joining us?'

'I'd love to,' said Bea, beaming, 'but I'm taking the wagon to the school again this afternoon, so I've got to dash. Are you coming to book club next week?' Bea asked.

'Definitely,' said Matt. We're really looking forward to it.'

'Perfect,' said Bea, 'your ticket includes the wine and cheese board, remember, so don't eat dinner before you come.'

'Got it,' said Matt, nodding.

'Oh, and make sure to bring garden chairs,' said Bea. 'And before I forget, the council have given permission for me to put a little free library on the green.'

'That's brilliant!' said Harry. 'What a great idea!'

'I've bought a kit online, so I'm building it myself – or trying to, at least,' said Bea, picking at the plaster on her thumb where she had hit it with a hammer. 'I thought we could have a little gathering to mark the opening? Maybe you could come along and cut a ribbon or something, Matt?

'I'd love to,' he said.

Bea felt her phone vibrate in her pocket. She smiled when

she saw it was a message from Lochlan: *Got a client dinner on the 13th, shall I book you in to the hotel? Miss you xx.*

Bea had almost forgotten about her trip to London. She quickly checked her calendar to make sure she was free, before sending a reply: *Perfect, love to xx.*

She tucked her phone back into her pocket with a thought niggling at her from the back of her mind.

The 13th? Why did that date sound so familiar?

Was she forgetting someone's birthday? Her parents wedding anniversary? There was nothing in her diary, but she couldn't shake the feeling that she'd forgotten something important.

When Bea pulled into the car park at the tiny primary school half an hour later, there was already a queue of people waiting for her, even though the school day didn't end for another thirty minutes.

'Hello!' Bea called, as she climbed out of the car and started unhitching the trailer. 'Just give me five minutes and I'll be ready for you.'

'I can't wait to look inside,' said the lady at the front of the queue. 'My son, Mason, told me all about your bookshop. He loves it! He's already given me a list of what to buy,' she said, waving a piece of paper in the air. 'Please tell me you've still got copies of *Dork Diaries*?'

'I do, yes,' Bea replied, opening up the wagon's doors.

'And do you have those cuddly Paddingtons? You'd sold out yesterday, and I promised Tiffany I'd get her one,' the woman behind her asked.

'Absolutely,' said Bea. 'I put a rush order in last night.'

'That's great,' replied the woman, relief flooding her face. 'Tiff will be thrilled!'

'If you can come inside in small groups, that would be great. I'm a little short on space,' Bea explained.

Where was Mrs Connolly when you needed her?

The queue seemed never-ending, not that Bea was complaining; as soon as one group of parents left, they were replaced by another, then the children started appearing once the school bell sounded.

'Bea! How's it going?' Rose asked, squeezing into the trailer. 'All okay?'

'Yeah, good thanks,' said Bea, handing over a cuddly Hungry Caterpillar to a delighted child.

'Sorry, I meant to escape from class in time to meet you, but things got hectic,' Rose explained. 'I'll be outside, but if you need me, just shout.'

'Will do,' said Bea, as she moved on to serving another customer.

'This bookshop is just adorable,' said a woman, handing her a stack of books to scan. 'I may have gone a little overboard,' she continued, sheepishly, 'but Tilly wanted one of almost everything!'

'Sounds like you've got a real bookworm on your hands,' said Bea, smiling at the little girl who was clutching her mum's hand tightly.

'Oh, absolutely! Tilly loves reading. I'm Tasha, by the way,' said Tasha, tapping her card to pay. 'I work at Pashley

Manor. We're having a garden party in September – it's invitation only, but there's going to be stalls selling local produce, arts and crafts, that kind of thing. Your wagon would fit in perfectly. Would you be interested?'

'Oh, yes, please, that sounds amazing! I'm trying to book in as many local events as possible,' said Bea, grinning broadly.

'Here's my card,' said Tasha, handing Bea a cream, embossed business card. 'My email's on there – drop me a line and I'll send you a booking form.'

'Thank you!' said Bea, handing Tasha's purchases across. 'I'll do it as soon as I'm home.'

'Great,' said Tasha. 'I'll see you soon, then.'

'See you!' said Bea, tucking Tasha's card safely into her back pocket. 'And thanks!'

A pitch at Pashley Manor's garden party could really help put Bea's Book Wagon on the map. It was exactly the kind of break Bea was hoping for, she just never expected it to come from a visit to the local primary school.

CHAPTER 25

How? How had she forgotten something so important? Bea realized as soon as she'd woken up the next morning that the thirteenth was the date of Nathan's big night, and she'd promised to be his plus one.

'I'm an idiot,' she groaned, burying her face into the pillow. Lochlan had sent the hotel reservation details through to her and her stay was booked and paid for.

'Oh, God,' she moaned, massaging her temples. Whatever she did, she was going to upset either Lochlan or Nathan.

'What are you going to do?' asked Jess, as Bea explained her cock-up over coffee that morning.

'I don't know,' Bea groaned, her head in her hands.

'Flip a coin?' Jess suggested half-heartedly. 'Whatever you do, you're going to have to let one of them down.'

'I know,' said Bea, an uncomfortable, nauseous feeling rising in her stomach. 'But who?'

'The trip to London to see Lochlan does sound amazing ... but Nate has done a lot for you recently,' Jess reminded Bea. 'Do you really want to let him down for a guy you barely know? If things with Lochlan don't work out, you might regret—'

'That's kinda the point, though,' said Bea. 'It's such early days with Lochlan, I really don't want to mess it up.'

'So, go to London. Nate will understand.'

'Do you think?' Bea asked.

'Sure,' Jess nodded. 'Listen, I could offer to go to the awards thing in your place, that might soften the blow a bit. At least he won't be alone?'

'Ooooh, would you?' Bea asked, relieved to have a get-out strategy.

'Yeah, no problem.'

'Okay,' said Bea, forcing a smile. 'Nathan won't mind as long as he's got someone with him.' But if that was true, why did she feel so wretched about it?

'What's the date again? I'll just check I'm actually free before you tell him—'

'No!' said Bea, her tone sharp. 'I can't. You're right. I can't let Nate down, not after everything he's done for me.'

'Okay, so what about Lochlan?'

'I'll message him and explain what's happened. I'm sure he'll be okay, and I can rearrange for another date. He's going to be in London for a while longer. It'll be fine.'

'Wow!' said Jess, sinking back into her chair. 'I'm proud of you, you know. You're actually taking my advice, and passing up a night in a swanky hotel for some local award that Nate probably won't even win . . .'

'Mates before dates,' said Bea, firmly. 'Isn't that what you're always telling me?'

'Okay, well, there's no time like the present,' said Jess, picking up Bea's phone. 'Might as well call Lochlan now; get it over with.'

'You're right,' said Bea, before hitting the call button. Maybe Lochlan would be in a meeting and she could just leave a message?

He answered on the second ring.

'Hey, gorgeous,' he said in a sexy voice. 'How's things?'

'Yeah, good,' she said, feeling a little shaky.

'I can't wait for you to get here. I've managed to get us the honeymoon suite for the night—'

'I'm so sorry, Lochlan, I can't come,' Bea blurted out.

'Why not?' he asked, sounding stunned.

'I've messed up my dates, I'm so sorry, but I'd already agreed to go to something else that night, I'd forgotten to put it in my diary . . .'

'Okay . . .' he said, slowly. 'But it's all arranged and paid for already, Bea. It's taken quite a lot of effort, and all my colleagues want to meet you. I've got a big client dinner – can't you just pull out of this other thing? This is important to me. How's it going to make me look when I tell people you're not coming?'

Something in his tone made her frown.

'I can't, I'm sorry. It's Nathan, he's up for a business award and he'd asked me to go with him first. It's a big deal, Lochlan; a black-tie event at The Grand in Brighton. If he wins then—'

'Hang on, you're dropping me to go on a date with Nathan?' Lochlan asked, incredulous.

'God, no, it's not a date,' Bea replied, quickly, desperate to reassure him, 'nothing like that. It's just, he's helped me so much with the book wagon, now it's my turn to support him, and I'd already said yes, you see—'

There was silence at the other end of the line.

'Lochlan? Are you still there?'

'Yes,' he whispered. 'I'm just not sure what you expect me to say.'

'It's fine, you don't need to say anything. Just know that I'm really sorry,' said Bea.

'Is there something going on between you and Nate? Because if there is—'

'God, no!' she said, mortified. 'But I made him a promise and I don't want to break it. It wouldn't be fair. I'd still love to come to London some other time, though? Can we reschedule?'

Lochlan didn't answer.

'Look, I'm really sorry, I'm not sure what else I can say.'

'Neither am I,' he said, his tone clipped. 'Just don't make a habit of letting me down, Bea, it's not a good look.'

'Okay,' she whispered, stung by his words. 'We can do it another time, though?'

'Sure,' he said, with less enthusiasm than she was hoping for. 'But Bea?'

'Yes?'

'Don't leave it too long.'

'I won't,' she said, closing her eyes. 'Send me some dates and I'll check my calendar properly this time.'

'Fine,' he said, dropping the call before Bea had a chance to reply.

CHAPTER 26

The day of the first book club had finally arrived, and, in typically English fashion, the weather forecast was for sunshine and showers. Bea was tracking the clouds on her weather app with a dedication that bordered on obsession.

'What do you think, Arch? Will it stay dry until ten?' Bea asked, pacing the living room.

'Seriously, if you ask me about the weather one more time, I swear I'll—'

'Okay, okay,' said Bea, chewing her thumbnail, 'point taken. But the Met Office is saying rain at eight, and the BBC is showing nothing until ten, see?' she said, shoving her phone under his nose.

'I don't know what to tell you,' said Archie, stifling a yawn. 'Now, can I please just eat my dinner in peace?' he said, winding spaghetti around his fork and shoving it into his mouth.

'Yeah. Sorry,' said Bea, apologetically. 'I guess there's nothing I can do about it anyway; it'll either rain or it won't.'

'Exactly!' Archie agreed. 'Oh, did I tell you? Josh and Claire are going on another date. Can you believe it?'

'Wow, that's great!' Bea was pleased her book speed-dating had brought them together.

'He said he's planning on taking her to Comic Con in the autumn, so he must be serious. I don't think he can believe his luck,' Archie chuckled.

'I bet! Right, I'm going, I want to set up before Phoebe and Nathan arrive,' she said, checking the weather apps one more time.

'Okay, well, good luck. I hope it goes well,' said Archie, his mouth full of spag bol.

'Thanks.'

'Oh, and if there's any cheese left, make sure you bring it home,' he said, wiping tomato sauce from the corner of his mouth.

Bea had done everything she could to prepare for tonight: she'd made sure the books in the wagon looked their best, set up the bean bags and deckchairs outside, lit some citronella candles and turned on all the fairy lights. Even though Nathan was supplying the food, she'd filled some pretty glass bowls with crisps and nuts, set out the chilled wine Phoebe had delivered the previous day with elegant plastic recycled picnic glasses, and Tori had given her a plate of cupcakes from the café to wish her luck. She had a few moments to herself before Nathan and Phoebe were due to arrive, so she sat in one of the deckchairs and took a deep breath.

A lot was riding on tonight being a success. The tickets weren't cheap, so she hoped everyone coming would think it was worth it and come again.

She turned her head when she heard the hum of a van crossing the green. Nathan was first to arrive, and as he climbed out of his truck he said, 'Looks like the rain's holding off.'

'Ssssh!' Bea hissed, 'don't jinx it.'

'Where do you want this?' he laughed, lifting a pile of foil-covered trays from the back of the van.

'Over there, please, next to the wine,' she said, pointing at a trestle table she'd laid with a pretty vintage lace curtain to hide the legs.

'Sure,' Nathan replied, uncovering the platters one by one.

'Ooooh, these look good,' said Bea, reaching to grab a small chunk of his famous blue cheese.

'Don't even think about it,' he said, batting her hand away. 'These are for paying guests.'

'Uh, but I'm starving,' she complained.

'Knew you would be,' he said, pulling a bag of walnuts from his back pocket and tossing them towards her. 'That's why I brought you these,' he said, winking.

'Yes! Thanks, Nate,' said Bea, tearing open the bag and shoving one into her mouth. 'Here's Phoebe!' she spluttered, trying not to choke as Phoebe struggled towards them, a heavy box in her arms.

'Hello, you two,' said Phoebe. 'Did someone order more wine?'

'Yes! And lots of it,' said Bea, taking the box from her and carefully stashing it under the table. 'Thanks so much for this.'

'No worries, I've been looking forward to it. Although, I have to admit, I haven't actually read the book,' said Phoebe, looking mortified.

'Oh, don't worry about that,' Bea replied. 'There won't be a test!'

'I meant to, but then, *life*,' Phoebe said with a grimace, 'and by that, I mean mum duties got in the way.'

'It's not a problem, it's just great to have you here,' said Bea.

'And even better to have the wine,' Nathan teased.

'Oi!' Phoebe chastised him. 'How long have we got to set up?'

'Thirty minutes until everyone should start arriving,' said Bea, looking at her watch again.

'Plenty of time,' said Phoebe. 'I'll get a few of these chilled bottles opened, and we'll be good to go.'

Bea had almost forgotten how nervous she was until she saw Tori and Joyce walking across the green towards the wagon, fold-up chairs under their arms.

'Here we go,' Bea said to Nathan and Phoebe. 'Tori! Joyce! Hello, thank you so much for coming.'

'Wow, this all looks gorgeous,' said Joyce, admiring the twinkling fairy lights and candles. 'Very cute.'

'Thanks,' said Bea, proudly.

'Let me get you both something to drink,' said Phoebe, springing into action. 'Red or white?'

'Oooh, white, please,' said Tori, setting up their chairs next to one of the beanbags.

'Me too,' said Joyce.

'Arthur!' called Bea, rushing to relieve him of the chair he was carrying. 'You made it!'

'I wouldn't miss it, my dear,' he said.

'Wine?' Phoebe asked, as Bea flipped open his heavy-duty camping chair.

'Yes, please. I'm staying at my son's, so I can have a glass or two, and he can drive me home in the morning,' said Arthur, a mischievous glint in his eye.

'Good plan,' said Nathan, approvingly.

'You must be the cheese man?' asked Arthur, with a nod of recognition.

'I am, but I also go by Nate,' chuckled Nathan, offering out a hand to Arthur. 'Although "The Farmer" is fine, too.'

'Good to meet you. Bea has been telling me all about this cheese of yours. I can't wait to try it,' said Arthur, shaking Nathan's hand firmly.

'It's delicious, believe me,' whispered Bea.

Beth, Maggie and Jess were the next to arrive, followed by Violet, Simon and Anya, Matt and Harry, Rose, Jake and Jean, as well as a few faces Bea couldn't put names to, but she thought she recognized from the WI meeting, the school or the Cosy Cat.

When everyone was settled in with a glass of wine or elderflower cordial, Bea took a deep breath.

'Hello, everyone!' she said. 'Thank you so much for coming to the first meeting of Bea's Book Club.'

A small round of applause reverberated around the circle.

'I'm hoping the weather holds out for us tonight, but, if it doesn't, Violet has kindly allowed us to use the village hall. So, if it does start raining, grab whatever you don't want getting wet and make a dash for it.'

'Fingers crossed it stays dry,' said Jess.

'So,' Bea continued. 'First of all, I hope you all received your copy of the book in the post?'

Everyone nodded.

'Perfect! And now you've had a chance to read it, I hope you enjoyed it, but if you didn't, that's okay. We're not all going to love the same books, and this club is all about trying things we might not usually read and sharing our thoughts. There's only one rule: be open and listen to everyone's opinions, even if you don't agree with them.'

'Isn't that two rules?' Harry pointed out.

'I suppose it is,' said Bea, laughing. 'Okay, so Book Club only has *two* rules! We're going to start by talking about what we thought about *The House by the Bay.* Then we can have a break to eat, and we'll finish off with some questions I've put together for us to discuss. How does that sound?' Everyone murmured their agreement.

'Oh, and I'll be coming round to top up your drinks, so just give me a nod if you'd like a refill,' Phoebe added.

'Perfect, thanks, Phoebe. Does anyone have any questions before we get started?' Bea asked. 'Nope? Okay, then, let's start! Violet inspired the pick of our first book: Kate Fisher's *The House by the Bay*. I've always loved Kate's books; she's such a phenomenal writer and this one didn't disappoint. I thoroughly enjoyed it, couldn't put it down in fact, so I really hope you all felt the same.'

There were a few murmurs of 'Absolutely' and 'Loved it!' from the group.

'I loved the love story between Jane and Damian; it was heartbreaking and uplifting at the same time, and that secret he was keeping, well . . . I didn't see it coming at all,' said Bea. 'Tori, what did you make of it?'

'I was exactly the same, I couldn't put it down. I haven't read anything by her before, but I'll definitely be reading her other books if this one's anything to go by,' said Tori.

'You're in for a treat,' said Violet, 'they're all just as good, if not better. My favourite's *The Garden of Dreams*. That was her debut.'

'I loved the setting. Portofino almost seemed like a character in its own right, if that makes sense? I fell in love with it,' said Rose.

'I hate to say it, but I didn't really like it,' said Harry, apologetically.

'That's okay, Harry. What was it you didn't like?' Bea asked.

'I just found it a little slow, and there was way too much historical detail for me. It just didn't hold my interest nearly as much as I hoped it would,' Harry explained.

Bea heard a tiny huff of annoyance from Violet.

'I can understand that,' said Bea. 'If you're not a fan of historical fiction, it might not be for you.'

'I think that's all it was, just not my bag really,' said Harry, casting Violet an apologetic look.

After a healthy debate, the consensus seemed to be that the majority of members had enjoyed the book, with a couple of exceptions, but no one completely hated it, so Bea was pleased.

'How do you think it's going?' Phoebe asked Bea, as she topped up everyone's glasses while they grabbed a cheese board and sat down to eat.

'Good, I think,' said Bea, watching Nathan chatting to Arthur, his eyes glinting with amusement in the light cast upon him by the flickering candles. Violet was deep in conversation with Tori, her face relaxed and happy.

The evening light was now fading and the fairy lights around the wagon were twinkling like tiny stars, giving the evening a magical feel. The sound of conversation and laughter was humming in the air – it was exactly what Bea was hoping for.

'Everyone seems to be enjoying themselves, and I've heard nothing but good things about your wine!' said Bea.

'I've sold all of the extra bottles I brought with me tonight, and Arthur wants to book in for a vineyard tour with his son!' Phoebe said.

'Amazing! I'm glad it's been worthwhile, Phoebe, that's

great,' said Bea. 'Right,' she said, glancing at her watch, 'I'd better crack on if we're going to try and be done by ten.'

'I'll go around and give everyone a top-up,' said Phoebe, bottle in hand.

With their stomachs now full of cheese, and with the wine flowing freely, Bea noticed that everyone seemed a bit more relaxed and more willing to share their opinions than they had been initially.

'Now, before we finish, I've got a favour to ask,' said Bea, resting a pile of cards she'd grabbed from inside the wagon in her lap. 'I've put these together for you,' she said. 'They're "Bea's Book Club Recommends", and I'd love for you to have a think about a book you'd like to recommend for the shop, and I'll order a copy from my wholesaler to display alongside a review from you, if that's okay?'

'What a lovely idea,' said Jean, stashing a card in her handbag.

'Can it be any book, or does it have to be a new release?' Joyce asked.

'Anything you like, as long as it's still in print,' said Bea.

'I'll put my thinking cap on,' said Arthur.

'There's no rush, take your time, and if you can drop them back to the Cosy Cat, I can collect them from there. If that's okay, Tori?' said Bea.

'Fine by me,' said Tori.

'Great! And we also need to pick our book for next month. Any suggestions?' Bea asked, looking around the circle.

'I've got one,' said Matt, quickly. 'How about *Frankenstein* by Mary Shelley?'

'Oooh, yes, I've not read that in years!' said Violet.

'I don't think I ever have,' said Jake, 'but it sounds good to me.'

'Okay, great! Looks like we've got our next title sorted then!' said Bea. 'We should get some great debates out of that one.'

'I'll put my order in now, please, Bea. Two copies for Jake and me,' said Rose.

'Don't worry, I'll do tickets the same as tonight, so a copy of the book is included in the price, unless people would prefer just cheese and wine tickets?' Bea asked. 'And then you could borrow a copy of the book from the library?'

'Oh no, I want a brand new copy, if that's okay, so I can start a collection at home. "Bea's Book Club picks". It's got a certain ring to it, don't you think?' declared Violet.

'Excellent, thanks, Violet!' said Bea, brightly. 'But I think I'll do two tiers of tickets anyway. One with the book and one without, so people can choose. Thanks so much for coming along this evening, everyone, I really hope you've enjoyed it, and I hope to see you all back here in July on the last Thursday of the month.'

'It's been a brilliant night,' said Jess, 'thanks for organizing it, Bea. I've really enjoyed it,' she continued.

'Well done, Bea,' said Tori, standing up and giving her a hug. 'See you at work tomorrow.'

'I'll see you tomorrow too,' said Jess, 'Gotta run, I'm meeting Archie at the pub and I'm already late.'

'Are you?' said Bea, taken aback. 'He didn't mention it.'

'See you,' said Jess, hurrying off across the green before Bea could say another word.

'I'd best be off too,' said Violet, turning to go.

'Bye! And thanks again for letting me use the green, I really appreciate it,' said Bea, folding up her deckchairs and stowing them in the boot of her car.

'Night, everyone,' she called to the rest of the group, as they began packing up their belongings before making their way home.

'Before I go,' said Rose, placing a hand on Bea's arm and making her jump. 'I just wanted to thank you for whatever you said to Billy the other day at school. He won't stop talking about that book you gave him.'

'*War Horse*?' said Bea, beaming.

'Yes, that's the one. He absolutely loved it. His mum bought him the follow up, *Farm Boy,* and he's been bringing it in for guided reading. His teacher's thrilled.'

'That's so lovely to hear. I'll have a think about what to recommend him next time I visit,' said Bea.

'Excellent! See you soon, and thanks for tonight, it was great,' said Rose.

'Oh Christ, is that rain?' asked Nathan, his palms suddenly outstretched.

'I think so, yes,' said Bea, pulling up the hood of her sweater.

'Better get a move on then,' said Phoebe, throwing the empty bottles and rubbish into bin bags.

'Shit,' said Bea, as the raindrops started to fall.

Bea, Nathan and Phoebe packed away as quickly as they could, as the rain started to hammer down upon them. When they'd finally got everything cleared up, they didn't stop to say a proper goodbye to each other, they just climbed into their respective vehicles and waved farewell.

Bea was soaked through to the skin, but she'd be back home soon enough and was looking forward to a hot shower, clean pjs and a glass of wine.

Bliss.

Phoebe gave her horn a little toot as she pulled off the green, and Nathan wound down his window, yelling, 'After you,' and waving his arms at Bea with a flourish. She smiled, put her foot on the accelerator and set off.

Bea flicked her wipers to full speed. She could barely see out the window now, the rain was so heavy.

The journey back to Meadowgate Mead took her down a winding lane that led out of the village, so she slowed down, dropping into a lower gear. She could just about make out Nathan's headlights behind her in her rear-view mirror when, all of a sudden, she was dazzled by a flash of lights that appeared to be speeding directly towards her on the wrong side of the road.

She pumped her brakes, tried to slow down, but, with the other car heading directly for her, she had no choice but to swerve to try to avoid a collision.

Bea screamed as the car flipped on its side, her head thumping hard against the window as it crashed to the ground. She felt something hot and sticky flowing down her cheek as her vision began to fade, her consciousness gradually slipping away.

She was out cold.

CHAPTER 27

Nathan couldn't believe what he was seeing. One minute he was following the red glow of the horsebox's rear lights, the next Bea's car had swerved off the lane sharply, flipping up and onto its side, before coming back down to earth with a thud in the ditch. He slammed on his brakes as he saw a pair of oncoming headlights hurtling towards him, the other vehicle coming off the road behind him. He didn't think, he just yanked on his handbrake, jumped out of his truck and sprinted towards Bea's car.

Smoke was pouring from the engine, the windscreen smashed, the airbag deployed. The horsebox was on its side, back doors open, books all over the road and in the ditch.

It was carnage.

'Bea!' he yelled, banging on the driver's-side window. He couldn't see a thing. 'Bea!' he shouted again.

There was no response.

He peered through the windscreen. He could see her. Her head was slumped forward, resting on the steering wheel, her hair soaked in blood and falling across her face.

He pulled his phone from his pocket, his hands shaking as he dialled 999.

'Is she breathing? Does she have a pulse?' the emergency response operator asked after taking his details.

'I don't know, I can't get to her.' Nathan tried the car door again, but the impact had jammed it shut. 'Hang on,' he'd said, throwing the phone to the ground, pulling off his sweatshirt and wrapping it around his arm. He slammed it hard against the driver's side window, which shattered, covering Bea with shards of glass.

'Shit,' he muttered. 'Bea? Bea?' he said, desperately. 'Come on, wake up,' he pleaded, through gritted teeth. He laid a hand on her neck and felt for a pulse, relief flooding through him when he felt it thrumming steadily beneath her skin. 'Yes,' he said, retrieving his phone. 'I can feel it, she's got a pulse.'

'That's good, really good,' said the call operator.

'Should I get her out? The engine might explode!'

'No, absolutely not, she could have a spinal injury. You need to wait until the ambulance and fire crew are with you. What about the other vehicle. Are the occupants okay?'

'I don't know,' said Nathan, 'I haven't checked.' He didn't want to leave Bea's side.

'I need you to take a look.'

'Okay,' said Nathan, using every ounce of strength he possessed to tear himself away from Bea. He jogged back down the lane towards the other car where a man was sat on the grass verge looking dazed and confused.

'Are you hurt?' Nathan yelled.

'I—I don't know. I don't think so,' the man whispered, shaking.

'Is there anyone else inside?'

'No, j—just me,' he stammered.

'Emergency services are on their way,' Nathan explained. 'The other guy's okay,' he said into the phone, rushing back towards Bea.

He ripped off his T-shirt and placed it gently between her head, which was gushing with blood, and the steering wheel. 'You're going to be fine, Bea, just fine. I've got you, okay?' he whispered, sweeping the hair off her face. 'Hang on, I can hear the fire engine,' said Nathan, turning towards blue lights flashing in the distance. 'They're here,' he said down the phone, 'help's here.'

'Good. I'm going to leave you with the crew now, Nathan. You take care.'

'Okay, thanks,' said Nathan, hanging up. 'We're here!' he shouted. 'Over here! We need help!'

'Nathan?' a familiar voice cried.

'Leo, thank God!' said Nathan. 'It's Bea, she needs help. *Now*!'

'Okay, we've got you, mate,' said Leo, resting a comforting hand on his shoulder. He dropped to his knees and opened a medical bag. 'Ambulance is right behind us. How long has she been out for?'

'I don't know, it feels like for ever – maybe ten minutes? I don't know,' said Nathan, running a blood-soaked hand through his hair.

'Let's get a neck brace on her and get her on a spinal board,' said a female officer, crouching down to look through the side window.

'Bea,' said Leo, taking her hand gently, 'Bea, we're going to get you out, okay? I need you to wake up, though,' he said, securing the neck brace and placing an oxygen mask over her face. 'Come on, Bea, time to wake up,' he continued.

Bea murmured softly.

'You've been in accident, Bea, but we're getting you out, okay? You're doing great,' Leo continued.

Bea emitted a long, loud groan, her head lifting slowly.

'I need you to keep nice and still for me, okay, Bea? Nice and still,' said Leo quickly.

'Nathan?' said Bea in weak voice.

'Welcome back,' said Leo, gripping her hand again tightly. 'Nathan's here, and we're getting you out, okay? Just a few more minutes. Stay with us.'

'Okay . . . ' Bea croaked, her breathing fast and shallow.

'I need you to step back, Nathan,' Leo said, 'just while we get her out, okay?'

'Okay,' Nathan nodded, wringing his hands. He felt completely powerless. All he could do was watch as the fire crew took the car door off and gently moved Bea on to the spinal board.

'The ambulance is here now,' said Leo, nodding towards the two paramedics waiting patiently to transfer Bea onto a stretcher and whisk her off to hospital. 'You going with her?' he asked.

'Yes,' Nathan nodded, 'I'm not leaving her.'

'Okay. Give me your keys, I'll get your truck moved out the way.'

'Cheers, mate,' said Nathan, climbing into the ambulance.

'Right then, Bea, this is where you leave us,' said Leo, giving her hand a last squeeze. 'You're in good hands.'

'Thanks, Leo,' she whispered.

The doors banged shut and the sound of sirens pierced the night air.

Bea groaned as she tried to sit up,

'Owww!' she said, a sharp pain searing down her left side.

'It's okay, sweetheart, don't try to move.' Bea's mum reached for her to try to keep her still.

'You're all right, love. We're here.' Gordon took her hand to reassure her.

'Where am I?' Bea asked, confused, slowly opening her eyes. She winced at the bright lights. 'What's happening?'

'You're in hospital, love,' said Carol. 'You were in an accident.'

'An accident?' Bea repeated. 'No, I was at book club, it was raining and then . . .'

And then, what?

'And then . . . well, I don't know what happened. *Ow*,' she repeated, clasping her side.

'You've got a couple of broken ribs, but you're going to be okay, Bea, I promise,' said Gordon, squeezing her hand again.

'What happened? I can't remember . . . .' said Bea, trying to sit up.

'Here, let me,' said Carol, propping an extra pillow behind her. 'Is that better?'

'Thanks, Mum,' said Bea. 'I'm thirsty,' she said, aware of how dry her mouth was.

'Here,' said Gordon, pouring a glass of water from the jug on the bedside cabinet. 'And a straw might help,' he said.

'Thanks,' said Bea, leaning forward as he held up the glass for her. 'Uh,' she moaned, raising a hand to her mouth, her lips felt swollen and sore. 'What accident?'

'A car accident, sweetheart,' said Carol.

Bea tried to remember. 'It was raining . . . and there were lights coming towards me . . .'

And then? Nothing.

The next thing she could remember was waking up here in a hospital bed.

'The main thing is you're going to be okay. You'll be sore for a few weeks, while those ribs heal, but the doctors are confident there's no lasting damage,' said Gordon.

'Was there another car involved? What happened? Are they okay?' Bea asked, anxiously.

'Yes, the driver's fine, he's already been discharged. One of the bloody Fallon boys. Over the limit, too. The police want to speak to you, once you're feeling up to it,' said Gordon.

'Oh, okay,' Bea nodded. She felt so confused. Why couldn't she remember what had happened?

'The doctor said you can go home in a couple of days. They need to keep you under observation for a while; you took a pretty nasty bang to the head and it needed stitches,' Carol explained.

'Hang on,' said Bea, any colour she had draining from her face. 'I was towing the horsebox. What's happened to it? Is it damaged?' she asked, pulling at her dad's arm.

She saw her parents throw each other a worried look.

'What happened to it?' she asked again.

'It took a bit of a battering,' Gordon whispered. 'Nothing that can't be fixed,' he added quickly, 'but it's going to take time.'

'What?' said Bea, her heart pounding. 'But I've got bookings, commitments . . . what am I going to do?'

'Don't worry about that now, just concentrate on getting yourself better,' said Carol, patting her arm gently. 'You're okay, and that's the most important thing. It could have been so much worse.'

Bea knew her mum was right. Broken ribs and a few stitches was getting off lightly, she could have been seriously injured, or worse still . . .

'We'll figure everything out once you're home. We'll get on to the insurance and it'll all be fine,' said Gordon.

'Oh no!' Bea groaned.

'What is it, sweetheart?' Carol asked, her voice filled with concern.

'The insurance,' Bea whispered. 'On the horsebox.'

'Yes?' said Carol.

'You do have insurance, don't you?' Gordon asked, his voice serious.

'Well, no. It's not a legal requirement and I was trying to save money,' Bea muttered, a tear rolling down her cheek. 'But the accident wasn't my fault, if the other driver was over the limit and on the wrong side of the road, I can claim on their insurance?'

'Ah,' said Gordon, screwing up his face. 'He was driving without insurance, love. The police are going to charge him, but that doesn't help you with the horsebox.'

'Oh, God,' said Bea. She felt physically sick.

'Forget about all that for now,' said Carol, waving a hand. 'Just focus on getting better and coming home.'

'But, Mum, I—'

'I mean it, Bea. I don't want you thinking about it right now. Just get some rest, okay?' said Carol.

'Okay,' Bea repeated.

'Now, your Dad and I need to go home to see to Wordsworth, but Archie's on his way with Jess. They'll be here soon,' said Carol.

As her parents left and Bea closed her eyes, laying her

head back on the pillow, rest was the furthest thing from her mind. If she didn't have the money to get the book wagon back on the road, her fledgling business was ruined, and then what was she supposed to do?

CHAPTER 28

Nathan had lost count of the number of times he'd checked his phone, but there was still no news of Bea. He'd called Carol from the ambulance and she and Gordon were waiting for them in A&E when they pulled up. They'd insisted he go home; there was no point in all of them waiting, and they promised to update him as soon as there was any news.

Bea had drifted in and out of consciousness throughout the journey. It was awful seeing her like that, knowing there was nothing he could do. What if she had internal bleeding? What if her head injury turned out to be serious? Life-threatening, even?

He hadn't slept a wink, his stomach churning as he kept replaying the scene in his head over and over: the flashing blue lights, Bea's upturned car, the sight of her lying motionless.

At 8am, he couldn't wait any longer. He pulled on his trainers, grabbed his car keys and was about to drive back to the hospital to find out how she was for himself, when a call from Carol flashed on his screen.

'How is she?' he answered, his grip on the phone tightening.

'She's going to be okay,' said Carol, and Nathan could hear the relief in her voice. 'She's got a concussion, a couple of broken ribs and some minor wounds, but apart from that, she's fine. She had a lucky escape.'

'Thank *God*.'

'She's worried about the wagon, though. She isn't insured,' Carol sighed.

'Shit! I hadn't realized.' Nathan knew Bea had tried to save money, but he thought she'd have taken out insurance given the cost of her stock alone.

'The other driver was one of the Fallon boys. You know them?'

'Yep,' said Nathan, 'they've always been trouble. Their dad caused all those problems for Rose and Scout a couple of years back.'

'Well, he didn't have any insurance and was over the limit, too. He'll be charged, but that doesn't help Bea,' Carol sighed. 'I don't want her worrying about that now, though.'

'No, of course not,' said Nathan. He knew Bea would be devastated, heartbroken. He didn't want that. 'What if I get it towed here? We can store it in the barn again, and I can see what needs fixing?'

'If you don't mind, that would be one less thing to worry about. Thanks, Nathan.'

'No worries. I'd like to visit later, if you think she's up to it?'

'She's resting right now, but if you leave it until after lunch, I'm sure she'd love to see you.'

'Okay, great. I'll be there,' he said, relief coursing through him that Bea was okay, even if the wagon wasn't.

He pulled out his phone and scrolled through to find Leo's number. The first thing he needed to do was to get the book wagon up to the farm and see exactly how bad the damage was.

Bea's pain medication had kicked in, so she was starting to feel better, if a little woozy, but she couldn't stop thinking about the book wagon.

How bad was the damage? Not knowing was killing her.

Archie and Jess had been to see her before lunch, Jess armed with a bag of pastries from the Cosy Cat and a family-size box of Maltesers, because Bea needed 'the essentials'. Archie had tried to make her laugh with stories about how bad the food in the hospital canteen was, which made her ribs hurt so much she'd begged him to stop. They'd both been worryingly evasive when she'd asked them about the book wagon, casting furtive glances at one another, neither of them looking her in the eye.

After pushing aside an unappetizing lunch of a limp cheese and tomato sandwich *(thank God Jess had brought supplies!),* Bea heard a familiar voice approaching her bed.

'Someone's looking better than the last time I saw them,' said Nathan, beaming at her.

He looked exhausted, with dark circles under his eyes and the distinct appearance of someone who hadn't slept.

'Nathan!' Bea cried, trying, and failing, to pull herself upright. 'Owww,' she winced.

'Here, let me,' said Nathan, rushing to help her sit up. 'Better?'

'Much. Thanks,' she said, forcing a pained smile.

'How are you feeling?' he asked, pulling up a chair at the side of the bed.

'Not too bad,' she said with a wince. 'The ribs are the worst. Who knew breathing could hurt so much?'

'Christ, Bea,' said Nathan, taking her hand, 'you gave me a scare last night. I was bloody terrified,' he said, blinking back tears.

'I don't remember a thing,' she said, squeezing his hand back. 'Which is probably a good thing, I'm guessing?'

'Too bloody right it is,' Nathan replied, shaking his head.

'I'm just glad you were there. The paramedics said you made the 999 call, stayed with me . . .' now it was her turn to fight back the tears.

'Yeah, well . . .' he said, his voice catching, 'like I was going to do anything else.'

'The wagon, though? Have you seen it?"

'Yep,' he nodded solemnly. 'It's at mine. Back in the barn.'

'And?' she asked, quietly.

'It's not that bad . . . there's damage, of course, the inside is . . .'

'What?'

'There's work to do, that's all,' he shrugged noncommittally. 'Best not to think about that now,' he said, trying to reassure her.

'You sound like Mum,' said Bea, slumping back into the pillows. 'Trouble is, I can't think of anything else.'

'No, I don't suppose you can.'

'Did Mum tell you? About the insurance? The other driver?'

'Yep. That whole family has a lot to answer for, always causing trouble. If I come face to face with Trevor . . .' he trailed off, his jaw clenched shut.

'Let the police deal with him. I'm more concerned with how I'm going to get the wagon fixed, Nate,' she whispered, her voice catching.

'Hey,' said Nathan, jumping up and cradling her in his arms, her head resting on his shoulder. 'It'll be okay. We'll sort it. It'll all be okay, Bea.'

'Promise?' she asked, as he wiped a tear from her cheek.

'Promise,' he nodded. 'It's going to be fine.'

'Sorry,' she sniffed, 'I'm a mess.'

'Don't be silly,' he said, passing her a tissue from his pocket. 'You've been through a lot in the last twenty-four hours, it's okay not to be okay right now, you know.'

'All right,' she said, blowing her nose hard. 'Thanks, Nate.'

'Listen, I've brought something that might cheer you up . . .'

he said, picking up a package from the floor where he'd left it. 'I know it's not your birthday until next week but—'

'You've brought me a present?' asked Bea.

'I have. I thought it might keep you occupied,' he said, passing her a book-shaped package, carefully wrapped in silver paper.

Bea tore open the wrapping paper and gasped at the antique copy of *Northanger Abbey* inside. The jacket was bound in red leather, the pages edged in gold. Bea carefully flipped open the front cover and saw that it was an 1898 illustrated edition, with beautiful pencil drawings.

'Nate,' she said, breathlessly. 'This is . . .' she couldn't find the words to express how she felt.

'Is it okay?' he asked, nervously. 'I know you love Austen and I thought . . . You don't have it already, do you?'

'A collector's edition of one of my favourite novels of all time?' she laughed. 'No, I absolutely don't,' she said. 'I love it, Nate, thank you.'

'There is nothing that I would not do for those who are really my friends,' he said, quietly.

'You remembered?' Bea murmured. She had quoted Isabelle Thorpe's words constantly in sixth form.

'As if I'd forget,' he murmured.

'It's perfect, *you're* perfect. Thank you.'

They looked at each other, their eyes locking. Bea could feel her heart rate increasing, her pulse thrumming. Did she really mean that? Was Nate *perfect for her?*

She swallowed hard. She couldn't think right now. All

she could do was focus on his face, those green eyes, his dark hair—

'Lochlan!' said Bea, her eyes wide with shock as she saw him out of the corner of her eye. 'Aren't you supposed to be in London?'

'Hey, gorgeous,' said Lochlan. He was carrying a huge bunch of flowers. 'Jess called last night and told me what happened, so I drove straight back this morning.' He cast a nod of acknowledgement towards Nathan. 'Bloody hell! Your face,' he said, examining her stitches. 'Will it scar?'

'It looks worse than it is,' said Bea, placing a hand to her head self-consciously. 'Nathan's been great, he was with me last night, at book club. He called the ambulance. If it wasn't for him, I'd have . . . well, who knows?'

'Christ!' said Lochlan, running a hand through his hair. 'Thank God you were there, mate,' he said, reaching across the bed to shake Nathan's hand.

'Not a problem,' said Nathan, 'I'm just glad she's okay.'

'He's just being modest,' said Bea, reaching out to squeeze Nathan's hand, 'if it wasn't for Nate—'

'Yeah, well, like I said, lucky you were there,' Lochlan replied, with a smile that didn't quite meet his eyes. 'Anyway, I'm here now and we've got a lot of catching up to do, so . . . '

'Oh, Nate, you don't have to go, it's fine, please stay?' said Bea, quickly.

'No, Lochlan's right. You need to rest. Take care of yourself, Bea,' Nathan said, leaning down to plant a kiss on her cheek.

'I'll see you soon, okay?' said Bea, as he walked away.

'Alone at last,' said Lochlan, sitting on the edge of the bed. 'God, I've missed you,' he said, tracing a finger along a bruise on her cheek. 'A car accident? I just can't believe it. Thank God it wasn't more serious,' he said, a shadow crossing his face.

'I know,' Bea whispered. This wasn't quite how she'd pictured their reunion, her lying in a hospital bed. 'Thanks for coming, though, you didn't need to—'

'Of course I did. As soon as Jess called, I dropped everything, got straight in the car, cancelled all my meetings, I'll be here all week—'

'But Jess doesn't have your number?'

'Ah, she tracked me down on the firm's website. Very clever.'

'Thanks for coming, that's sweet,' she said.

'I know we've not seen much of each other these past few weeks, but I'm here now, okay?'

'Okay,' she nodded.

But, as Lochlan pulled her to him, hugging her close despite the pain in her ribs, Bea's gaze lingered on the empty chair where Nathan had been sitting just moments ago, and a wave of sadness washed over her.

CHAPTER 29

Bea persuaded Nathan to take her straight to see the wagon the moment she was discharged from hospital, but when she saw the extent of the damage, she was plunged into a deep despair.

The inside of the book wagon was a complete wreck. The bookcases that he'd spent hours building were battered and broken, all the lamps, decorations and stock smashed, torn and damaged, the paintwork scuffed and tattered, the walls dented and misshapen. Jess's beautiful hand-written signage was now barely legible.

It looked in worse shape than when Bea had first collected it from Charlotte, all those weeks ago.

She was right back to where she started, but, worse than that, she had no money to repair the damage. All her savings were gone and any profit she'd made had been ploughed straight back into buying stock that was now ruined.

It felt like her dream was over; that this was the end of Bea's Book Wagon. The worst of it was, she had been *so* close to making her business a success.

Bea didn't leave the house the first week she was home; whether it was her sadness at the state of the wagon or the shock of the accident, she couldn't tell. Lochlan had barely left her side. He hadn't actually cancelled all his meetings, but he was doing them virtually, on Zoom, from her kitchen table, and he'd been attentive and patient, trying to lift her spirits with candlelit takeaways in the living room and marathons of her favourite boxsets.

Physically, Bea was recovering well. The pounding headache she'd had since the accident was gradually starting to clear and her bruises were fading, but her ribs still hurt. Laughing and sneezing were excruciating, the latter she'd found out the hard way when her hay fever kicked in.

She was trying to keep herself busy with what stock she had left for the online shop and subscription boxes, but her heart wasn't really in it. She hadn't been back to see the wagon since the day she was discharged from hospital. She just couldn't face it.

She wasn't fit enough to paint, sort or repair anything, so she'd called the organizer of the Cherrydown fête and cancelled her pitch. All she wanted to do was eat a vat of Ben & Jerry's and spend her days on the sofa watching black and white movies with Lochlan.

Anything else felt too painful.

*

When Nathan saw Bea's face as she assessed the damage to the wagon, it almost broke him. It was as if she had just crumbled right there in front of him. He'd never seen her look so sad and he couldn't blame her, it looked a total mess. Bea was usually the first to look on the bright side of life, but not this time. This time it was different. It was as if all the fight had gone out of her, but he was damned if he was going to let her give up.

'Okay, everyone! There's a reason I asked you all here tonight,' said Nathan, looking around the Apple Tree at all the familiar faces of his friends and neighbours.

'I thought you were going to buy us all a round, mate?' joked Jake, putting his arm around Rose.

'No, sorry,' continued Nathan, clearing his throat. 'I'm sure you all know what happened to Bea?'

'Terrible business,' Jean tutted. 'And right after book club, too.'

'That damn Fallon boy,' agreed Joyce.

'I'm sure you've all heard that the wagon's been badly damaged and Bea doesn't have the money to fix it,' said Nathan.

'Oh no!' wailed Violet, 'that's a terrible shame, she's worked so hard.'

'She has,' Nathan agreed. 'But she's got broken ribs and no insurance money. She can't fix the bookshop on her own . . . but we can!'

'What do you mean?' asked Joyce.

'Well, if we all pitched in, did what we could, we'd have

it finished in no time. It's a big job for one person, but all of us working together?' said Nathan.

'Greg and his lads will help, won't you?' said Joyce, nudging Greg in the side.

'Oh, yes, happy to,' said Greg.

'Count me in,' agreed Jake with a nod.

'Me too,' called Leo.

'And me!' Pete chorused.

'And I'm sure we can get the WI ladies to make new cushions and bunting,' said Violet. 'Can't we, Jean?'

'Oh, absolutely,' Jean agreed.

'Excellent!' said Nathan. 'I knew you lot would be up for it, but we're against the clock.'

'How'd you mean?' asked Joyce.

'Well, she was booked in for next Saturday at the Cherrydown fête and I was hoping—' said Nathan.

'We could get it done by then?' suggested Tori.

'No, by Friday actually. It's Bea's birthday and I thought—' said Nathan.

'It would be the perfect present?' said Jean.

'Exactly,' said Nathan, 'I know it's a lot to ask,' he added quickly. 'But Jess and Archie are up at the farm already getting started.'

'We'd better drink up, then,' said Leo, downing the remains of his pint, 'so we can join them.'

'What? Now?' said Tori, eyes wide.

'No time like the present,' said Jake, with a nod of agreement.

'Honestly, guys, I can't thank you enough,' said Nathan. 'Can I ask one last favour?'

'Name it,' said Beth.

'Don't breathe a word of this to Bea. I want it to be a surprise,' whispered Nathan.

'Ooooh, I do love a secret,' said Maggie, her eyes sparkling as she picked up her bag and followed the others out the door. 'And this is a pretty big one.'

CHAPTER 30

'I know it's my birthday, Jess, but I'm *really* not in the mood,' sighed Bea, as she flicked through the TV guide.

'Oh, come on,' pleaded Jess, 'It'll do you good to get out.'

'Jess is right,' Archie said, switching off the TV. 'You've been stuck in this house for a fortnight now and it's not good for you.'

'It's fine,' said Bea, shaking her head, '*I'm* fine. Anyway, Lochlan's coming over in a bit.'

'Well, that's easily fixed,' said Jess, pulling her phone out of her bag. 'Lochlan, hi!' she said, brightly when he answered. 'Do you fancy meeting us at the pub tonight for Bea's birthday?' She paused. 'Excellent! See you there at seven? Perfect,' she nodded. 'See?' she said, turning back to Bea. 'All sorted.'

'There's no point in arguing, is there?' Bea sighed, heaving herself up from the sofa.

'Absolutely none,' said Jess. 'Come on, I'll help you get ready.'

'I'll meet you there,' said Archie, casting a sideways look at Jess. 'I can get a couple in with the lads first.'

'See you there, Arch,' said Jess. 'Come on,' she continued, taking Bea's hand and heading for the stairs. 'Let's get you birthday-ready!'

Bea couldn't believe how packed the Apple Tree was. It was almost as though everyone from the village was there.

'Happy birthday, love,' said Beth, as Bea and Jess waited at the bar to get served.

'Thanks,' said Bea, smiling.

'It's good to see you out and about, dear' said Jean, as Beth handed her a tray of sherries.

'Thanks, Jean,' said Bea, 'I hope those aren't all for you?' she chuckled.

'Oh no, dear. WI night out,' Jean replied, her eyes glinting mischievously, 'it's been known to get a little messy.'

'Jean's a dark horse, isn't she?' Bea whispered, once she was out of earshot.

'I know, right?' Jess sniggered. 'I hope I'm half as much fun when I'm eighty.'

'Course you will be,' said Bea. 'I bet you'll still be causing havoc at *ninety*.'

'Let's hope so,' said Jess, as Beth handed her two large glasses of prosecco. 'Cheers!' she said, raising her drink in the air. 'To the birthday girl.'

'They're on the house,' said Beth, holding up a hand as Jess reached for her purse.

'Aw, thanks, Beth, that's really kind of you,' said Bea.

'Right, let's go and find the others,' said Jess, determinedly.

'Good luck!' said Bea, attempting to push her way through to the back of the pub. 'It's absolutely rammed in here tonight. It's never this busy, even on a Friday—'

'Course it is. You're just not normally here on a Friday,' Jess replied, casually, as she spotted Archie, Lochlan, Tori and Leo sitting at the large round table right at the back of the pub.

'Bea!' called Lochlan, standing up kiss her. 'Happy birthday!'

'Thanks,' she said, giving him a peck on the cheek. 'Thanks for coming out, everyone.'

'How are you feeling?' Tori asked, hugging her gently. Bea winced. 'Oh, God, sorry,' Tori apologized, her face flushing hot. 'Ribs still sore?'

'A bit, yeah,' said Bea, 'it's fine though,' she said, sitting down next to Lochlan.

'We're missing you at work,' said Tori, sipping her negroni.

'I'll be back next week, I think,' Bea replied quickly.

'Oh God, that wasn't a hint,' said Tori, looking mortified. 'Take as long as you need. Whenever you're feeling up to it. Mum and I are coping just fine.'

'Thanks, Tori,' said Bea.

'Well, you're definitely looking better than the last time I saw you,' said Leo. 'You had us all pretty scared that night, you know.'

'I'm just glad I got through it,' said Bea, her voice sticking in her throat.

'So are we,' said Jess, patting her hand. 'Anyway,' she continued, keen to change the subject. 'Shall we do presents?'

'Presents? You didn't have to—' said Bea.

'I'll go first,' Tori said, taking a pretty pink gift bag out from under the table.

'Ooooh, what's this?' said Bea, pulling the tissue paper out. 'Oh, wow! It's gorgeous, I love it!' she continued, unwrapping a silver bookmark engraved with the message: *A new chapter.* 'It's beautiful, Tori. Thank you!' said Bea.

'I'm glad you like it,' said Tori.

'I'm next,' said Jess, pulling a gold-edged envelope from her bag. 'Happy birthday, Bea.'

Bea carefully prised the envelope open and slid out an embossed gift voucher for a spa day at Rye's most exclusive hotel.

'Jess!' Bea shrieked, grabbing her friend's arm. 'Bayview Sands! That place is super posh, I've always wanted to go!'

'I know!' Jess laughed, 'I'm coming too,' she said, pointing at the voucher. 'You deserve a day of pampering after everything you've been through.'

'It's brilliant, Jess, thank you!' said Bea, 'I can't wait!'

'My turn . . .' said Lochlan, reaching into his pocket. 'I hope you like it.'

Bea recognized the robin's-egg blue of the Tiffany bag instantly, and she let out a little gasp of delight. When she'd lived in London, she'd pause outside the Old Bond Street store whenever she passed by, admiring the sparkling diamonds in all shapes and sizes, never daring to venture inside. And now, there was a Tiffany & Co package in front of her, waiting to be unwrapped.

'Go on then, open it,' said Lochlan, a little impatiently.

Her heartbeat quickened as she wondered what was inside. A bracelet? Earrings? *A ring?*

She gulped. Surely not.

She tugged at the blue ribbon and pulled out a large, square box. Okay, so definitely *not* a ring.

She paused before lifting the lid to reveal a beautiful circular pendant necklace. It was stunning.

'Bloody hell, Bea, that's gorgeous,' said Jess, peering over her shoulder.

'Let's see,' said Tori, and Bea tilted the box towards her. 'Wow.'

'Do you like it?' Lochlan asked.

'Like it?' Bea replied, her voice shaking. 'Lochlan, it's beautiful, I love it . . .'

'Here, let me put it on,' said Lochlan, taking the necklace from the box and fastening the chain around her neck.

'How does it look?' she asked, flicking her hair back off her shoulders.

'Gorgeous,' Lochlan said, as she kissed him hard on the mouth.

'Bloody hell, you two,' said Archie, looking away. 'Get a room, would you?'

'It looks stunning, Bea,' said Jess, leaning in to hold the pendant. 'It really suits you.'

'Thanks,' said Bea.

'That's totally beaten my spa voucher,' Jess grumbled.

'And my bookmark,' said Tori, sitting back in her chair and crossing her arms.

'How do you think I feel?' Archie complained.

'Why, what did you get?' Leo asked, taking a sip of his pint.

'He offered to unload the dishwasher for the rest of the month!' Bea laughed, giving her brother a playful nudge in the chest.

'Oh, Arch,' said Jess, wincing, 'that's pretty shabby.'

'Oh, come on! I've been too busy at Nate's—' he started to explain.

'I didn't know you were doing work for Nate,' Bea said, eyes narrowed.

'Oh, it's nothing really,' said Archie awkwardly. 'I've been helping him out with some, erm . . . calving,' he mumbled.

'Isn't it a bit late in the year for that?' Bea asked, confusion etched on her face.

'Oh no,' Leo piped up, 'Jake's been the same too, absolutely chocka.'

'Oh, okay,' said Bea, unconvinced. 'Where is Nate, anyway? I thought he was coming tonight?'

'Speak of the devil,' said Archie, jerking his head towards the door as Nathan walked in.

As Bea turned to look, she realized the pub was completely empty, even Beth and Pete seemed to have vanished from behind the bar.

'Where's everyone gone?' asked Bea, even more confused now.

'There's one more present outside for you,' said Nathan, grinning so widely that he reminded Bea of the Cheshire Cat.

'But you've already given me a present; that gorgeous book—' said Bea.

'Ah, but this isn't just from me . . .' said Nathan.

'No, we all helped,' said Archie, standing up.

'What?' asked Bea, shaking her head in puzzlement. 'Helped with what? I don't understand . . .'

'Come outside and see for yourself?' said Jess.

'Do you know anything about this?' Bea asked, turning to Lochlan.

'Nope,' Lochlan replied. 'I'm as much in the dark as you are. Let's go see what the mystery is, shall we?' he suggested, taking her by the hand and leading her outside.

There, on the green, everyone who had been in the pub, together with her mum and dad, Arthur, and what looked like the whole WI, were gathered.

'We've got a surprise for you, love,' said Carol, beaming at her daughter as everyone stood aside to reveal the wagon, standing proudly in the middle of the green looking as good as new.

'What on earth?' said Bea, stunned, rushing towards it. 'But I don't understand,' she said, shaking her head. '*How*?' she stammered, resting her hand on the pastel blue paintwork.

'It was Nathan's idea,' said Gordon, clapping him on the back. 'He knew you'd need a helping hand getting the book wagon back on track.'

'I didn't want all your hard work to go to waste, Bea. I didn't want you to lose it,' said Nathan. 'Not because of some stupid accident . . .'

'None of us did, darling,' said Carol, taking Bea's hand and squeezing it gently.

Bea looked at Nathan, her eyes filling with tears, her heart fit to burst. He'd done all this, for *her*?

'It wasn't just me, though,' Nathan explained. 'It was a team effort.'

'Once everyone knew what had happened, they wanted to help, Bea. All of us did,' said Tori.

'We couldn't bear to see you give up,' said Rose, nodding.

'We all wanted to get Bea's Book Wagon back on the road,' said Violet, her eyes misty with tears. Jean passed her a tissue, to pat her cheeks dry.

'I . . . I don't know what to say? I just can't believe it,' said Bea, her hands shaking, her heart pounding. 'You've done all this in just a couple of weeks?'

'We have,' said Jean, proudly. 'We couldn't all help with the building work, but us ladies from the WI made you some new bunting and patchwork cushions.'

'And some matching reading quilts,' added Clara.

'I found you some lovely antique lamps,' said Arthur. 'Got them for a song, too,' he chuckled.

'And I ordered you some new fairy lights; we've got the same ones in the salon,' said Claire. Bea noticed she was holding Josh's hand.

'Thank you! Thank you, all,' said Bea, half-crying, half-laughing. 'You're all . . . amazing! I don't know how to thank you!'

'Come inside and take a look,' said Jess. 'Everything's as good as new.'

'We repaired what was salvageable,' said Nathan, gently, 'and anything that couldn't be fixed, we've replaced.'

'Oh. My. God,' said Bea, breathlessly, as she walked inside. The interior of the wagon looked just as good as its freshly painted exterior: the bookcases were back in place, painted in the same shade of cream she had originally chosen, the shelves were full of books, there were new beanbags, deck-chairs and patchwork rugs, together with the cushions and bunting made by the ladies of the WI. Her wall hangings were back in place, too, with new lamps, new artwork . . . new *everything.* It was perfect.

'It's incredible, it looks . . .' said Bea, trailing off.

'Okay?' asked Nathan, nervously.

'Okay?' said Bea, throwing her arms around him, ignoring the pain in her ribs. 'It's spectacular!'

'Good,' said Jess, looking relieved, 'because you're off to Cherrydown fête tomorrow!'

'Oh no, I cancelled that,' said Bea.

'Yeah, and I phoned them back a couple of days ago and rebooked your pitch,' said Nathan, sheepishly.

'You did?' said Bea, eyes wide.

'Yeah,' Nathan nodded. 'Once I knew the wagon was going to be ready in time. I hope that's okay?'

'*Okay*?' Bea laughed, 'it's brilliant. Thank you!' she said, hugging him again. When she looked up, she noticed Lochlan was watching her intently from his spot on the green, his arms folded, eyes narrowed.

'Oh and there's one more surprise,' said Jess, pointing towards a corner of the green illuminated by a Victorian street lamp.

'Oh my God! I don't believe it! It that the little free library?' asked Bea.

'It is!' Matt confirmed, 'Harry and I finished it off for you. I hope you don't mind?'

'Of course I don't mind, it looks amazing!' said Bea.

'Everyone donated a book too, so there's enough to keep it going for a while, I think,' said Harry.

'That's brilliant, thanks so much!' said Bea, her heart fit to burst as she realized how much time and effort her friends and neighbours had put in to help get her back on her feet. She knew she'd never be able to repay their kindness, but she hoped she'd find a way to thank them for making this the best birthday ever.

CHAPTER 31

It took Bea days to get over the shock of seeing the wagon fully restored, but there was one person she owed a debt of gratitude to more than most: Nathan. It had been *his* idea to rope everyone into helping, he'd co-ordinated the whole thing and had been at the centre of all it, and she hadn't been able to stop thinking about it. To stop thinking about *him*.

They were just friends, she knew that, and, anyway, she was with Lochlan now. Any confusing feelings that she had for Nathan were simply driven by a sense of nostalgia, nothing more. Things had been over between them for years, and she was fine with that. More than fine.

The Cherrydown fête had gone well. Luckily, Jess and Archie had gone with her, and she'd needed their help more than she'd realized. Lifting and carting stock around was a challenge while her ribs were healing, and Matt and Harry had surprised her by turning up to give them a much needed lunchbreak. They had all mucked in to help her set up and pack away and, by the time she made it back home, she was exhausted.

Exhausted, but elated.

The bookshop had been as much of a hit in Cherrydown as it had in Blossom Heath, and she was back doing what she loved. She had confirmed a date for her first book club in Cherrydown, too, as well as regular visits to Cherrydown and Appleton primary schools. It felt like those dark clouds that had descended in the days after her accident had finally lifted.

'Bea!' said Tori, as she returned to the Cosy Cat for her first shift since the accident. 'It's great to have you back! How are you feeling?'

'Good, thanks,' Bea replied, 'I really missed this place.'

'Aw, that's good to hear,' said Tori.

'So, what's been going on?' Bea asked, tying a Cosy Cat apron around her waist.

'Well, Amos and Treacle have both gone off to new homes, so we've got a couple of new additions from Izzy,' said Tori, scooping up a ginger cat that was circling her legs meowing loudly. 'This little fella is Gizmo.'

'Aw, hello, Gizmo,' said Bea, stroking him gently.

'And that's Ginny, asleep on the windowsill,' said Tori, nodding towards a small, black cat who was snoring loudly. 'But other than that, it's just same old same old. Oops, here's Anya, right on time,' continued Tori, popping Gizmo back down on the floor.

'Hi, Anya!' Bea said brightly, before noticing Anya's tear-streaked face. 'Oh my god, what's wrong? What's happened?'

'It's my Mum. She's had a fall,' said Anya. 'It sounds like she's going to be okay, but we're definitely going to have to move back to Scotland now.'

'Oh, Anya,' said Bea, resting a hand on her arm, 'I'm so sorry.'

'I just don't want Mum to be on her own anymore,' said Anya, in a quiet voice. 'It's as simple as that.'

'I'm so sorry, that's tough,' said Tori.

'Is there anything we can do to help? If you need someone to mind the shop for a while—' asked Bea.

'Thanks, that's kind of you, but no. We've made the decision,' said Anya. 'We're going to shut the shop permanently at the end of this week and head straight back to Scotland at the weekend. Mum still lives in our family home; it's huge, so we can move in with her.'

'It sounds like you're doing the right thing, but I'm sure that doesn't make it any easier,' said Tori. 'Let me get you a coffee. What do you fancy?'

'Something sweet, thanks' said Anya.

'I'm going to really miss you, you and Simon have been so kind to me since I moved back here,' said Bea. 'And I'll miss the shop, too.'

'Thanks, Bea. Maybe we can find another shop to open in Scotland. But I'm gutted to be leaving Blossom Heath, I love it here,' sniffed Anya.

'There you go, one vanilla latte,' said Tori, handing Anya

a takeaway cup and brown paper bag. 'And a couple of cinnamon buns, on me.'

'Oh, thanks, Tori,' said Anya, 'that's really kind of you.'

'And if there's anything we can do to help, just shout, okay?' said Tori.

'Actually, there *is* something ...' said Anya. 'Could you spread the word that we're having a closing down sale?' she continued wryly, heading for the door. 'Starting today.'

'God, that's such a shame,' said Bea, once Anya had left.

'I know, I can't quite believe it,' replied Tori, exhaling.

'I wonder who'll take over the shop?'

'Hmmm ... I don't know, but I bet it'll go pretty quickly. There's not been a vacant lease come up for a few years. I think the last time was actually when Simon and Anya opened the Pink Ribbon, and that's got to be five years ago now.'

'What was there before?' Bea asked, curiosity getting the better of her.

'Erm ... let me think,' said Tori, drumming her fingers on the counter. 'Oh, it was an old-fashioned haberdashery store, you know the ones. Mum used to get name tags and new buttons for my school uniform from there. Then Mrs Simpson, the old lady who ran it, retired, and there was no one else to carry it on, so the lease came up. She'd been there donkey's years, I think, since before I was born.'

'I guess we'll just have to wait and see ...' said Bea, an idea starting to form in her mind.

*

Bea couldn't stop thinking about the Pink Ribbon. It was still early days for Bea's Book Wagon, but she couldn't shake the feeling that there was an opportunity here for her. She'd only just got the wagon back on the road, but the business was thriving. The online store was already turning a profit and she'd had loads of sign-ups for her subscription boxes, but . . . a *shop*? There was so much more to consider: rent, utilities, taxes, fitting it out . . . it was much more involved than a mobile bookshop, so much more of a *risk*. And then there was the question of cost. Refurbing the wagon the first time had wiped out her savings and she hadn't been able to afford to fix it herself after the accident. No, it was just a silly pipe dream, there was no way she could take on such a huge commitment, not yet anyway. But . . .

Tori had told her shops rarely became available in the village. If she didn't go for it now then she might not get another opportunity. Maybe she could get a small business loan, find a backer? A Kickstarter campaign even? Surely it couldn't hurt to just make some enquiries? Find out how much the rent was and if she'd have to pay a deposit? What were the business rates? She was due to go to an antique sale in Rye with Arthur that afternoon, so maybe she could pick his brains, see what he thought of her idea. It couldn't hurt.

Bea knocked on Arthur's bright red front door just after lunch and smiled at his dark grey trousers and matching waistcoat, despite the heat of the warm July day.

'Beatrice!' he said, beaming at her. 'Right on time!' he said.

'I'm so looking forward to this!' said Bea, taking his arm as they walked down the steps from his house. 'I've never been to a proper auction before.'

'You're in for a treat!' Arthur replied, leaning heavily on his walking stick. 'There's no buzz quite like it. Even after all my years in the business, I still get as excited as a child on Christmas Eve!'

'I wonder what treasures we'll find?' she asked.

'That's exactly the point, you never know. It could be a colossal waste of time or we could find a hidden gem,' said Arthur. 'I'm sure we'll find some books, though, there always are some.'

'I hope so,' Bea replied, excitement fizzing in her stomach at the prospect.

When they arrived at Atkins Auction House, Bea couldn't believe just how many antiques there were under one roof.

'Here,' said Arthur, picking up a copy of the auction catalogue and handing it to her. 'This will give us a detailed description of every lot. Mark out anything you fancy and we'll track it down and take a look. Why don't we start with a wander first, though? See what catches our eye?'

'Good idea,' Bea agreed, heading straight for some boxes of books she'd spotted in the far corner.

'Lot number thirty-two,' said Arthur, examining the catalogue. 'Assorted books. Fiction. Sold as seen. There's not much to go on there.'

'So, is that all four boxes?' Bea asked, crouching down to rummage through the books on top of each box. 'They're not in great condition . . .'

'Yes, looks like all four boxes make up a single lot,' Aruthur confirmed. 'See anything you like?'

'Not sure,' said Bea, as a woman pushed past her. 'There's too many here to see properly, but it could be worth a punt? There are some eighties editions of Dickens and Hardy, which could be interesting.'

'But not worth much, I wouldn't have thought. The guide price is between twenty and fifty pounds if you want to risk it?'

'I think I might,' said Bea, standing up, her knees creaking. 'As long as I break even. And I'm desperate to bid on something,' she giggled. 'What about you? Have you seen anything you like?'

'There's a 1920s umbrella stand that would be perfect for my walking sticks. I'll give it a go, see if it's my lucky day,' said Arthur, his eyes twinkling.

'Oooh, looks like they're getting ready to start, I'll find us some good seats,' said Bea, heading to the rows of plastic chairs that were starting to fill up.

'You go ahead, my dear, I'm right behind you.'

Bea sat at the end of the aisle a few rows from the front so Arthur could get out easily if he needed to. As he settled himself next to her, he handed her a card with her bidding number on it.

'You're forty-eight, I'm forty-nine. When you're ready

to place your bid, hold up your number. If you win, the auctioneer will write it down, then we go and pay. It's quite straightforward, really,' Arthur explained.

'Got it,' said Bea, enthusiastically, getting swept up in the excitement.

The auctioneer worked through the lots one by one and Bea was surprised by the fast pace of it all. He was a real showman, whipping the crowd up into a frenzy and tossing his gavel into the air for dramatic effect every time he closed the bidding. Bea could see how easy it would be to get carried away and bid much more than she'd intended.

Arthur's umbrella stand was up next and he got his first bid in early. In the end, it came down to him and just one other bidder, but Arthur snuck in a last-minute bid just before the final gavel sounded, securing the umbrella stand for ninety-five pounds.

'That was impressive,' said Bea, patting his arm.

'You have to wait until the last second and just when they're about to drop the gavel, in you pounce with your final bid,' he whispered, tapping his nose. 'Works every time.'

When Bea's book lot came up, she found she was the only bidder. She raised her hand once making an opening bid of twenty pounds, and the next thing she knew it was going once, going twice, sold . . . to her!

'Well, that was a bit of a let-down,' she complained to Arthur. 'I was hoping for a spectacular bidding war,' she admitted, feeling a little disappointed.

'Never mind, my dear! It's still your first auction purchase.

Let's pay our dues and then perhaps we can stop for a cup of tea on the walk home? If you have time, that is,' Arthur asked, looking hopeful.

'That would be lovely, and I did want to pick your brains about something, actually,' said Bea.

'I'm all ears,' he said, pushing himself up from the chair, 'let's go crazy and get cake too!'

'Let's!' Bea agreed with a nod, taking his arm as they walked slowly to the cashier's desk.

CHAPTER 32

Arthur was brimming with enthusiasm and advice when Bea shared her idea for the bookshop, and he'd patiently talked her through some of the pros and cons of running a physical shop; what pitfalls to look out for and what the benefits could be. And, despite feeling awkward, the following morning Bea decided Arthur was right, so she took a deep breath and set off to the Pink Ribbon.

'Hiya!' called Bea, feeling a little nervous as she walked through the door. She knew how sad Anya was to be closing the shop, and the last thing Bea wanted was to upset her and Simon before they'd even had a chance to pack up.

'Hi, Bea!' said Simon from behind the counter, knee-deep in boxes.

'How are you doing? It looks hectic . . .' said Bea, glancing around. There were '50% off everything' signs everywhere, and Anya was carefully bubble-wrapping some of the larger vases and bowls before boxing them up.

'Oh, you know,' said Anya, with a deep sigh. 'Just getting on with it, really.'

'The sale's going well, though,' said Simon. 'We've shifted quite a bit of stock already.'

'That's great news,' said Bea, brightly. 'I could do with some new candles actually.'

'Help yourself, there's still loads left over there,' said Anya, pointing to a shelf in the corner.

'I also wanted to give you this,' said Bea, getting a copy of Jane Austen's *Sense and Sensibility* out of her bag. 'This book has given me some comfort in the past, and I thought it might do the same for you.'

'Thanks, Bea,' said Anya. 'That's really thoughtful of you.'

'Actually,' Bea continued, feeling even more nervous than before. 'I wanted to talk to you both about something, if you've got time?'

'Course!' said Simon. 'I could do with a break from all this, to be honest,' he said, gesturing at the pile of boxes next to the counter.

'Well . . .' Bea said, hesitantly, her jaw muscles tightening. 'I really hope you don't think I'm being insensitive, but Tori and I were talking about what might happen to the shop once you've left – what kind of business might take over – and, well, erm,' Bea continued, 'I was wondering if perhaps . . . if *I* could . . . *maybe* . . . look into opening a bookshop,' she finally blurted.

'Oh, wow!' said Anya, clearly shocked.

'I feel awful even asking, given everything you're going

through, but my friend Arthur thought I should pick your brains, seeing that you've been here for years,' Bea said, her face flushing hot.

'Well, for what it's worth, I think a bookshop here would be great. Someone has to take it over, and I'd much rather it be you than a stranger. I know you'd look after the place,' said Anya, looking around the shop fondly.

'Really?' said Bea, relief flooding through her.

'I agree,' said Simon, nodding. 'But what will you do with the wagon? You worked so hard doing it up,' he continued.

'I'd still use it for events and fêtes, that kind of thing, and I'd need it for my school visits, too, now they've become a regular thing,' Bea explained.

'Ah, well it's great that you can still make use of it. Do you want us to go through some of our costs? So you know what to expect?' Anya suggested.

'If you don't mind, that would be really helpful,' said Bea, relived. 'I don't have a clue what to expect, to be honest.'

'Why don't you come up to the flat?' said Anya. 'Simon can manage here for a bit. I'll run through everything with you and give you the landlord's details so you can get in touch with him direct. We've been really lucky, actually; Mr Pritchard's a nice guy,' said Anya.

'Thanks so much,' said Bea. 'Even some rough figures will be a good starting point. It might all come to nothing, but I feel like I've got to—'

'Try?' said Anya.

'Exactly,' said Bea.

'Come on, let's go,' said Anya, heading towards a door at the back of the shop.

'Can I just pay for these, please, Simon?' Bea asked, on her way past the till, handing two huge vanilla-scented jar candles to him.

'Of course,' said Simon, 'I'll wrap them up for you.'

As Bea followed Anya up the stairs to the flat above the shop, she felt as though every step was taking her one inch closer to making her dream of opening a bookshop a reality.

Bea was excited when she picked up the phone to call Lochlan that evening. Actually, excited didn't even cover it. She was *ecstatic.* Going through the figures with Anya had been a revelation. Yes, it would be a stretch, but if she managed to secure a small business loan, maybe, just maybe, she could make it work.

'Hey, babe,' he said, picking up on the first ring. 'How's things?'

'Good! Great, in fact,' said Bea, struggling to contain the excitement in her voice. 'How's London?'

'Yeah, it's going good. Clients are happy, boss is happy,' he said. 'I can't wait to show you the site; the building work is right on schedule, and believe me that *never* happens. The views from the penthouse flat are something else. You can see right across London. You'll love it.'

'Wow, sounds brilliant,' said Bea, imagining herself wandering around the development in a hard hat and fluorescent tabard.

'How's your day been?' he asked.

'Pretty exciting, actually,' she paused, nervous all of a sudden. Would Lochlan think she was crazy to take on a shop?'

'Oh yeah, what's happened?'

'Well, you know the Pink Ribbon, the gift shop on the green?'

'Erm, not really, but carry on.'

'Well, the owners, Simon and Anya, are moving away, so the shop and the flat above are going to be vacant, and . . .' she trailed off. 'I'm not sure yet, but I'm hoping I might be able to take over the lease and open a bookshop!'

'Wow! Open an actual shop?' said Lochlan, and she could hear the surprise in his voice.

'Yes! I know it's a big step, but, well, it seems like too good an opportunity to miss.'

'No, I get that. Sounds, erm . . . interesting,' he paused.

'It is. Imagine what I could do there? Author talks, signings, poetry readings, children's events! The sky would be the limit,' said Bea, her mind fizzing with ideas.

'Sure, so it's the shop and one flat, yeah?' he asked.

'No, there are two flats: Anya's and the one on the top floor. Anya said the lease is coming up for renewal on that one too. Why?' she asked, confused at Lochlan's sudden interest in the building.

'So the *whole* building's potentially empty?' he asked.

'Well, maybe, but I'm only interested in the shop, obviously.'

'Yeah, sure. Makes sense. What do you need two flats for?'

'Well, exactly. Like I said, I'm not sure if I can make it work, but I'm going to try,' said Bea, hoping for his support. 'What do you think?'

He paused before answering.

'I think you should go for it!'

'Really?' said Bea, relief flooding through her. She realized that his opinion mattered to her.

'Absolutely. This time next year you could have shops all over the country!'

'I'll settle for just one in Blossom Heath,' Bea laughed. 'You don't think I'm crazy then?'

'No way! You're ambitious, Bea, it's an attractive quality,' he said, huskily. 'God, I can't wait to see you,' he groaned. 'Remind me when your trip is?'

'In three weeks, but you're back before then, right?'

'Yes, the weekend after next and then I'm driving you back to London with me, yes?'

'Yes, and I promise I won't cancel this time,' Bea laughed.

'I should think not,' he teased, but Bea detected a harsh edge to his tone.

'Okay, well, I'll speak to you soon, take care,' she replied, feeling a little unsettled by his words.

'You too,' he muttered, before hanging up.

Bea couldn't pinpoint exactly what it was, but something about their conversation hadn't felt right, somehow. Lochlan had seemed more interested in the building being vacant than her idea of opening a bookshop, and she couldn't help but feel that Nathan would have reacted differently.

But there was no point comparing the two. Lochlan was the man she was seeing and Nathan was just a friend, wasn't he?

CHAPTER 33

Bea practically skipped back to the car after her meeting with the small business advisor at the bank. She was doing it, *really* doing it! She had wasted no time in getting in touch with Mr Pritchard and expressing her interest in the shop. Malcolm, as he'd told her to call him, had been every bit as lovely as Anya had described. He was thrilled with the idea of the Pink Ribbon becoming a bookshop, and was happy to keep the rent fixed at the same price Anya was paying. Bea would have to pay the first two months in advance, plus a security deposit, but, he assured her, he'd be happy to draw up the paperwork as soon as she had her finances in place. So, as long as the bank agreed her loan application, the shop was as good as hers.

Mrs Watson, the branch manager of the Barclays in Hastings, had talked Bea through the paperwork she needed to complete and confirmed that, if successful, it was likely she would have an agreement in principle by the end of the week. As Bea climbed into the car, her phone began vibrating and she smiled when she saw it was Jess calling.

'So, how did it go?' she asked, as soon as Bea had accepted the call.

'Good, I think. I've submitted the application and they reckon I should have the offer within a few days.' Bea grinned.

'That's bloody brilliant news,' squealed Jess. 'When can you move in?'

'Well, I need to have the money, first, before the landlord will draw up the paperwork, so it's not going to happen overnight.'

'God, I can't wait! Are you going to start telling people?'

'Well, I've already told you, Mum and Dad, Archie, Tori, oh, and I'm telling Nathan tonight before the awards thing.'

'Oh yeah, I'd forgotten about that. I really hope he wins.'

'Me too. It feels like there's a lot going right now for all of us really. I can't believe it's only a few months since I was stuck in that shitty temp job.'

'God, I know, right?' Jess agreed. 'Well, have fun tonight, and wish Nate good luck from me.'

'Will do, speak tomorrow,' said Bea.

Bea pulled up at Three Acre Farm, just after six-thirty, checking her makeup in the rear-view mirror and smoothing out the edges of her lipstick one final time before getting out of the car.

'Stay there,' said Nathan, striding towards her in Archie's borrowed tux. 'There's cow muck all over the yard and I don't want you ruining that outfit,' he said, admiring the long midnight blue satin dress she was wearing.

'Me neither,' Bea agreed, 'it took me hours to look like this.' She did a double-take when she saw just how good he looked, too.

He looked nothing like the Nathan she was used to, Nathan the farmer in his dirty jeans and checked shirts, his hair an untamed mop of tangles, his face always sporting a few days' worth of stubble. The Nathan standing in front of her was clean shaven, well-groomed and *devastatingly handsome.* There was simply no other way to put it. Her heart did an unexpected flip.

'Wow! Don't you scrub up well?' she said, planting a kiss on his cheek.

God, he smelled good.

'You're not looking so bad yourself, Miller,' he said, stepping back to take in the full effect of her dress.

Miller? Nathan hadn't called her by her surname, his pet name for her, in years. She felt her stomach somersault in spite of herself.

For goodness sake, Bea, get a grip.

'How are you feeling about tonight?' she asked.

'Oh, you know,' he shrugged, 'either way it's a free night out, I guess.'

'Exactly. Try not to think about it too much, we'll just have fun.'

'I'm planning on making full use of the free bar, seeing as you're driving,' he said with a cheeky grin.

'Hey, it's your night, that's why I offered to drive.'

'Shall we hit the road?' he asked with a smile that showed off his dimples.

'Let's do it!' said Bea, climbing back into the car and pulling on her seatbelt. 'Brighton here we come!'

'Wow, this is gorgeous,' said Bea, as they walked through the entrance to the Empress Suite at the Grand Hotel. There were uniformed waiting staff handing out champagne cocktails, and the organizers came straight over to shake Nathan's hand and congratulate him on making the shortlist.

'We're so pleased to have you as one of our finalists,' said an elegant woman, with perfectly straight, perfectly white teeth. From the name tag she was wearing, Bea could see she was Cece Smith from the East Sussex Chamber of Commerce. 'There's been some stiff competition this year.'

'Thank you, I'm chuffed to be here,' said Nathan, shaking her hand enthusiastically.

'I've had some of your cheese before, and I have to say it's out of this world,' said Cece, miming a chef's kiss.

'Thank you,' replied Nathan, with a shy smile.

'Do you sell direct, by any chance?' Cece asked.

'Not at the moment, I'm afraid, no. I have thought about opening a shop on the farm, but it's not very practical, really, I'm too busy with the animals to staff it myself and we're quite a bit off the beaten track anyway,' he explained.

'That's such a shame. I'm sure lots of people would travel to buy direct from you, rather than at a marked-up retail price,' said Cece.

'Maybe,' said Nathan, nodding. 'It's definitely something to think about.'

'You should, and if you need any help, we at the Chamber of Commerce are always here for any guidance you might need,' said Cece. 'Lovely to meet you in person, Nathan. Have a wonderful evening, and best of luck!'

'Thanks,' said Nathan.

'She seemed nice,' said Bea. 'I wonder if she knows who's won?' she whispered.

'Maybe, but I'm sure she's nice to everyone,' Nathan replied, replaying Cece's advice in his mind.

'Shall we head to the bar or sit down?' Bea asked, scanning the seating chart by the entrance to find their table number.

'Bar! I need a proper drink,' he chuckled, draining his champagne cocktail. 'What do you fancy?'

'Just orange juice for me, thanks.'

As Nathan headed to the bar, Bea found them a couple of bar stools to sit on.

'Why I am so bloody nervous?' he laughed, returning with a pint in one hand and tumbler of juice in the other. 'I can't stop sweating!'

'It is pretty warm in here, to be fair,' said Bea, fanning herself with her spare hand. 'It's just the adrenalin kicking in, you're going to be fine.'

'I didn't realize there were going to be so many people

here,' Nathan said, looking anxiously around the function suite. 'There's bloody hundreds of them,' he continued, taking a healthy glug of his lager. 'I'm kinda hoping I don't win. The thought of getting up in front of this lot is terrifying,' he said.

'Hey,' said Bea, resting a hand on his shoulder. 'Forget about everyone else; you're never going to see any of them again anyway, so who cares what they think? Even if you make a total idiot of yourself and fall off the stage, who cares?'

'Jesus! I hadn't even thought about fall—'

'I'm just saying, it doesn't *matter*,' said Bea, squeezing his hand. 'You're Nathan Chambers. You make the best cheese in Sussex! You've got this, okay?'

'Okay,' Nathan nodded, some of the colour returning to his cheeks. 'What's going on with you, anyway?' he asked. 'Tell me something to distract me.'

'Well,' said Bea, realizing she hadn't let go of his hand yet. 'I *have* got some news, actually.'

'Go on?' said Nathan, gazing up at her with his bright green eyes.

'I've applied for a bank loan to get the lease on the Pink Ribbon, to open my own bookshop!'

'Oh. My. God. That's brilliant news!' said Nathan, leaning in to hug her and almost toppling off his bar stool.

'Steady,' said Bea, grabbing his shoulders to keep him upright.

'Woah!' he chuckled, holding on to her for support. 'I hate bar stools!'

'I know, right?' Bea agreed. 'Try hoisting yourself up on one in heels and a dress!'

'Rather you than me!' he said, his eyes dancing with amusement. 'Your own bookshop though, Bea? That's massive,' he said.

'It's not finalized yet, I'm waiting to hear about the loan, *but*, if I get it, the landlord's promised me the lease at the same rent Anya was paying.'

'I'm so proud of you,' he said, placing his hand on her knee. Electricity coursed through her. She stared into his eyes and found she couldn't – and didn't *want* – to look away.

'Bea, listen—'

'Ladies and gentleman!' a voice announced over the tannoy system. 'Please take your seats! The East Sussex Business Awards 2025 are about to begin!'

Nathan snatched his hand back, standing up abruptly. 'Shall we?' he asked, holding an arm out for her to take.

What had he been about to say?

'Let's,' she replied, and it felt like the most natural thing in the world to loop her arm through his and lean in close.

According to the order of service, Nathan's category was going to be one of the last to be announced. The ceremony was being compèred by a local radio host, Mike Gibson, who did a great job of keeping the guests amused with funny anecdotes during the lull between awards presented to other category winners. The dinner itself was delicious and Bea had enjoyed every mouthful of the three-course meal, although she noticed that Nathan barely touched his food. It wasn't until coffee was being served that Mike finally announced the next category, 'Best Local Food Supplier', and Bea watched the colour drain from Nathan's face.

'So, folks,' said Mike, microphone clutched in his hands, 'the nominees are . . .' The LCD screen behind the stage flashed the logos of all the nominees in order. 'Manor Park Dairy, The East Sussex Brewery Company, Sizzling Hog. And Three Acre Cheeses.'

Bea cheered at the top of her voice at the mention of Nate's cheese company.

'And the winner is . . .' said Mike, pausing for dramatic effect as he opened the envelope, 'Three Acre Cheeses!'

'*Whaaaat*?' whispered Nathan, looking stunned.

'Yessss!' cried Bea, grabbing his hand, 'You've won!'

'Three Acre Cheeses?' Mike repeated. 'Where are you? Come on up!' he said, his eyes squinting in the bright light to scour the room.

'Go on,' said Bea, nodding encouragingly. 'It's you, Nate!'

'Bloody hell!' he said, getting to his feet and heading to the stage.

The applause was loud as Nathan climbed the steps, and Mike clapped him on the back and handed him an oval-shaped, glass award. The look on Nathan's face was priceless; Bea didn't think she'd ever seen him look so flabbergasted. He pulled a piece of paper from his pocket as Mike handed him the microphone, urging him to say a few words.

'Wow,' said Nathan, puffing out his cheeks. 'I genuinely didn't see this coming. I don't know what to say . . . I honestly didn't think I had a chance in hell of winning,' he continued, much to the amusement of the crowd, 'but I would like to say a huge thank you to everyone that voted for me, and congratulations to all of the other businesses who were shortlisted.' He paused. 'I'd also like to say thank you to someone very special, who is here with me tonight.'

Bea felt her heart pound in her chest.

'Bea,' said Nathan, his eyes locked on hers. 'This is for you.'

Bea could feel tears stinging the back of her eyes as Nathan returned to the table, and, when he finally sat down, she thew her arms around him and pulled him in close. 'I knew it! I knew you'd win!' she said, holding his face and kissing him hard on the cheek.

'I can't believe it,' said Nathan. 'I need a drink,' he said, reaching for the last wine bottle in the ice bucket on the table before realizing it was empty. 'Champagne?' he said to Bea, wiggling his eyebrows.

'I can't, I'm driving,' said Bea, kicking herself that she hadn't suggested they book a taxi instead.

'Sod it!' said Nathan, 'let's get a cab home tonight and I'll drive you back tomorrow to pick up the car. What do you reckon?'

'Are you sure?' said Bea, a smile curling at the corners of her mouth. 'It'll cost a fortune in an Uber.'

'Abs-a-bloody-lutely! It's not every day I win a business award!' Nathan grinned.

'True,' said Bea, with a shriek of delight.

Once all the winners' photographs had been taken, the music ramped up and almost everyone made a beeline for the dancefloor, Bea and Nathan included. Nathan took off his jacket and threw it down next to the DJ stand, along with Bea's heels, which, despite looking good, were instruments of absolute torture.

As 'Mr Brightside' by The Killers faded out, it was replaced by Florence and the Machine's 'Cosmic Love'.

Bea murmured, 'I love this song.'

It seemed like the most natural thing in the world when Nathan pulled her in close to him and they started to move together as the music played on. Bea could feel Nathan's heart pounding against her chest, her skin tingling where his touched it.

She lifted her head, they locked eyes, and Bea felt something pass between them – a moment of intense tenderness.

She shut her eyes, lips parted—

'And that's all we've got time for this evening, folks,' Mike Gibson's voice rang out through the tannoy, bringing them back to reality with a thud as the music stopped abruptly. Bea took a step backwards, blinking, confused, embarrassed.

'Sorry,' she apologized. 'I need the loo.'

'Bea, wait!' Nathan called after her, as she darted off the dance floor.

But she couldn't stop, couldn't turn back. Guilt warmed her neck as she dashed into the bathroom and locked the door behind her, dropping her head in her hands.

What the hell had just happened? Had she just been about to *kiss* Nathan?

CHAPTER 34

Bea woke up the next morning with a ferocious hangover. Pulling off her eye mask, she reached for the glass of water on her bedside table and drank thirstily, draining the glass in seconds.

What a night.

She'd slept fitfully, replaying those moments with Nathan over and over again: the slow dance, their bodies pressed up close, desire coursing through her veins, their lips moments away from touching.

If the music hadn't stopped, who knows what would have happened? Would they have kissed? Did she, somewhere deep, deep down, *want* to kiss Nathan?

Her thoughts then turned to Lochlan. She tried to imagine his face if he found out what had happened. But did anything actually happen?

God, she was confused. She needed to clear her head and work out how she felt. And if she was going to do anything about it.

Nathan sat at the kitchen table staring at his award, a mug of coffee in his hands, thinking about Bea. She'd looked incredible last night. He'd almost managed to forget she was with Lochlan when they were dancing; he'd almost *kissed* her. But how would that have turned out?

She'd have been horrified, and the last thing he wanted was to jeopardize their friendship. She meant far too much to him to risk losing her.

But he couldn't stop thinking about her. The more time they spent together, the more he realized that his feelings towards her had changed.

He loved her.

There was no point denying it, to himself at least. He'd wanted to tell her last night, as he was sure she'd felt the spark between them, too, but today, when they'd driven back to Brighton to collect her car, she'd acted like it hadn't happened, and he could see that she wasn't interested in him at all, not like that.

He'd just have to try to move on.

'Any news from the bank yet?' Tori asked, as another busy shift at the Cosy Cat drew to a close.

'Nope, not yet,' replied Bea, shaking her head. 'The lady said it could take anywhere from a week to ten working days.

Waiting's the worst, though. You should see how many times I'm checking my email.'

'Believe me, I get it. I remember waiting to hear from the council about this place. I was so busy making plans for the cats to arrive, but everything was dependent on whether I got a yes from them first. It was agonizing.'

'I won't leave you in the lurch, though, if I do get the loan,' Bea said, quickly. 'You've been so good to me, and I'll stay here until you find someone else.'

'Don't you worry about that,' said Tori, waving a hand. 'Mum's happy to step up temporarily, and I'm sure we'll find a replacement soon enough. It won't be the same as having you here, though, we'll miss you.'

'Well, if the bookshop does go ahead, I'll only be across the green, so I'll be in every day for coffee … lunch … snacks. You'll see more of me than you do now!'

'I'll hold you to that,' Tori chuckled.

'Sorry to interrupt,' said Violet, who had just finished eating the last scone from a cream tea she was sharing with Jean. 'Can I settle up? It's my turn to treat Jean.'

'Of course!' said Tori, ringing up their bill. 'I hope everything was okay?'

'Delicious as always,' said Jean, joining Violet at the counter. 'Although, I don't think I'll be needing any dinner this evening,' she said, patting her stomach.

'You know, it's been lovely seeing you two in here together so regularly, you didn't used to—'

'Get on?' ventured Violet.

'Oh, gosh, no, I didn't mean that,' said Tori, her cheeks colouring.

Bea could tell Tori thought she'd well and truly put her foot in it.

'You're absolutely right, my dear. Violet and I have history. It's common knowledge, you may as well say as much,' said Jean, matter-of-factly.

'It's all her doing,' said Violet, pointing in Bea's direction.

'*My* doing? What on earth did I do?' Bea muttered, confused.

'It's that book club of yours,' said Violet. 'Turns out Jean and I are both huge Kate Fisher fans.'

'And that's not all we've got in common,' said Jean. 'Is it?'

'No, it isn't. Baking, gardening, jigsaws – the list is endless,' Violet explained.

'We just had to get past our differences to see how similar we both are, and we have Book Club to thank for that,' Jean nodded. 'Same time next week, Violet?'

'Absolutely,' Violet agreed, putting away her purse as the two friends headed for the door.

'Bye then, ladies, see you next week!' Tori called after them.

'Well, I didn't see that coming, did you?' said Bea, flopping down in the nearest chair.

'No, absolutely not,' Tori agreed. 'Never in a million years would I have put those two together.'

'Just shows you, doesn't it?' Bea continued. 'If it hadn't been for a shared love of books, they might never have re-solved their differences and become friends.'

'That's very true! I'm glad they're getting along, it's just a shame they didn't realize it years ago,' said Tori, wiping down the counter. 'Anyway, isn't it next weekend that you'll be away with Lochlan?'

'Yeah, I can't wait,' said Bea, her pulse rising at the mention of his name.

'That necklace he got for your birthday was stunning.'

'I know—'

'Oh, to be young and in love.'

'Hang on, no one said anything about being in love yet,' Bea insisted, wondering why that word bothered her so much.

'Okay, okay, sorry,' Tori laughed. 'Just getting ahead of myself. I didn't mean anything by it.'

'Wait – did you hear that?' Bea asked.

'What?'

'I've got an email,' said Bea, thrusting her hands into her pockets to find her phone. 'It's from the bank,' she whispered, holding the phone at arm's length. 'You look.'

'You got it!' squeaked Tori, opening the message and scanning the confirmation.

'Oh. My. God,' said Bea. 'I've got the loan!' the colour draining from her face.

'Yes, you got the loan!' Tori repeated, pulling Bea into a hug. 'Congratulations! I'm so pleased for you!'

'I can't believe it,' murmured Bea, before she burst into tears.

*

It took several days for the news to sink in that Bea's Bookshop was going to become a reality. Once she had stopped crying, Bea had called Mr Pritchard, who was having the contracts drawn up and was going to meet her at the shop first thing on Saturday to sign the paperwork. She wouldn't officially get the keys for another couple of weeks as the lease still belonged to Simon and Anya, and, although they had already left for Scotland, they had some remaining stock to clear out. But once the papers were signed, Bea could finally start making plans.

News about the new bookshop had spread throughout the village, and everywhere Bea went people stopped to tell her how much they were looking forward to opening day. Lochlan sent the biggest bunch of flowers she had ever seen with a card that read, *I knew you could do it, Congrats! xx*.

And despite not seeing him since the morning after the awards, Nathan sent a cheese hamper with extra bags of walnuts that somehow meant even more than the flowers.

More personal. More thoughtful. More Nathan.

Mr Pritchard was already at the shop waiting for her when Bea arrived early on Saturday morning to sign the paperwork.

'Morning, Mr Pritchard,' she said, swinging open the door, the bell tinkling above her head.

'Ah, Bea, you're here,' he said, sounding different in real life. Anxious, nervous, worried. Not as he had on the phone at all.

'Is everything okay?' Bea asked, frowning as he started pacing backwards and forwards across the shop floor.

'I'm afraid there's no easy way to say this . . .' He drew in a long, deep breath. 'I've had a cash offer for the shop and both the flats that's too good to turn down.'

'What? But . . . I don't understand, we've got an agreement,' she said, shaking her head.

'Well, technically, we haven't, not until the paperwork is signed,' he explained, unable to look her in the eye.

'But . . . but, I've got the bank loan, it's all agreed, and the paperwork is here, I'll just sign it now. Please, Malcolm, we had a deal,' she pleaded, picking up the lease agreement that was on the counter.

'No, no, that's not—' said Mr Pritchard, making a grab for it.

'Hang on, is this the cash buyer?' she said, staring at the name on the contract.

EliteHaven Homes.

She shook her head. 'Is this them? A developer is buying the whole building? My *boyfriend's* firm is buying it?'

'Oh, erm, I don't know about that,' said Mr Pritchard, stumbling over his words. 'But, yes, EliteHaven Homes have made the offer and I've accepted.'

'But, what about the bookshop?' said Bea, reeling.

'I know, I know,' said Mr Prichard, looking at the floor. 'And believe me, I feel awful. I've got no idea how they even knew the building was available, I hadn't advertised it, and as far as I was aware you were the only person who knew the leases were up for renewal.'

Bea's stomach hit the floor.

She thought she might be sick and placed a hand on the counter to steady herself.

She knew exactly how EliteHaven Homes had known the shop was available. Because she had told Lochlan.

'Are you okay?' Mr Prichard asked, genuine concern etched on his face.

'I . . . I . . . I'm not sure,' said Bea. She felt like she'd been hit by a truck.

There must be some kind of explanation. There's no way Lochlan would have done this to her, surely? It was too awful to contemplate that he'd used the information she'd shared with him to steal her dream from under her nose.

'And there's nothing . . . nothing I can say to change your mind?' she murmured, tears stinging the back of her eyes.

'I don't think so,' Malcolm said, shaking his head. 'Unless you can match their cash offer?'

'What if I increased my rent? Could I have it then?' she asked, and she could hear the desperation in her voice.

'Is that an option? Could you do that?' Mr Pritchard asked.

'No,' she whispered, hanging her head. 'No, I—I don't have that kind of money.'

'Then I'm afraid there's nothing to be done,' he said, apologetically. 'If your situation changes, then do let me know. It's not a done deal with the developer until the deeds are transferred, so never say never,' he said, trying to soften the blow.

They were hollow words, she knew that.

'Right, yes . . .' replied Bea, despondently. She knew there was no way she'd be able to compete with Lochlan's cash offer, whatever it was.

'And for what it's worth, I'm sorry, Bea. That's why I wanted to keep our appointment. I wanted to tell you in person, not over the phone,' he said, shuffling his feet. 'I felt I owed you that much at least.'

'It's fine,' said Bea, quietly.

It absolutely wasn't fine. It was *far* from fine. But what else could she say?

'I appreciate you telling me face to face.'

As Mr Pritchard locked up the shop behind them, Bea was focused on just one thing: Lochlan had betrayed her, and she had to know why.

CHAPTER 35

Bea hurried away from the shop, tears flowing freely down her face. She wiped them away with the back of her hand and took a deep breath. *Lochlan had done this?* Her shock turned to anger. How could he? And why had he sent her flowers if he was just going to go behind her back and buy the building? She shook her head. It made no sense. She sat heavily on one of the benches by the duck pond and tried to calm down.

'Bea?' asked a hesitant voice. 'Are you okay?'

She looked up to see Katerina standing in front of her, cup in hand.

'Oh, Katerina, hi,' Bea said, in a wobbly voice. The last person she wanted to see, mid-meltdown, was a world-famous author.

'Is everything all right?' Katerina asked, her face full of concern.

'Oh, I've just had a bit of a bad news, it's nothing really, but thank you,' said Bea, trying, and failing, to smile.

'It doesn't look like nothing,' said Katerina, sitting down next to her.

'No, actually, it isn't,' Bea sniffed, 'it's pretty catastrophic,' she sobbed, unable to hold back the tears, covering her face with her hands and letting them fall.

'Here,' said Katerina, pulling a pack of tissues from her bag and handing one to Bea. 'Is there anything I can do?'

'Not unless you can find out why the guy I'm seeing has gone behind my back and scuppered my plans to open a bookshop?' said Bea.

'You were going to open a bookshop? Here in the village?' Katerina asked.

'I was, yes,' Bea nodded. 'I went in today to sign the lease, but . . .' she hesitated. 'It turns out the company he works for has made a cash offer to the landlord, so the deal's off.'

'Oh, Bea, that's awful. I'm so sorry,' said Katerina, patting her hand. 'God, men are shits sometimes,' she added.

'Yeah, they really are,' agreed Bea.

'But a bookshop, though? That sounds exciting!'

'I know, it would have been great,' said Bea, mustering a weak smile.

'*Will* be great,' Katerina cut in, a determined look on her face. 'This is a setback, it's not the end. There'll be other shops, other men, too, for that matter.'

'Well, I suppose I do still have the loan . . .' Bea muttered.

'And you're right, the old Pink Ribbon isn't the only shop in the only village in Sussex.'

'Exactly. You've had a shock, of course, finding out what this *man* – and I use that word loosely – did,' said Katerina, a look of disdain on her face. 'What's his name, by the way?'

'Lochlan,' said Bea. Even saying his name made her angry all over again.

'Terrible name,' said Katerina, twitching her nose. 'I'll name my next villain after him.'

Bea couldn't help but smile at the thought of Lochlan appearing in K. L. Fletcher's next bestseller.

'As I said, you've had a shock and you're entitled to feel upset . . . *betrayed*. But don't let it linger. Take a beat, move on, and when you *do* open your bookshop – and I've no doubt you will – let me know. I've got good contacts in the industry: editors, authors, agents, movers and shakers, people who owe me a favour. I'll get them all down here for the launch and do a signing event for you.'

'Really?' Bea asked, surprised. 'I thought you didn't do public appearances?'

'I don't, but I'll make an exception for you,' said Katerina, patting Bea's shoulder. 'I'm very fond of you, Bea.'

'Wow, gosh, I don't know what to say, but thanks,' said Bea, 'that would be amazing!'

'Now, I really must go, I'm on a deadline,' Katerina said, getting to her feet.

'How's the word count going?' Bea asked, curiosity getting the better of her.

'Good. Better than good, actually. Strange as it sounds, being here has helped me find my mojo again.'

'That's brilliant news!' said Bea, smiling.

'Well, my editor certainly thinks so! Now, what's your plan? You can't sit here moping all day.'

'No, I know,' Bea agreed. 'My courage always rises at every attempt—'

'To intimidate me,' said Katerina, finishing the quote from *Pride & Prejudice*.

'I need to talk to Lochlan,' Bea said.

'You give him hell,' said Katerina.

'Oh, don't you worry,' Bea replied. 'I intend to.'

Bea didn't even know if Lochlan was back from London yet, as she pulled up outside his house less than half an hour later. But she couldn't wait, she had to find out what the hell he had done. Part of her was hoping that it was all just a misunderstanding and there was an innocent explanation for how EliteHaven Homes had found out about the Pink Ribbon, but she knew, deep down, there wasn't.

She jabbed her finger on the gate buzzer with force.

'Hello?' he answered.

'It's me,' said Bea, her voice flat and emotionless.

'Bea!' he replied, sounding genuinely pleased she was there. The entrance gate creaked open, and, as Bea pulled up at his front door, she saw him leaning casually in the doorway, seemingly without a care in the world. That is, until he saw the look of thunder on her face.

'Hey, what's up?' he asked.

'What's *up*?' Bea shouted, furious. 'I've just been to sign the lease on the shop.'

'Ah,' he said, his usual confidence slipping. 'So, you know, then?'

'Yeah, I know,' she mimicked his tone. 'I know you've gone behind my back and offered the landlord cash.'

'It's just business, babe,' he shot back, stepping towards her.

'Just business?' she said, recoiling. 'And don't you fucking dare call me "babe", you fucking arsehole.'

'Hey, calm down, Bea, this has got nothing to do with . . . *us*', he continued, 'it doesn't change things.'

'Are you insane? It changes *everything*.'

'It's just a shop. There'll be others,' he scoffed.

'It isn't just a shop, Lochlan. It's my dream and you've just . . . trampled all over it.' She couldn't believe he was gaslighting her like this.

'Do you think I got where I am today by letting my heart rule my head? No. Success in business is about making tough decisions, and sometimes you have to upset people along the way, that's just how it is . . .'

'*People?*' Bea repeated, her eyes blazing. 'Is that what I am to you . . . *people*?' She couldn't believe what she was hearing.

'Of course you're not "people",' he conceded, his tone softening. 'But you're not going to let something as silly as this ruin what we have, are you?' he demanded, flashing her his best smile.

The smile that used to make her heart swell. But not now, not today, not ever again.

'God, you're not even going to apologize, are you?' she asked, her hollow laugh louder than she expected.

'It's business,' he repeated. 'I could turn that building into six luxury apartments and I'd make a killing, too.'

'Luxury apartments? That's your plan? You'll never get it through planning—'

'Don't bet on it,' he said, slyly.

God, he disgusted her now. What had she ever seen in him?

'Listen, try to get it all in perspective: we'll have a great time in London—'

She cut him off sharply,

'I wouldn't go to London with you if you were the last man on earth,' she said, her fists balled at her sides. 'We're done, Lochlan. I don't ever want to see you again.'

'Oh, come on, babe, don't be stupid—'

'*Stupid*?' she repeated, rage bubbling up inside her.

'I didn't mean—'

'Oh, and you can have this back,' she said, yanking the necklace from her neck and throwing it at him. 'Tiffany isn't really my thing, after all. Turns out I'd much rather have a book,' she said, the memory of the beautiful gift Nathan had given her flashing into her mind.

'I can't believe it,' said Jess, pulling Bea into a tight hug. 'What an absolute arsehole!'

'I just didn't see it coming,' said Bea, pulling a woollen throw around her shoulders as she snuggled down on the sofa back at home. Even though it was a warm summer's day, Bea couldn't stop shaking.

'Well, of course you didn't! How were you to know what a sneaky, manipulative git he would turn out to be,' said Jess, through gritted teeth.

'Here, take this,' said Archie, passing them mugs of hot chocolate. 'I've put extra sugar in yours, Bea,' he nodded, 'you know, for the shock.'

'Thanks, Archie,' said Bea, appreciatively.

'If I ever see him again . . .' Jess said, her eyes flashing.

'I just want to move on and forget him,' said Bea, her eyes hot with rage.

'That's going to be hard to do once they start work on that building,' said Archie, brows furrowed.

'God, I'd not even thought about that,' Bea groaned, pulling the blanket more tightly around her.

'Surely he won't get planning permission, though? I'm pretty sure that building's Grade II listed,' said Jess.

'Maybe we could start a petition, or something?' said Bea, resting her mug on the arm of her chair. 'I could talk to Violet now she's chair of the parish council?' she suggested.

'That's a great idea! She hates change, and luxury flats being built right next to her cottage? I don't think so!' said Jess.

'She's always been a great supporter of the wagon, too,

so I'm pretty sure she'd rather I open a bookshop than EliteHaven Homes build flats there,' said Bea.

'Why don't you go and see her now?' suggested Archie, giving Bea a gentle nudge. 'I'm sure this is just a setback, that's all. It's not over till the fat lady sings, remember?'

'You're the second person to say that to me today,' said Bea, thinking of Katerina's advice earlier.

This is just a setback, that's all.

And, as Bea sipped her hot chocolate, she knew that things weren't over yet. She would find a way through this . . . *she had to.*

CHAPTER 36

Nathan was furious over the way Lochlan had treated Bea. Sure, he'd never liked the guy; he was far too cocky and full of himself, trying to impress everyone with his flash car and tailored suits. He'd never trusted him. But to pull a stunt like this? It was low. Beyond low. What a snake. And after everything Bea had been through, too.

Where did that leave him, though? With Lochlan out of the picture, surely this was his chance? He might not get another. The door was open for him to be honest with her. He was in love with her, for God's sake, shouldn't he just tell her?

Sometimes you just had to take a leap and jump in head first . . .

It wasn't that easy, though, was it? Bea must be in turmoil right now, and the last thing he wanted to do was add to her problems. Neither of them had brought up their near-kiss, and, if she felt anything for him, surely she would have said something by now?

He didn't want to risk ruining their friendship; he couldn't lose her, and telling her how he really felt could do exactly that.

As much as he wanted to be there to comfort her, he knew he needed to give her space; to stay away. He couldn't trust himself not to blurt something out, something that could jeopardize their friendship for ever. If he declared his feelings and she didn't reciprocate, their friendship might never recover, and that was a risk he just wasn't willing to take.

As hard as it was, staying silent was his only option.

As it turned out, Jess was absolutely right about Violet. Once Bea had explained Lochlan's plans for the building, Violet had mobilized the full force of the parish council to fight EliteHaven Homes. She called an emergency council meeting and started going to door-to-door with an army of volunteers, collecting signatures for a petition to block the development.

Bea hadn't heard a word from Lochlan since their showdown. Apparently, he'd been seen leaving Blossom Heath on Sunday evening, so she figured he'd gone to London as planned, just without her. Lochlan had swept her off her feet and she'd been so caught up in their whirlwind romance, the dinners, his good looks, the whole *idea* of him, that she'd been blind to who he really was: smarmy, flash, selfish and a little controlling. She'd done what she'd always done, been swept away in her own fantasy, and now she was left feeling . . . well, a little silly and a *lot* mad.

Bea distracted herself by planning more events for the wagon. The Christmas season wasn't that far away, and she wanted to secure pitches so she could forward forecast her income during the winter months. The business was still viable, even without a physical shop, so she needed to pick herself up, dust herself down and strike while the iron was hot.

Having secured slots at seven upcoming markets, including the pitch at the Pashley Manor garden party in September, Bea turned her attention to sorting out and cataloguing the stock she had stored in the garage. With so much going on, she hadn't even had time to look through the boxes she'd bought at auction, but there was no time like the present, she thought, taking a pair of scissors to open them up.

Most of the books were either too damaged to be saved or would be going straight to the charity shop, but there was a small pile of old classics from the seventies and eighties that she thought she might be able to sell online, rather than in the wagon.

It wasn't until Bea got to the bottom of the last box that she spotted something special: a copy of Agatha Christie's *The Mysterious Affair at Styles.* It was protected by a clear, plastic jacket and she could tell from the cover that it was an old edition. She flipped it open carefully to read the title pages and discovered it was published in 1920, and was a first Canadian edition.

Her heart was racing as she quickly typed the details into Google on her phone and waited, holding her breath, for the search results to load. Her first instinct was right, if this was genuine, it was a find. Reading on, she discovered that the Canadian edition had preceded the UK release in 1921, and was considered highly collectable.

Could this be the real thing? It was definitely plausible; she could easily see how it could have sat in someone's attic for years, simply overlooked and forgotten. She knew exactly who could help her with this; she just hoped he was at home.

'Beatrice!' said Arthur, greeting her with a smile as he opened the front door. 'This is an unexpected pleasure.'

'Arthur, great, you're here,' Bea replied, breathlessly, exhausted by running from where she'd had to park the car.

'Are you okay? You seem a little flustered.'

Bea nodded. 'Yep, but I really need your help with something,' she said, holding her side where a stitch had rooted itself under her ribs.

'Come in, come in,' he said, standing aside. 'I was just about to have some tea, would you like a cup?'

'I'd love one, thank you.'

Once settled in the living room, Bea told Arthur all about what had happened with the bookshop and Lochlan, and how she'd only just got around to going through the boxes from the auction.

'And look,' she said, passing him the Christie novel. 'It

could be nothing, but, then again, it might be something,' she continued, hopefully, 'And I thought, if anyone could help me, it would be you.'

'I'll certainly do my best . . .' said Arthur, putting on his spectacles. 'Well, well, well,' he chuckled, reading the title page.

'It is a first edition, isn't it?' asked Bea, on the edge of her seat.

'It certainly looks like it,' Arthur agreed, running his hand over the cover.

'That's what I thought, too,' said Bea, quickly. 'I'm pretty sure it's a first Canadian edition, published the year before the UK one.'

'Let me make some calls. I know a couple of excellent book dealers that might be able to help.'

'Really? That would be great,' Bea replied. 'I know it's the first Poirot novel and a bit more obscure than some of her others, but I don't know if that would have an impact on the value?'

'I'm afraid I wouldn't really know. Maybe? Let's talk to the experts. Are you happy to leave it with me for a few days?.'

'Of course! Thanks, Arthur.'

'My pleasure, my dear' said Arthur. 'You never know, this could be just what you need to help get that bookshop plan of yours back on track.'

'Well, the landlord did say to contact him again if my circumstances changed . . .'

'There you are then,' said Arthur, brightly. 'Leave it with

me. I'll get in touch with my contacts and as soon as I've got any news, I'll let you know.'

'Thanks, Arthur, you're a star.'

'What time do you finish?' asked Nathan, leaning on the counter at the Cosy Cat the following afternoon.

'In about half an hour, why?' said Bea, glancing up at the clock on the wall.

'Fancy spending the afternoon with me?' he asked.

'Doing what?' Bea asked, intrigued.

'It's a surprise,' said Nathan, jiggling his eyebrows comically.

'You can head off now if you like,' Tori called on her way to the kitchen, balancing a tray of crockery in her hands. 'It's pretty quiet, and Mum will be back soon, anyway.'

'Are you sure?' Bea asked, already untying her apron strings.

'Absolutely. Go have some fun,' said Tori with a smile.

'Thanks, Tori, I'll see you tomorrow,' said Bea, dashing to the door.

Bea climbed into the passenger seat of Nathan's truck and popped her sunglasses on. It was a glorious sunny day, a stark contrast to all the rain they'd had recently, and she was determined to enjoy her afternoon.

'Any news from Arthur yet?' Nathan asked, fastening his seatbelt.

'Yeah. One of his dealer friends came over to take a look at the book this morning and apparently he confirmed it's genuine. He's going to reach out to some of his clients who he thinks might be interested in buying it.'

'Bloody hell, that's great news!'

'I know. I don't want to jinx it, but he thinks I might get a couple of grand for it!'

'That's amazing!'

'I know, right? I'm thinking about contacting Mr Pritchard again and offering to pay more rent up front for the shop.'

'Ah, you might want to hold fire on that,' said Nathan, smiling. 'That's kind of what today's about. I've got something I want to show you . . .'

'Really, what?' Bea asked, curious.

'If you can wait five minutes, you'll see.'

'Five minutes? Where are we going, then?' said Bea.

'Just five more minutes,' he repeated, eyes focused on the road ahead, smiling.

'God, you're infuriating,' Bea groaned, tapping her hand impatiently against the dashboard.

CHAPTER 37

'The vineyard?' Bea said, her forehead wrinkling in confusion. 'I don't get it,' she continued, unfastening her seatbelt and getting out of the car.

'All in good time,' Nathan smirked, opening the door to the barn and nodding hello to Phoebe, who was waiting inside.

'Hey, Phoebe! How are you?' said Bea, giving her a hug.

'Good, thanks, you?' asked Phoebe.

'You know, coping, but I'm a little confused as to why Nathan's brought me here and what it's got to do with the bookshop?' said Bea, turning back towards Nathan.

'Ah, he hasn't told you then?' asked Phoebe.

'Told me what?' Bea said, flicking her gaze between them both.

'I thought we should wait until we got here,' Nathan explained.

'Will someone *please* tell me what's going on?' said Bea.

'Well, hopefully this should help make things clearer,' said Phoebe, opening the door for Bea to follow her inside the barn.

'Okay . . .' Bea said, looking around at the display of wines, cheeses *and* books, expertly decorated with fresh flowers and fairy lights, it looked . . . *beautiful*.

'Go pretty well together, don't they?' said Nathan.

'This looks wonderful, but I'm still not sure I understand . . .' said Bea, trying to put the puzzle together.

'Well, Book Club was such a success, it got us thinking,' said Phoebe.

'Remember when I was chatting to Cece at the awards? And she said a farm shop would be a great place for me to sell my cheeses?' said Nathan.

'Yeah,' said Bea.

'And I've got a similar issue here; it's a trek for people to come and buy from us direct,' said Phoebe. 'So—'

'What if Bea's Bookshop wasn't just a bookshop, but we sold cheese and wine, too? cried Bea, realization dawning.

'Bingo!' said Nathan, grinning widely.

'That's genius! We could pair wines with books, you know, like you do with food? This steamy romance goes perfectly with a full-bodied red—' said Bea.

'And a crisp white sauvignon with a thriller!' added Phoebe.

'*But*,' said Bea, her face falling a little. 'I didn't get the lease on the shop, remember?'

'Correction,' said Nathan. 'You don't have the lease on the shop *yet*.'

'I'll do my best to win Mr Pritchard over, but he was pretty keen on selling to EliteHaven when I saw him. I've got more money now, but that might not change anything,' said Bea.

'It's got to be worth a try?' said Phoebe. 'And Nathan and I can help with the deposit, seeing as we'll be selling our stock too, that way you can make Pritchard an even more compelling offer.'

'Definitely!' Bea agreed. 'Are you both sure you want to do this, though? It's a big step.'

'Yes!' they chorused.

'And remember, Pritchard isn't flavour of the month, thanks to Violet, so that might help,' said Phoebe.

'Speak of the devil,' said Bea, showing them a message from Violet which read: *Beatrice, can you meet me at Primrose Cottage urgently? I've got news I think you'll want to hear.*

'I wonder what that's about?' asked Phoebe.

'I guess there's only one way to find out. Nate, can you drop me back there?' Bea asked.

Bea tapped the heavy, brass door-knocker twice and Violet opened the door almost immediately, as though she had been stood behind it waiting for Bea to arrive.

'Bea,' said Violet with a nod, 'thanks for getting here so quickly. Come through.'

'Thank you,' said Bea, bending down to pat the little pug excitedly bouncing around at her heels.

'Rolo, do calm down,' said Violet, grabbing his collar and shoving him out of the way.

'Oh, it's fine, he's a sweetheart,' said Bea, taking a seat in an armchair in the lounge. 'You said you had some news?'

'Yes, well,' Violet started, clapping her hands together. 'As you know, all of us at the parish council were horrified by Malcolm's plans to sell the Pink Ribbon building to a developer. It's made him very unpopular. Flats on the green! Can you imagine? His wife is mortified; she's a member of the WI and she's disgusted by the whole thing.'

'That's kind of her,' said Bea. It wouldn't make any difference, but she was grateful to hear that the little community supported her.

'EliteHaven Homes has made an approach to the council and they have been told, unofficially, of course, that gaining planning permission to develop the site would be difficult, *very* difficult indeed,' Violet explained.

'So, have they withdrawn their offer?' Bea asked, hopefully.

'I'm afraid not,' said Violet. 'However . . .'

However sounded promising.

'I wouldn't be surprised if Mr Pritchard was having a change of heart,' Violet continued. 'I think if you made another approach and upped the rent, what with the money from that Agatha Christie book you found—'

'You know about that?' Bea blinked

'Of course I know about that,' said Violet, rolling her eyes. 'I know everything that goes on here.'

'So, you think if I increase my offer, I might get the shop after all?'

'I do. If I were you, I'd send Malcolm another email *now*; strike while the iron's hot,' Violet said, banging her hand down on the coffee table, making Bea jump.

'Okay, on it,' said Bea, pulling out her phone and typing furiously.

'Now, can I interest you in a slice of lemon drizzle cake?' asked Violet. 'Homemade, of course,' she added quickly. 'It won 'Best Sponge' at the village fête. All this scheming gives me quite the appetite.'

'Oh, yes, please,' said Bea, hitting send and looking up from her phone. *There, done.* 'And, me too!'

CHAPTER 38

As it turned out, Arthur's dealer contact found two potential buyers for the first edition of *The Mysterious Affair at Styles,* resulting in an exciting auction, much to Bea's surprise. In the end, a buyer actually *from* Canada had sealed the deal, with a bid of £2,100, and the money was immediately wired through to her bank account.

Mr Pritchard got back to her and they arranged a meeting at the shop for Thursday, which Bea took as a good sign. Phoebe, Nathan and Bea met up again to discuss the logistics of how running a shop together might work, just in case Mr Pritchard had changed his mind, and they agreed it made sense for Bea to take care of the day-to-day running of the business, with half the space dedicated to book stock, while Nathan and Phoebe would share the other half for wine and cheese. Phoebe and Nathan would each pay a quarter of the monthly rent and Bea would pay the remaining fifty per cent. One thing Phoebe and Nathan wouldn't negotiate on was the shop's name.

'But it wouldn't be just a bookshop anymore, we need a name that reflects all three of our businesses,' Bea had protested.

'Absolutely not,' Nathan had replied. 'This was your idea, it's still your bookshop Bea, it would just sell cheese and wine as well.'

'Exactly,' Phoebe had agreed. 'It's Bea's Bookshop, or we're both out.'

On Thursday morning, Mr Pritchard pulled open the door of the old Pink Ribbon with a sheepish smile.

'Here we are again, eh, Bea?' he said.

'Yes, thanks for seeing me. You said to contact you if my circumstances changed,' she said quickly. 'Well, I've raised some extra cash, so I could pay six months' rent in advance now. I know it's not the same as buying the building outright, but I'd be working with two other local businesses: Three Acre Cheeses and Cherrydown Vineyard. We'd stock books, wine and cheese, you see, and I think we could create something really special here, a place for the community to—'

'Let me stop you there,' he said, holding up a hand.

Oh God, she was wasting her time, wasn't she? There was nothing she could say to change his mind. What was she thinking?

'I've rejected the offer from EliteHaven Homes.'

'*What*?' replied Bea, her eyes wide with shock.

'My wife made her views on the matter *very* clear. The lease is yours if you want it. I've got the paperwork here ready for you to sign,' he said, tapping his fingers on a folder resting on the counter.

'Sorry,' she said, shaking her head. 'Did you say the shop's mine?'

'I did, yes,' said Mr Pritchard, beaming as he took a pen from his top pocket and handed it to her.

'Gosh,' was all Bea could say in response.

'Now, if you'd like to sign here,' said Malcolm, pointing to a dotted line on the bottom of page six, 'and here,' he repeated, turning to the final page of the contract.

Bea leafed through the lengthy document; it was a lot to take in.

'Do you mind if I take this home, give it a proper read through?' Bea asked. 'I'm sure everything's in order, but I'd like to share it with Nathan and Phoebe before I sign, if that's okay?'

'Of course, take your time, there's no rush. Pop it back to me when you're ready. And if you've got any questions, just ask, you know how to contact me.'

'Brilliant, thanks,' said Bea, shoving the contract into her bag.

'I want you to rest assured, though, Bea. I won't be going back on my word this time, the shop's officially yours,' he said, holding out a hand for her to shake. 'Congratulations!'

'Thank you,' said Bea, relief flooding through her.

It was official. Bea's Bookshop was about to become a reality and there was only one person she wanted to run to and tell: *Nathan.*

Nathan. It had always been Nathan – how had she not realized it before? It seemed so obvious to her now. She'd been telling herself for months they were just friends, that there was nothing more to it than that; she loved him like a friend, that was all. But that wasn't true. She knew if she was being honest with herself, the signs had been there all along, ever since she came back from London. That day at the fête when they'd been locked in the wagon reminiscing about their first date, their first *kiss*. The way his eyes crinkled when he laughed, the feelings that had stirred when her skin touched his, the way that, no matter how down, depressed or hopeless she felt, he could always make her laugh. It was the *little* things, but those little things were *everything.*

She realized now that she'd been scared to admit it to herself, frightened that he wouldn't feel the same. What if she told him how she truly felt and he rejected her? How could their friendship recover from that? *Could* it recover from that? And how would she be able to deal with the pain of not being with him?

'Hello, love,' said Maggie, as Bea barged into Harrison's. 'Everything all right? You look—'

'No. Yes. Sorry. I just wondered if Jess was here?' Bea asked, her face flushed.

'Jess? Yes, she's out the back,' said Maggie, with a worried look on her face.

'Bea! How'd it go?' Jess asked, running out of the store room.

'How'd what go?' Bea asked, pressing the heel of her hand into her temple.

'Er . . . at the shop? With Mr Pritchard?' Jess laughed.

'Oh, yeah, good, the shop's mine,' Bea said, distractedly.

'Oh, that's brilliant news, I'm so happy for you,' said Jess, a smile lighting up her face.

'Yeah, thanks, Jess, me too,' Bea agreed.

'So . . . why do you look so *miserable*?' Jess asked, her eyes searching Bea's face.

'Can we talk? In private?' Bea asked, looking sadder than Jess thought she'd ever seen her.

'Of course, we'll go upstairs,' said Jess.

'So, what's wrong?' Jess asked, as soon as they were sat in the living room in the flat above the shop.

'Okay . . .' said Bea, taking a deep breath. 'The shop's mine, I've got the lease and everything, but I realized the only person I wanted to tell was . . . *Nathan*.'

'Well, that makes sense, he's going to be involved in the shop too . . .' Jess trailed off. 'Hang on,' she said, realization dawning. 'That's not the reason, is it?'

'No,' said Bea, shaking her head. 'The thing is, Jess . . . well, I think I might have feelings for Nathan,' she blurted out quickly. There. She'd finally said it out loud.

'Course you do!' said Jess, grinning. 'I mean, it's bloody obvious.'

'You mean, you *knew*?' said Bea, 'but how could you? Even I didn't know until about ten minutes ago—'

'Well, it's been pretty obvious for ages: you're into him, he's into you,' said Jess, crossing her legs. 'It's perfect.'

'He's into me?' Bea stammered. 'Jess, are you *sure*?'

'Course! I'm telling you, he's got feelings for you too, Bea. I promise.'

'God!' said Bea, sitting back in her chair.

'It was a relief when you finally dumped Lochlan, I was beginning to think you'd never see what he was really like, to be honest.'

'But why didn't you say anything, Jess? If it was obvious he wasn't right for me?'

'You had to figure it out for yourself, Bea, you were so wrapped up in him, but I knew you'd get there *eventually*.'

'So, what do I do now? Tell Nathan how I feel? Just like that?' Bea asked, panic rising in her chest. 'I'm not sure I can just blurt it out. We're such great friends, I don't want to risk losing him.'

'Yes, but,' said Jess, taking her hand, 'if you don't try you'll never know.'

'True,' Bea whispered.

'While we're admitting things . . .' said Jess, chewing her bottom lip. 'I've got something to tell you, too.'

'What?' Bea asked.

'Well, Archie and I have been on a few dates. It's not that serious, but, well, I do kinda like him . . .' Jess admitted.

'I knew it!' said Bea. 'I did wonder if there was something going on, but Nathan convinced me I'd got it wrong.'

'Well, you were spot on. He persuaded me to read *Firestarter* after your book speed-dating thing and then we watched the film together, and things kind of went from there.'

'But you *hate* horror?' said Bea, laughing at the thought of Jess hiding behind a cushion watching the Stephen King classic with her brother.

'Turns out, not when I'm watching it with Archie. Horror is pretty cool, actually. You're not annoyed, are you?'

'Annoyed? Course not, why would I be? I think it's brilliant news! I'm happy for you both.'

'Thanks, Bea,' said Jess, hugging her friend tightly. 'So, are you going to talk to Nate?'

'I guess I have to really, don't I?' Bea nodded. 'It feels bloody terrifying though.'

'Well, no one said it was going to be easy, did they?'

'No, I guess not,' said Bea, squeezing Jess's hand. 'I suppose I just have to hope you're right, otherwise I don't know what I'm going to do.'

When Bea pulled up at Three Acre Farm, she was fizzing with nerves. Sue was hanging washing on the line in the September sunshine and she waved when she saw Bea jump out of the car.

'Hey, Sue!' called Bea. 'Is Nathan about?'

'Sorry, love, you've just missed him,' replied Sue.

'Ah, okay. Do you know where he is?' Bea asked.

'No, sorry, he's on a date! You should have seen him, all suited and booted,' said Sue fondly, proud of the man her son had become. 'Off somewhere fancy for lunch, I think.'

'On a date?' Bea repeated, blinking.

'Yes, with Cece. I think you met her at that awards thing in Brighton. Lovely young lady she is, and so pretty.'

Cece? The drop dead gorgeous Cece from the Chamber of Commerce?

'Oh, right,' said Bea, her heart breaking into a thousand tiny pieces. 'Do you know when he'll be back?'

'Your guess is as good as mine. Do you want me to tell him you're looking for him?'

'No, don't bother,' said Bea, her tone sharper than she'd intended.

'You okay, love?' Sue asked, taken aback.

'Yeah, I'm fine, sorry. I've got to go,' said Bea, climbing back into her car. 'Take care,' she called, gripping the steering wheel tightly and pulling out of the yard.

Bea couldn't stop her hands from shaking as she drove home. After *everything*, she'd left it too late ... Nathan was seeing Cece and there was nothing she could do about it.

CHAPTER 39

Bea glanced down at her phone. *How did it go with Pritchard? N xx.* She put the spoon back in the tub of Ben & Jerry's she'd been eating and wiped the tears from her eyes. She knew she should have messaged Nathan – and Phoebe come to think of it – to tell them they'd got the shop, but she hadn't been able to face it.

All she could think about was Cece. Gorgeous, perfect, beautiful Cece.

Her phone pinged with another message: *Hey, Miller, call me when you get this. Where are you? Mum said you dropped by, is everything okay?*

She typed out a reply: *Sorry, yeah, the shop's ours xx*

Nathan's reply was instant: *Brilliant! Apple Tree tonight? 8pm?*

She wasn't sure she could face seeing him yet, not after finding out about Cece. Why hadn't he told her himself? It was bad enough knowing she'd missed her chance with him, but to find out through his mum was awful. Bea dropped her head into her hands and carried on sobbing. *What was she going to do?*

She thought back to everything she'd been through over the last few months: leaving her job, risking all her savings to buy the wagon, the accident, Lochlan. Despite it all, she was still standing, still *thriving*. She'd overcome all the challenges of the past few months and, if she'd learnt anything, it was that when life gets you down, you have to pick yourself up and keep on going. It may have taken her a while to see clearly, but she knew now, for certain, that what she wanted was Nathan, so she'd just have to go and fight for him.

Bea didn't think she'd ever felt so nervous before in all her life, as she walked into the Apple Tree that night. Her palms were clammy, her pulse racing and her legs threatening to give way. After polishing off the whole tub of ice cream, she'd taken a hot shower and spent the afternoon thinking about how badly this conversation with Nathan could play out, but in the end she knew, regardless of the result, she had to tell him how she felt.

She ordered a whisky from Pete, downed it in one, and was just about to order another when she felt a gentle tap on the shoulder and turned round to see Nathan, *her* Nathan, behind her.

'Hello, you,' he said, leaning down to kiss her on the cheek.

He looked gorgeous, and Bea took a nervous swallow.

How was it she'd never noticed how cute his dimples looked when he smiled? He was so familiar to her, but now she saw him clearly. The most handsome, kind, thoughtful and caring man she'd ever known.

Oh, Nathan, she thought. *Why did it take me so long to see you?*

Gathering herself, she replied, 'Hey, yourself! Good day?'

'Yeah, fine, good, just the usual, really. So, do you know when we'll be able to open?' he continued, catching her off guard. So he wasn't going to mention his date, then, she thought.

'Erm . . . no, not yet. There's so much to do, we need to sit down properly, work it all out. We'll need to add shelving, of course, but I'm going to speak to Greg about that. Then there's the colour scheme to think about. I thought I might paint it in the same pastel colours as the wagon? What?' she asked, suddenly aware of his eyes upon her.

'I dunno,' he shrugged, his green eyes dancing with mischief. 'It's just you. You light up when you talk about your business. Honestly, it's so sweet.'

Bea reached for her empty glass again, her fingers brushing his. Their eyes locked and she felt something flicker between them. The knot in her stomach was tightening – this was it, this was the moment to tell him how she really felt . . .

'Listen, Nate, I—'

'Bea! I've just heard the news about the shop, my dear!' Bea looked up and there was Jean, beaming widely, looming over her. She cursed her timing.

'It's brilliant news, isn't it?' said Nathan, smiling warmly.

'Oh, absolutely! I'm so pleased for you,' said Jean.

'Thanks,' said Bea, flatly, all the spark having left her.

'Looking forward to the launch party!' called Jean, heading for the bar.

'Great, thanks,' Bea replied.

'Sorry, were you going to say something?' Nathan asked, his boyish grin wide.

Her heart flipped.

'Yeah, so . . .' she started. 'The thing is, Nate, I—'

'Congratulations, Bea! Tori told me about the shop,' called out Rose, walking into the pub with Scout.

For God's sake.

'Thanks,' Bea replied, momentarily distracted by the always-excitable Border Collie.

'I don't suppose you've seen Jake, have you?' Rose asked.

'Yeah, I saw him head to the beer garden,' said Nathan, helpfully.

'Ah, brilliant, thanks,' said Rose. 'By the way, did I tell you we're off to Portofino in October? It sounded so wonderful in that book we read for Book Club, and Jake surprised me and booked it!'

'Wow! I can't believe it!' said Bea.

'Me neither, I can't wait. We're going to try to find that secret beach that Damian takes Jane to,' Rose grinned. 'Anyway, see you later.'

'Do you fancy going for a walk?' she asked Nathan, quickly, before anyone else interrupted her.

'What, now?' Nathan replied, surprised. 'Don't you want another drink?'

'Nah, I'm fine,' said Bea, trying to sound casual. 'Come on, it's a nice night,' she added.

'Sure, okay, a walk sounds great,' said Nathan, downing the dregs of his pint. 'Lead the way.'

When they finally made it outside, having been stopped by other well-meaning well-wishers, the cool night air was a blessed relief.

'News certainly travels fast, doesn't it?' she said, looping her arm through his as she always had done. His warm skin against hers felt incredible, and she took a moment to collect herself.

'Around here it does, yeah,' Nathan chuckled.

They walked in silence, the stars bright as diamonds high in the night sky.

'Wow, it's chilly,' said Bea, rubbing her arms

'Here, take this,' he said, giving her his jacket. 'You know, if you look up, that's Orion's Belt,' he continued, pointing in the distance, his hand brushing her cheek.

Her skin tingled where he touched it.

'And see that trio of stars there?' he said, 'that's Alnitak, Alnilam and Mintaka. It's crazy, really, they look so close, but they're actually light years away.'

'They're beautiful,' she whispered, her breath caught in her throat. 'Listen, Nate, there's something I want to talk to you about . . . I know my timing's not great, as you're seeing Cece, but if I don't say it now I'll always—'

'Sorry, what?' he said, his gaze moving from the sky to rest on her face.

'Cece? Your mum said you were seeing her—'

'Well, that explains a lot,' he said, laughing. 'I'm not *seeing her*,' he said, making air quotes. 'I'm helping her out with a project she's working on. She's asked me to be a mentor, that's all. That's Mum putting two and two together, but it was just a business meeting, nothing more.'

'So you're not . . .' said Bea, relief flooding through her.

'No, we're not,' he replied, emphatically.

'Oh,' Bea murmured.

'Oh?' he asked, his face searching hers for an answer.

'Well, you see, the thing is,' she said, stepping towards him.

This was it. She *had* to tell him. It was now or never.

'The thing is, Nate . . . well, the thing is, I've realized something. I've realized that our friendship isn't . . .' she stuttered, somehow more nervous now she knew he wasn't going out with Cece than when she thought he was.

'Isn't what, Miller? Spit it out, for God's sake.' he chuckled, absolutely not getting the hint at all.

'It isn't, well . . . what I mean is . . . Oh god, this is so hard!' she gulped. 'Okay, I've got feelings for you, Nate, like, real feelings. There. I've said it.'

His mouth dropped open in surprise.

'I think there's something there. I felt it. In Brighton, you know? I was scared, I think, scared of ruining our friendship,' she said, on a roll now and powerless to stop. 'But I think you felt it, too? *Feel* it, too?'

He stepped towards her, nodding slowly, his eyes sparkling.

'I don't want to lose you, Nate, but I can't not tell you how I feel, you know?' she said, squeezing her eyes shut, letting out a very deep, very slow breath.

Silence. Not a word. She could hear him breathing, but you could have heard a pin drop.

'You're not going to lose me,' he said, finally, and when she opened her eyes, he was smiling. 'I feel the same, Bea. I have for months and it's been killing me.'

'You *have*?' she gasped.

'God, yes! But what with Lochlan and the accident, it just never felt like the right time, and I wasn't prepared to risk losing you as a friend in case you didn't feel the same way,' he admitted, sheepishly.

'I know,' she said, closing the space between them. 'But I think it's a risk we have to take, don't you?' she murmured.

'I think so,' he said.

And, when his lips finally touched hers, they were soft and warm, and she pulled him close, never wanting to let go.

Book Club Recommends

The Mysterious Affair at Styles by Agatha Christie

A classic whodunit! This is Christie's first Poirot novel and it doesn't disappoint! This English country house murder mystery has all the genius plot twists you'd expect from Christie (which I never see coming!), and it's the perfect introduction to the greatest fictional detective ever written: Hercule Poirot. Have you got what it takes to crack the case before the murderer strikes again? A must-read for all crime fans!!

Recommended by Bea

My Favourite Mistake by Marian Keyes

Is Marian Keyes the queen of the laugh-out-loud romcoms? Absolutely! This book was hysterical and had me belly-laughing from start to finish. Out of all the Walsh sisters, I think

Anna might be my favourite, and I found myself cheering her on as she navigated her way through life. The banter throughout is witty and full of grit, and you don't need to have read any of the other Walsh books to dive straight into this one - so what are you waiting for? It's five stars from me.

Recommended by Jess

What If I Never Get Over You by Paige Toon

Paige Toon delivers yet again! I've been a Paige Toon fan for years, but I think this might be my favourite novel to date; I couldn't put it down! This sweeping love story was uplifting, but at the same time heart-breaking, and there were so many twists and turns that I just didn't see coming! Ellie and Ash are such engaging characters and their 'right place, wrong time' romance had me hooked from the very first page. It's an easy five stars.

Recommended by Rose

All Creatures Great and Small by James Herriot

Herriot was my favourite author as a kid and, since joining Bea's Book Club, I've been rediscovering the joy of reading and revisiting his books. Do I love them just as much as the first time around? Yes!!! Rose even got me a signed edition of *All Creatures Great and Small* for my birthday. If you're an animal lover, this book is a must-read! The stories of the animals (and their owners) Herriot meets in his job as a Yorkshire vet offer the perfect mix of humour, heartbreak and nostalgia. If you're looking for your next page-turner, you've found it!

Recommended by Jake

Firestarter by Stephen King

This book is hot stuff! I've been a Stephen King fan for most of my life and I've lost count of the times I've read this novel. It's got everything you'd expect from a good thriller: mystery, conspiracy, a brilliant villain, and it'll have you gripped right from the start. Fast-paced with a great plot, *Firestarter* deserves a flaming five stars!

Recommended by Archie

Before We Say Goodbye by Toshikazu Kawaguchi

A magical café with a secret menu offering time travel? Where do I sign up! I loved this book, and when Bea asked for my pick for book club, it was a no brainer! This story really got me thinking: if you could go back in time for just one moment, where would you go? This novel is the fourth in the series by Kawaguchi and I'd definitely recommend checking out the rest, they're all great. A truly heart-warming story with a very clever concept.

Recommended by Tori

The Cat Share by Angela Jariwala

When Bea told me about a book with a cat called Fred who lands unexpectedly in the life of Ben the firefighter, I was sold! Ben's been finding life tough and Fred's arrival helps him feel less alone.

But when Fred arrives home one day with a note on his collar from Jenni, a furious neighbour accusing him of stealing her cat, things get complicated. I don't want to give away any spoilers, but let's just say Jenni and Ben might have more in common than they first thought!

Recommended by Leo

The Complete Cheese Pairing Cookbook by Morgan McGlynn

It's all about the cheese in this collection of cheese-pairing charts and recipes and I am here for it! This book has taught me loads about curating cheese boards and how the taste can change depending on what you pair your cheese with. I've certainly tried some more adventurous combinations since discovering this book and they've all gone down a storm. A must-read for any cheese-lover!

Recommended by Nathan

The Colour of Magic by Terry Pratchett

This is the first book in the Discworld universe and it's got it all: dungeons, trolls, dragons, wizards, you name it! It's an adventure-filled rollercoaster ride, perfect for fantasy fans. The only drawback is you'll become so hooked on Pratchett's books, you'll have to buy them all. If you're pushed for time like me, the audiobooks are a lifesaver, as you can listen on the go.

Recommended by Lochlan

The Diary of a CEO by Steven Bartlett

As a managing director that's going places, Bartlett's wisdom has undoubtedly unlocked my potential and helped me to see things from a different perspective. I love him on *Dragon's Den*, and this book is like having the man himself in your pocket, dishing out advice! The interviews with industry leaders were inspiring. With Bartlett in my ear, I doubt I'll be at Hobbs & Partners for much longer: Brendan Fuller is moving on up, people, so watch this space!

Recommended by Brendan

The Killing Floor by Lee Child

Well, isn't that Jack Reacher chap a marvel? When I watched the TV show with my son, I just knew I had to seek out the books, and I wasn't disappointed. This is the first of twenty-eight in the series (can you believe it?), and it's a great introduction to the Jack Reacher character. Jack goes for breakfast at a local diner and, before he's had a chance to enjoy it, he's arrested for murder! What are the chances? A well-written, brilliantly thought-out story.

Recommended by Arthur

Pride and Prejudice by Jane Austen

Is the love story between Elizabeth Bennett and Fitzwilliam Darcy the greatest ever told? There's a simple answer to that: yes. Elizabeth is a heroine with fire in her belly and you can't help but admire her from the get go. Austen tackles the issue of a woman's role in a society that has strict social rules, with a leading couple who both challenge and change one another. This book is a classic for a reason and it's no surprise it came in at number two on the BBC's Big Read list.

Recommended by K. L. Fletcher

You Are Here by David Nicholls

Beth has been bending my ear about reading this since the *One Day* series on Netflix, and I have to say I thoroughly enjoyed it! A well-crafted, later-in-life love story that had me laughing out loud (even though I don't usually like romances). Anyone who, like me, has ever done any proper country walking in the fickle English weather will totally relate!

Recommended by Pete

It Ends With Us by Colleen Hoover

Where do I even start? This book quite literally broke my heart! It's a powerful, thought-provoking read, that deals with some difficult subject matter (domestic abuse) and I found myself staying up late each night just to keep reading. You'll need tissues as the ready as you follow Lily's story, but I promise you'll be ordering the next instalment immediately! Unputdownable!

Recommended by Beth

Murder in my Backyard by Ann Cleeves

Inspector Ramsay is a captivating character and, in this novel, the seasoned detective moves to an idyllic village in Northumberland, but it's not long before he finds himself embroiled in a fresh murder inquiry. If you enjoy a good police procedural with a twist you'll never see coming, I can heartily recommend this book!

Recommended by Ted

The Women Who Wouldn't Leave by Victoria Scott

The perfect read! I found myself rooting for Connie and Matilda from the start as they fight to save the community they love from a mercenary developer (sound familiar?). This is a story of courage, demonstrating the power of community in fighting the good fight, which felt very relatable given that I live in Blossom Heath! If you're looking for a feel-good, uplifting read that's utterly heart-warming, you'll love *The Women Who Wouldn't Leave*.

Recommended by Maggie

The Reading List by Sara Nisha Adams

A gorgeous story about the power of books and libraries, that will help to remind you what it's like to discover a book you truly connect with. If you're an avid reader like me, add this to your TBR immediately! The Reading List is a book designed for readers: it's joyous and heart-breaking in equal measure, and has everything you'd expect from the perfect story. Love, resilience, friendship and bucket loads of emotion means five stars from me!

Recommended by Carol

We Solve Murders by Richard Osman

I was slightly apprehensive about leaving *The Thursday Murder Club* behind, but I needn't have worried as Osman's writing style and humour was just as brilliant as ever. *We Solve*

Murders is a cracking start to a new series:; it was witty and gripping and I've already pre-ordered the next one.

Recommended by Gordon

Black Beauty by Anna Sewell

As stories about horses go, this has to be the best one out there! Bea tracked down a beautiful clothbound vintage edition as a thank you for the horsebox, and I'm reading it to my girls at bedtime - they are loving it! Black Beauty is a colt with a strong spirit, but the kindest of natures. He is forced from a life of comfort into one of suffering and cruelty, but this horse is not one to give up easily; his will to survive is unbreakable. Black Beauty's story will melt the hardest of hearts and, although I can't promise you won't shed a tear while reading, I can promise that you'll fall in love with this book and you'll want to read it again and again (I know I do). Five stars.

Recommended by Charlotte

Room on the Broom by Julia Donaldson

This is my favourite book at school and I love it so much that Mummy bought it for me from Bea's bookshop! It's the best bedtime story EVER, and I love how it rhymes on every single page. My favourite character is probably the frog and I love it when they all get covered in mud! This book is funny because you think a witch would be evil, but she's actually not and she saves all the animals.

Recommended by Melody

Diary of a Wimpy Kid by Jeff Kinney

This book is a fun-packed adventure that's sooooo funny. It always makes me laugh and everyone at school loves it too. The cartoons are great and there's a film as well. Sometimes, I read it to my little sister and it makes her giggle like crazy. There are loads of *Diary of a Wimpy Kid* books, so you can read all of them if you like the first one. I've started my own diary at home, too, just like Greg in the book. I give this story top marks!

Recommended by Hazel

Dog Days by Ericka Waller

Woof, woof, woof, yap, yip, ruff, ruff. Woof, arf, woof, yip, yip, grrr. Wuff, yap, yap, bowwow.

Recommended by Wordsworth

***Tequila Mockingbird* by Tim Federle**

This is such a fun book and a great gift for any aspiring mixologists! Think cocktails with a literary twist and you're on the right track (the Gin Eyre has to be my favourite, closely followed by The Pitcher of Dorian Grey Goose). The book sets out everything you need: equipment, ingredients, techniques, to make the perfect literary cocktail (or mocktail). We've had a great time trying out some of the recipes (and accompanying drinking games!) at book club. A solid five stars from me.

Recommended by Phoebe

***Frankenstein* by Mary Shelley**

It's hard to believe that a horror story published over two hundred years ago is still relevant today, but that's exactly the case with Mary Shelley's thought-provoking tale. The novel deals with the central issue of the importance of human connection and, by the end, the reader is left asking, 'who is the real monster?' This is a story I've reread many times over the years; it's beautifully crafted, poignant and utterly enthralling.

Recommended by Matt

One Love by Matt Cain

Matt Cain is a genius! I absolutely loved this book and I couldn't stop reading. One Love is a dual timeline novel split between 2002 and 2022 and chronicling the 20-year friendship between Danny and Guy from when they first meet at university through to a weekend spent at Manchester Pride two decades later. A truly uplifting and authentic story brimming with love, laughter, kindness and friendship. This is one very special book indeed!

Recommended by Harry

The Forgotten Village by Lorna Cook

I do love a good historical romance with a dual timeline, and Lorna Cook always delivers. *The Forgotten Village* is the author's debut novel and it tells the story of a requisitioned village during the Second World War, which is hiding an awful secret. Melissa, the novel's present-day heroine, must uncover this secret if she is to find the truth about the village's past. This book combines history with a dose of mystery, and it had me on the edge of my seat throughout. I couldn't stop reading!

Recommended by Jean

The House by the Bay by Kate Fisher

I'm a staunch Kate Fisher fan and her latest novel, *The House by the Bay*, might just be her best book yet. This heart-wrenching love story takes place in the sumptuous setting of Portofino, and you can almost imagine yourself sat in a café by the Italian fishing harbour, sipping limoncello and watching the boats go by. With their parents set against their relationship, Damian and Jane's forbidden love is doomed from the outset, but when a big secret is revealed, the fates of everyone involved will be changed forever ... If you want to find out how, you'll have to read for yourself, as my lips are well and truly sealed.

Recommended by Violet

She Has My Child by Emma Robinson

I do love a tearjerker and Emma Robinson always does them brilliantly! A captivating story that will pull at your heartstrings and take you on an emotional rollercoaster of a ride. When one sister agrees to become the surrogate for another, tensions rise and, with a huge plot twist that will shock you to the core, the siblings are left wondering who they can really trust. Make sure you have tissues at the ready!

Recommended by Joyce

Restore – the art of caring for the things you love by Will Kirk

As Joyce will tell you, I'm a huge fan of *The Repair Shop* – those guys can literally fix anything, so I'm not surprised she bought this for my birthday and I loved it! Will is the king of all things woodwork, he's a real craftsman, and this book teaches you the basics so that you can get stuck in with your own restoration projects at home. It's full of hints and tips and easy to use hacks that will soon have you upcycling, recycling and perhaps even tackling some larger projects. The sky's the limit with a little help from Will!

Recommended by Greg

***Behind the Seams* by Esme Young**

I love *The Great British Sewing Bee*, and when I heard Esme had released a book, I ordered a copy from Bea immediately. I'm a keen seamstress (I made the bunting and cushions for the bookshop) and this was an informative and enjoyable read. I loved reading Esme's backstory and hearing more about the British fashion industry, I bet she was a real hoot in the sixties!

Recommended by Clara

***Matilda* by Roald Dahl**

Any book by Roald Dahl is always special, but *Matilda* is a firm favourite at the school and it's one of our most requested titles at story time. It's a book about loving books, sprinkled with a little bit of magic. Is there anything more inspiring for children and adults alike? Of course, I like to think I'm nothing like Miss Trunchball, the book's terrifying and cruel headteacher, who rules the school with a rod of iron. In fact, one of my favourite parts of the story is when Matilda runs Trunchball out of town, leaving the kind and gentle Miss Honey in charge. A beautifully crafted story with a cast of wonderful characters that conveys the incredible power of reading.

Recommended by Mrs Connolly

Hinch Yourself Happy by Mrs Hinch

When my girlfriend, Claire, brought me this book, I thought she was trying to send me a not-too-subtle message about the state of my flat, but it turns out Mrs Hinch is an absolute legend! Who knew? I've been following all her hints and tips, and my flat is now starting to feel like a proper home – I'm even following her on Insta, too.

Recommended by Josh

Onyx Storm by Rebecca Yarros

If you enjoyed *Fourth Wing* and *Iron Flame*, you're going to love this follow up. I'm totally obsessed with this book, it really is fantasy at its best, I didn't want it to end! It's got definite *Hunger Games* vibes, with some added spice and more mythical creatures than you can shake a stick at. I'm counting down to the next instalment, I just hope we don't have to wait too long!

Recommended by Claire

How to be a Domestic Goddess by Nigella Lawson

No one does comfort cooking like Nigella! This book has become my baking bible and I'm always referring back to it for my go-to bakes (the marzipan fruit cake is a firm favourite). The recipes are always a triumph and Nigella's tone of voice really shines through – it's like she's in the kitchen with you. You can keep your Mary Berry, it's Nigella all the way for me!

Recommended by Sue

Sense and Sensibility by Jane Austen

A timeless story, with a gorgeous cast of characters - I adored it! I've read a few Austen novels but never *Sense and Sensibility*, so when Bea gifted me a copy, I couldn't wait to dive in and I wasn't disappointed. Austen captures the importance of family just perfectly, and the bond between sisters Elinor and Marianne, although they're so different, is something quite wonderful.

Recommended by Anya

Daisy's Christmas Gift Shop by Hannah Pearl

I'm not usually one for a festive romance, but when Bea told me the main character in this book opens her own gift shop so she can spend her time helping customers find the perfect gift, I thought I'd give it a try and I'm glad I did! This was a really fun read and I quickly found myself caught up in the characters and enjoying all the twists and turns in the story. The plot has so many layers to it, there's drama, mystery and intrigue as well as romance, so there really is something for everyone. With it being set in a gift shop, I could totally relate to the character of Daisy and the joy she experiences helping people find the perfect present. It's definitely five stars from me.

Recommended by Simon

Wahaca: Mexican Food at Home by Tomasina Miers

If you're looking to cook up a bit of authentic Mexican spice at home, this book will show you how! It's got everything from breakfasts and dinners to puddings and cocktails, and the author's love of Mexican food comes across brilliantly. The recipes are easy to follow and delicious, so why not give it a try and add a little spice to your weekly menu?

Recommended by Tony

War Horse by Michael Morpurgo

When Bea told me I would enjoy this book I didn't believe her, as I don't like reading, but it was actually fun. I like the way they told the story, as if it was the horse talking, that was clever. Joey is a very brave horse, even though there is a war going on and I would definitely read more books by Michael Morpurgo. I give this four stars.

Recommended by Billy

ACKNOWLEDGEMENTS

Well, where to start? I can't quite believe we've made our third trip to Blossom Heath! These characters are starting to feel like old friends to me now, particularly Rose, who has been with me since page one of book one. I hope you enjoyed meeting this new cast of characters, especially Bea and her wonderful book wagon, just as much as I did creating them.

I want to kick off my acknowledgements with a huge thank you to all my amazing readers. There is nothing I love more than seeing how much you've enjoyed visiting Blossom Heath and meeting the characters I've conjured up, and I hope this return visit is everything you hoped for.

To my editor Sara-Jade Virtue at Simon & Schuster, thank you for believing in Bea's story from the first moment you read the synopsis. Your guidance and support has been invaluable and I can't thank you enough. To Louise Davies, thank you for guiding me through another copyedit so skilfully and, remember, you must try a pistachio latte (I will be checking up!).

I'd also like to thank my brilliant friend, Amanda Watson, and her gorgeous cheese business, Beau Fromage, which she runs from a refurbished horsebox, and was the original inspiration for the book wagon idea. Thank you for answering my (numerous!) WhatsApp voice notes asking all the technical questions – I now know exactly what a jockey wheel does and how to hitch a trailer thanks to you. You were an absolute star and nothing I asked was too much trouble, so thank you!

To my wonderful agent, Laura Macdougall at United Agents, a huge thank you for all your support in helping me to share Bea's story and always answering my (far too many!) questions so quickly and with such good humour.

To my brilliant Essex writer buddies from the RNA, hanging out with you all is such a tonic and I love how we get to pick each other's brains and offer support and advice when we need it. Writing can be a solitary career and I honestly don't know what I'd do without you lovely lot! A special shoutout goes to Fiona Collins, Lauren North, Lorna Cook, Emma Robinson, Carrie Elks, Lizzie Chantree, Carrie Walker and Lizzie Page for being your brilliant selves.

To fellow Simon & Schuster author, Eva Verde, how lucky am I that you literally live just around the corner? Our coffee catchups, train journeys and dedication to finding the best scones and jam Chelmsford has to offer are always a joy!

And finally, I can't write a bookshop book without mentioning all the marvellous local independent bookshops I've visited recently, all of which have helped to inspire Bea's fictional bookshop. To Olivia and the team at Maldon Books (who have an actual real-life book wagon in the summer months), Jo at Red Lion Books in Colchester, Andrew at Dial Lane Books in Ipswich, Kate at Harris & Harris Books in Clare, and Kathryn and William at Tea Leaves & Reads in Andover, thank you for always giving me such a warm welcome and for bringing books to the local community. There really is nowhere I'd rather be than a good bookshop!

Always By Your Side

'A warm, romantic story about community, friendship and following your heart, *Always By Your Side* is a feel-good delight, I adored it!' **HOLLY MARTIN**

When school teacher Rose loses her dream job at a London primary school, her self-confidence takes a knock. Worse still, her stockbroker fiancé, Ollie, sees it as the perfect opportunity for her to join his firm, which only adds to the feelings Rose has that their relationship might be coming to an end.

An unexpected phone call, and an elderly aunt who's taken a fall, means Rose must drop everything – including Ollie – and return to Blossom Heath, the Sussex village she grew up in.

With no job to rush home to, Rose decides to stay in Blossom Heath for the summer, trading London for the idyllic countryside. Here, Rose finds herself reconnecting to the village life of her childhood in more ways than one, including falling head-over-heels for local farmer, Jake.

So when her London life comes calling, Rose is faced with an impossible choice . . . to return to the high-pressure life of her past, or embrace the joy of a new life in the country.

Available in paperback, ebook and audio

SIMON &
SCHUSTER

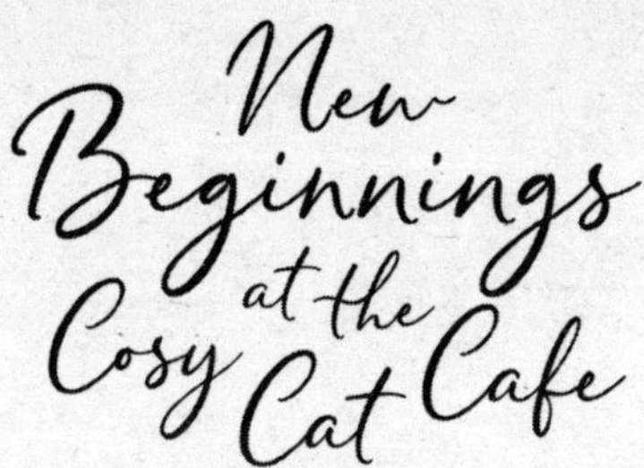

‘A truly heartwarming return to Blossom Heath!’ **HEIDI SWAIN**

New Beginnings at The Cosy Cat Café tells the story of Tori who, after being dumped and left stranded by her long-term boyfriend, Ryan, on a trip of a lifetime to Asia, returns home to the sleepy Sussex village of Blossom Heath with her tail between her legs and her dreams shattered.

Donning her frilly apron to help her mum, Joyce, behind the counter at the Cosy Cup Café, Tori starts to believe – with the help of a hunky fireman and a collection of rescue cats – that perhaps the secret to her future happiness might lie closer to home.

If you love your romance with a side order of cake, cats and cosy community dynamics, this is the purrfect uplifting, feel-good read from the winner of the RNA Katie Fforde Debut Novel of the Year 2023.

Available in paperback, ebook and audio

SIMON &
SCHUSTER